Praise for Juan José Saer

"Juan José Saer must be added to the list of the best South American writers."

—*Le Monde*

"To say that Juan José Saer is the best Argentinian writer of today is to undervalue his work. It would be better to say that Saer is one of the best writers of today in any language."

—Ricardo Piglia

"The author's preoccupations are reminiscent of his fellow Argentinians Borges and Cortázar, but his vision is fresh and unique."

—*Independent*

Also by Juan José Saer in English Translation

The Sixty-Five Years of Washington

Juan José Saer
Translated from the Spanish
by Steve Dolph

OPEN LETTER
LITERARY TRANSLATIONS FROM THE UNIVERSITY OF ROCHESTER

Copyright © Juan José Saer, 1986
c/o Guillermo Schavelzon & Assoc. Agencia Literaria, info@schavelzon.com
Translation copyright © Steve Dolph, 2010
Originally published in Spanish as *Glosa*, 1986

First edition, 2010
All rights reserved

Library of Congress Cataloging-in-Publication Data:

Saer, Juan José, 1937–
    [Glosa. English]
    The sixty-five years of Washington / Juan José Saer ; translated from
the Spanish by Steve Dolph. — 1st ed.
        p. cm.
    Originally published in Spanish as Glosa, 1986.
    ISBN-13: 978-1-934824-20-7 (pbk. : alk. paper)
    ISBN-10: 1-934824-20-8 (pbk. : alk. paper)
  1. Argentina—Fiction. I. Dolph, Steve. II. Title.
    PQ7797.S22435G5613 2010
    863'.64—dc22
                        2010029041

Printed on acid-free paper in the United States of America.

Text set in Granjon, an old-style serif typeface designed in the period 1928–1929
by George William Jones (1860–1942) and based on the Garamond typeface.

Design by N. J. Furl

Open Letter is the University of Rochester's nonprofit, literary translation press:
Lattimore Hall 411, Box 270082, Rochester, NY 14627

www.openletterbooks.org

To Michael, Patrick, Pierre Gilles, who practice three
true sciences, grammar, homeopathy, and administration,
the author dedicates, for the Sunday conversations, this comedy

but then time is your misfortune father said.

In another man devoured
my own death I don't see
but plagued by geometric flowers
I waste away the hours
and now they keep vigil for me

The First Seven Blocks

Suppose it's October, October or November, let's say, in 1960 or 1961, October, maybe the fourteenth or sixteenth, or the twenty-second or twenty-third maybe—the twenty-third of October in 1961 let's say—what's the difference.

Leto—Ángel Leto, no?—Leto, I was saying, has, a few seconds ago, stepped off the bus on the corner of the boulevard, far from the usual stop, compelled by the sudden desire to walk, to traverse San Martín, the central avenue, on foot, and to let himself get lost in the bright morning instead of shutting himself up in the dark mezzanine of one of the businesses where for the last few months he has patiently but impassively kept the books.

He has, then, stepped off, not without bumping into some passengers who were trying to get on and in his haste generating among them a momentary wave of vague protests; he has waited for the bus to pull away and move metallically down the boulevard toward the city center; he has crossed, alert, both sides of the boulevard separated

3

by the center median, which is half planted and half paved, avoiding the cars driving, placid and hot, in both directions; he has reached the opposite sidewalk, has bought a pack of Particulares and a box of matches at the cigarette kiosk that he has put away in the pockets of his short-sleeved shirt, has walked the few meters to the corner, where he has just arrived, turning the corner south on the eastern sidewalk, the shady side at that hour; and he has begun to walk down San Martín, the central avenue—its parallel sidewalks, as they approach the city center, begin to fill with businesses selling records, shoes, groceries, fabric, candy, books, cigarettes, and also with banks, perfume shops, jewelry stores, churches, galleries, and which, at opposite ends, when the cluster of businesses thins out and finally disintegrates, reveal the pretentious and elegant façades, including some—why not—residential buildings, many of which are decorated, beside the front door, with the bronze plaques that publicize their occupants' profession, doctors, lawyers, notaries, engineers, architects, otorhinolaryngologists, radiologists, dentists, accountants, biochemists, brokers—in a word, essentially, or in two better yet, to be more precise, every thing.

The man who gets up in the morning, who takes a shower, who eats breakfast and goes out, afterward, into the sun of the city center, comes, without a doubt, from beyond his bed, and from a deeper and heavier darkness than his bedroom: nothing and no one in the world could say why Leto, instead of going to work this morning, like every other day, is now walking easy and calm under the trees that amplify the shade from the row of houses, down San Martín to the south. *He suffered so much*, said his mother Isabel during breakfast before she left for work; alone afterward, Leto poured a second cup of coffee and went to drink it in the rear courtyard. This *He suffered so much* was stripped of its representations while he walked around the cramped and blooming courtyard where in the shady corners grass and shrubs, flowerpots and planters retained the dampness of the morning dew, but its overall shape and its impalpable reverberations still preserved their fragile and distracted resonance. Maybe the damp and concentrated shade that persisted at the foot of the houses, on the central avenue, or that mix of damp and brilliance the foliage displays in spring, and which stands out in some front yards, is what recalls his mother's expression to Leto's mind once again, how it doubles as sincere gesture and set phrase. The morning humidity that persists in the rising but mitigated heat is absorbed, by association, into the persistent and well-framed image, strange but at once familiar, of his mother who, turning from the gas stove, bringing the steaming coffee pot in her hand, uttered, in a low and thoughtful tone, as though to herself, without the slightest connection to what she had been saying just then, that sentence: *He suffered so much*. In the early penumbra of the kitchen, the little blue flames joined into concentric rings continued burning behind her after she removed the coffee, the milk, the water, the toast, and turned toward the table with the steaming coffee pot. To Leto, the sentence that was just uttered and has dissipated in the kitchen has the characteristic ambiguity of many of his mother's assertions—he finds it difficult to understand its precise meaning; and when he raises his head, stifling his embarrassment and maybe even his shame, and begins to scrutinize Isabel's expression, his suspicions that this ambiguity is deliberate only increase, now that, against the backlight of the little blue flames, Isabel's now slightly thickened figure advances in silence, her eyes lowered, avoiding his gaze, disarming any inquiry. She has let her comment slip unexpectedly, during the routine exchange over breakfast in the kitchen, when phrases, spoken politely, out of courtesy, a dubious motive, have no more significance or extension than the sound of silverware striking plates. And Leto has begun to think, while he takes the first sip of black coffee and watches her sit, abstractedly, on the other side of the table: *It must be the hope of erasing her humiliation that makes her pretend he suffered so much*—but, and Leto raises his head again and fixes his eyes on the dumpy though still somewhat childlike face, which, with its eyelids lowered, reveals nothing: *Can she tell? Does she notice? Is she sounding me out? Is she testing me?* The hardest part, regardless, is, at a distance,

5

knowing how to reply. Leto would have been well-disposed and, above all, relieved, to give the response she is waiting for, if, just then, it were possible to know what she is waiting for, but, with a desperate insistence, she seemed to want him to guess it on his own, and does not give him, therefore, any help. Leto searches, hesitates, and then, unsure, though not without a degree of resentment, the way he reacts toward every comment of that kind, does not say anything. A somewhat hard silence follows, uncomfortable for them both, in which there is possibly deception and not even a little relief, and which Isabel breaks by emptying her cup of *café con leche* in one swallow and chewing, noisily, her last piece of toast, and afterward recur the opaque and customary comments furnished with ambiguity by their intonation alone, though issued from neutral and distracted lips. These comments also come, certainly, from farther away, farther back than the tongue, the vocal chords, the lungs, brain, and breath, from the far side of the depository of named and accumulated experience, from which, blindly groping, though believing to consider carefully, each person withdraws and expels them. In the silence that follows, including when, after brushing his cheek with her lips, closing behind her, softly, two or three doors, she has finally gone, before him, to work, her image, as strange as it is familiar, begins to unglue itself from its representations so as to disseminate itself more easily throughout his body, as though, in its ebb and flow, blood is able to reduce the impalpable to its material tenacity, metabolizing and distributing it to cells, tissue, flesh, bones, muscles. With his second cup of coffee in hand, while he observes the dampness of the morning dew that's yet to dissolve from the corners of the shade, Leto, though not his body, has now forgotten his mother, and it is this same humid shade persisting now, around ten, on the central avenue, which covers his body like the first invisible layer of the world and is likewise covered by the bright morning, that causes him again to remember her, to project her onto the unstable and inconstant little screen of images where he flashes, momentarily, the tiny spotlight of his attention. Without, as they say, a doubt, the same impulse that moved Isabel to utter her startling and mysterious comment, has caused him, suddenly, to get off the bus, cross the boulevard, buy the cigarettes, and begin walking, for no reason, to the south.

Every fifteen meters, a *tipa* tree rises at the edge of the sidewalk, and its branches almost touch those that, at the same height, grow from a tree on the opposite sidewalk. In the spaces between the trim branches, patches of blue sky can be made out, and on the street and the opposite sidewalk the bright stretches outnumber those in shadow. Puerile, in every color, at a constant speed, the cars run in both directions: those coming toward Leto on his side, and those that, likewise, follow his direction, alongside the other sidewalk. Flashes and shadows from leaves and branches alternate fleetingly over the chrome of the bodywork, over the painted molding and the glass, as they travel down the tree-lined street. Other pedestrians—not many, because of the distance from the city center as well as the relatively early hour—walk, alone or in groups, lost in thought or conversation, along the sidewalks. Another thirty meters and Leto will reach the corner.

It is, as we know, the morning: though it doesn't make sense to say so, since it is always the same time—once again the sun, since the earth revolves, apparently, has given the illusion of rising, from the direction they call the east, in the blue expanse we call sky, and, little by little, after the dawn, after daybreak, it has reached a spot high enough, halfway in its ascent let's say, so that, through the intensity of what we call light, we refer, to the state that results, as the morning—a spring morning when, again, though, as we were saying, it is always the same time, the temperature has been rising, the clouds have been dissipating, and the trees which, for some reason, had been losing their leaves bit by bit, have begun to bloom again, to blossom once more, although, as we were saying, it is always the same, the only Time and, so to speak, from equinox to solstice, it's the same, no? As I was saying, we call it *a* because it seems like there have been many, because of the changes, which we name and presume to perceive—a dazzling spring morning, forming for three or four days, since the end of the last rains

7

in September or October that wiped clean the final traces of winter from a sky that grew warmer and clearer each day. Leto feels neither good nor bad: he walks oblivious, in the morning, in the center of a material horizon that sends him, in constant waves, sounds, textures, flashes, odors. He is submerged in this horizon and is, at the same time, its center; if, suddenly, he disappeared, the center would change location.

For this reason, in order to prove that he suffered so much, some three months before she had found a lump in her right breast, *like the seed from a paradise tree*, and had begun to worry. Charo, the elder cousin who, lacking a boyfriend or husband, had acquired, at forty-five, an approximate understanding of nearly every illness in order to fill the cavity of any other curiosity or *sed non satiata*, had insisted that she make an appointment with a specialist—an *illuminary*, his aunt Charo had trilled, dithyrambic, though she was not, in reality, anything more than his second cousin. Leto thinks: *It wasn't wrong to have told Charo either. It's as if you were to suggest to a madam that you had some spare cash you'd like to spend on an escort.* Because of his international conferences, the dinner-conferences at the Rotary, and the rows of the cancerous and its candidates leafing through old magazines in the waiting room of his office, the specialist had only recently seen her, a month after her discovery, and after looking her over, examining her, carefully and skillfully, had told her, with distracted lightheartedness, that, *in his modest opinion, there was no reason to worry, and that a more meticulous exam or a biopsy were not justified.* The lump, *the size of a seed from a paradise tree*, according to Isabel, or *of an acorn*, according to Charo, who, for some obscure and undetermined reason, had also performed an examination, did not reveal itself to the fingers of the specialist, which, though they searched and searched again did not find a single notable hardness in Isabel's now, on the contrary, somewhat shapeless breasts—not in the right or the left. The specialist sat down at his desk and had begun to fill out a form, and, while she dressed, standing near the bed, Isabel had begun an inquiry full of allusions, to which the specialist would respond with ambiguous monosyllables, whose meaning, like those of the blotches in a psychological test, depended on what pre-existed in the observer. According to Isabel, upon seeing her come in, the specialist had given her significant looks, as she had presented herself with her married name, and her husband's case, so recent, and so sudden too, as often happens with young people, had probably not been forgotten. Because when she came in they had made her fill out a form where she wrote that she was born in Rosario, and since *he* would surely have come from Rosario for a consultation, the specialist could not have missed the connection. Of course, because of professional confidentiality— *yes, they have that categorical imperative*, Charo had confirmed—the specialist could not make it plainly known that he had been to see him during his frequent trips to the city and that, after having examined him, had found that incurable illness, but his responses, deliberately imprecise, were nevertheless significant enough to dismiss any of her leftover doubts. *But she's not too sure she'll be believed because she insists so much*, thinks Leto. That same night she had called Rosario to confirm it with Lopecito who, protective and attentive, had interrupted her revelations with a firm, *Don't waste your money. I'll call you back*, so they hung up and a minute later, when the phone rang from Rosario, she picked up, impatient and satisfied, conveying, in complete detail, the confirmation of her suspicions which, in a discreet but unmistakable way, the specialist had given her. Lopecito, who from the age of twenty-five had begun, in a tacit way, to court her, who had seen her marry his best friend, and who had even been a witness in the civil ceremony, who had seen her have two miscarriages in the second or third month before finally getting pregnant with Leto and bringing him into the light of the world, who had been the impassive confidant for the matrimonial lurch of both man and wife and who, the year before, had finally seen her widowed, being left in the awkward position of eternal pretender and of her husband's childhood friend whose world was coming up roses—Lopecito, no?—who between his distribution of two or three television brands and his duties as a member of the Rosario Central Festival planning committee, had found enough time to make their leaving Rosario possible without agreeing with the decision, the move, the costs, he had recommended her as a saleswoman in an appliance store and Leto as bookkeeper for two businesses in the city center, he had administered, through his relationships *downtown*, as he liked to say, her late husband's pension, and would come to visit them from Rosario every fifteen days, sleeping in a hotel so it would be clear to everyone that they wouldn't soil the memory of a loved one, likewise feeling enough devotion to Isabel to accept, despite representing in the eyes of the world the voice of moderation, each of her points of view, her discrete extravagance, her constant struggle to deny the obvious, her repeated interpretations among which the theory of an incurable illness *isn't even*, Leto thinks as he reaches the corner, *the least bit preposterous.*

The corner, where the two lines of cars driving on San Martín in both directions slow down, is particular in this way: because the cross street runs east to west, the shade of the row of houses disappears, and as there is nothing to intercept the rays of the sun shining above the street, the street and sidewalk are now filled with light, so as to make Leto's shadow, which has appeared in a sudden way, only slightly shorter than his body, project itself onto the gray pavement and fall to the west. When Leto is about to step off the gray sidewalk into the cobbled street, his shadow is broken by the cable guardrail and continues to be projected onto the even cobblestones of the street. The shadow moves forward, slightly oblique to the body, breaks again at the cable guardrail on the opposite sidewalk and when Leto's shoes touch the opposite pavement, continues to slide across the sidewalk until Leto enters the shade of the row of houses and his own shadow disappears. The square is deserted—not abandoned, but deserted—empty, without the presence of people (apart from Leto) who, like him, are also the center of a horizon that, as they move, moves with them. After walking a few meters under the trees, he sees appear, suddenly, on the next corner, a boy on a bicycle who has turned the corner of the cross street, advancing toward him on the sidewalk. It proceeds with that kind of undulation bicycles have when they are not moving very quickly, and whose equilibrium, which the cyclist recovers with every pedal stroke, is not the principal consequence but the transient and fragile phase of a more ample and more complete movement. The cyclist, no more than nine or ten years old, his legs barely able to reach the pedals when they are at the lowest point of their circular path, moves, in spite of his slowness, much more quickly than Leto, whose pace, neither slow nor fast, has not varied since he crossed the boulevard and began walking down San Martín. As he approaches—his velocity, while constant, is increased by Leto's opposite movement—Leto can hear, each time more clearly, the complex sounds issuing from the bicycle, metallic squeaking, the hum of rubber against the pavement, the stretching and creaking of leather, pedals, spokes, cables in an invariable sequence that repeats periodically because of the regularity of the movement. The bicycle passes between Leto and the row of houses, and the series of sounds, which had reached, arriving next to Leto, its maximum intensity, begins to diminish behind him until finally it is no longer heard. Leto does not even turn and, strictly speaking—as they say, no?—they have barely seen each other, moving in opposite directions and each taking his own horizon with him.

When he hears the second whistle, Leto realizes that, despite his distraction, he had also heard the first, and turns around. The thick arms, slightly elevated from the body, are buoyed in the air, and the head, which thinks itself elegant, and which certainly is, bobs a little, now that the Mathematician, in the stooped shoulders moving several meters ahead of him, has recognized Leto and begun to whistle so he'll stop and wait for him. At the moment he recognizes him, Leto thinks: *If he has just turned the corner, which is probably the case, since he lives on that street, he should have just passed the bicycle since, because it's out of sight, the cyclist must also have turned the corner.* The Mathematician, a head taller than him, arrives and holds out his hand. *What's up?*

he says. Without looking him in the eye, Leto responds vaguely. *Well,* he says, *we're walking along.*

The Mathematician lets a hesitant smile linger. To Leto, his white moccasins, like his tan, seem premature, but the Mathematician knows that he just returned from Europe, where he spent three months touring factories, beaches, museums, and monuments with the annual Chemical Engineering alumni group. *They're out of control since they saw* La Dolce Vita, he heard Tomatis say, with distracted disdain, the week before. And it was Tomatis, meanwhile, or so Leto heard him tell someone, who began calling him the Mathematician. *He's really not a bad guy,* he often says, *kind of a snob at worst, but, frankly, I don't know what kind of sick satisfaction he gets from the physical sciences. Haven't you noticed his tone when he talks to you about relativity theory? Because of his height he already has a tendency to look down on the world, but I'm just saying maybe it's not our fault that multiplying the mass of a body with the speed of light squared equals the energy needed for the complete disintegration of that body?* For a few seconds, the two young men, one tanned, blonde, tall, muscular, and handsome, dressed completely in white, including the moccasins he is wearing, sock-less, the other thinner, wearing glasses, with thick brown, well-combed hair, whose clothes are from first glance cheaper than the other's, fifty centimeters apart, they remain silent, without animosity but without much to say either, each of them lost in his own thoughts, an internal swamp that stands in sharp contrast to the bright exterior, from which it was costing them an indescribable effort to emerge and where, because of the tendency to perceive the foreign with a rose tint, as they say, they simultaneously think that other would never be trapped. Without noticing, Leto, who, not knowing what to do, reaches his hand into his shirt pocket to remove the cigarettes, thinks that, for some reason, he is excluded from many of the worlds the Mathematician frequents, that the Mathematician is a species of astral being who belongs to a galaxy where everything is precise and luminous and that he, on the other hand, slogs through a viscous and darkened zone, which he is seldom able to leave, while the Mathematician, in spite of his elegant head, which is full of recent and colorful memories of Vienna, Amsterdam, Cannes, Málaga, and Spoleto, feels like he has been floating in the stratosphere for three months and that Leto, Tomatis, Barco, the Garay twins, and everyone else has taken advantage of his absence to live it up in the city. Finally, and concentrating on the act of opening his pack of cigarettes, in order not to be obligated to raise his head, Leo murmurs: *And Europe, how was it?*

—I hate resorting to a platitude, says the Mathematician offhandedly, but she's a decadent old madam.

Leto does not suspect that, beneath the apparent disinterest and the generous estimation of those who have not traveled, the Mathematician fears that an over-admiring appreciation will disqualify him. And he hears him add: *Just now, I'm off to distribute the press release from the Association to the papers. Goes without saying that whorehouses don't figure in the expense report.* Without realizing that the Mathematician is holding his unlit pipe by the stem, in his right hand, which is hanging against the seam of his pants, and that because of this, with a wave of his free hand, he rejects his offer, Leto, after tapping the bottom of the cigarette pack to remove three or four from the opening he has made in the top edge, holds out the pack toward the Mathematician, offering him one. So that the reason for his rejection is clear, the Mathematician brings the pipe to his mouth and holds it pressed between his ultra-white and even teeth. *To stay so tan and so healthy,* thinks Leto, *he probably went rowing the day after he got back.* While Leto lights the cigarette, the Mathematician, taking advantage of his distraction, induces him, by taking a few steps himself, to keep walking. They continue—or they pass—thanks to the faculty they possess, who knows why, from one point to another in space, gaining ground, so to speak, although the points between those they cross are all, with the two of them between, in each of the points, and in all of them at once, in the same place. *No, seriously though*, says the Mathematician, *it's an experience one should have*—and what he calls experience are those

13

memories that, although fresh and colorful, are no more accessible to himself than a packet of postcards of Amsterdam, of Vienna, of Capri, of Cadaqués, of San Gimignano. Siena is a rosy mirage, floating in the warm fog of the afternoon; Paris, an unexpected rainstorm; London, a problem finding hotel rooms and some manuscripts in the British Museum. While he listens, Leto puts images to the names that echo in the warm morning, and these images, which he forms with assorted memories that have been rescued from disparate experiences and have no real connection to the names he hears, are neither more nor less pertinent or relevant than the Mathematician's memories, which are unable to render the thing more accessible even when they come from what the Mathematician could call his experience. The names of cities pass as though fixed to an endless mountain range or to a carousel, in the same way that, periodically, in spite of the variations and supplements, sooner or later the same names reappear in the memory of the Mathematician, who makes them sound to Leto's ears as though they came from an instrument: La Baule, even though it was the middle of summer the sea was frigid; Prague, a great portion of Kafka's work makes sense when you get there; Bruges, they painted what they saw; Paris, an unexpected rainstorm. Suddenly the Mathematician, who is walking closest to the wall, jumps sideways, pushing aside Leto who, staggering, stumbles a little but keeps walking: as they arrived at the corner, the Mathematician, concentrating on his story, was startled to see appear, abruptly, although always maintaining his placid and undulating pedaling, the kid on the bicycle who, in the time it took them to walk to the corner, has gone around the block. A furious, somewhat ostentatious silence interrupts, after the scare, the chain of recollections from the Mathematician, who stops and turns and sees move away, on the gray sidewalk, under the trees, the slow bicycle with its metallic, discrete, and complicated sounds. Leto, who has kept walking, gains a few steps on him and stops to wait, just beyond the oblique border of the shade of the houses. The Mathematician reaches him, smiling and shaking his head. *If he'd run you over*, says Leto*, he'd have stained your pants.*

—I'd kick him to pieces, says the Mathematician, showing with his playful tone that there's no way he would. He seems less like a flesh and bone person than one of those archetypes you see on billboards, those for whom every contingency inherent to humanity has disappeared. His physical appearance, perfected by his European tan and the whiteness of his clothing, is nothing but the consequence of his biographical perfections: in spite of having been a star on the university's rugby club, he has, as Tomatis puts it, *something slightly more dense filling his head than usually fills up a rugby ball.* Though more than a few hectares in the north of the province, near Tostado, belong to him, the Mathematician's father, a scrupulous *yrigoyenista*, abhors oligarchs and soldiers and is one of the old liberal lawyers whose name appears at the bottom of the *habeas corpus* appeals of almost all of the political prisoners in the city, and the Mathematician, unlike his older brother, who is also a lawyer but who has accepted official posts in almost every government—the Mathematician, I was saying, no?—has not only followed the liberal tradition of his father and his maternal grandfather but also, at some point, four or five years back, was a founding member of one of the Trotskyite or socialist reform groups that, after 1955, began to proliferate. But the Mathematician is a thinker and not an activist, a scrutinizer, not an organizer, and not a practician but a theoretician. He likes treatises more than gatherings and prefers futurist manifestos to the builders of the future. His engineering studies are, no doubt, the result of some familial strategy aimed at confronting, with the corresponding diploma, the national development that will one day obligate the heirs to move from passive ownership of the land to industrial investment. *They can be as liberal as you want*, Tomatis likes to say, malevolently, *but they don't do anything without a motive.* The Mathematician, who possibly intuits skepticism or mistrust in Tomatis's wit, continues impassively in the role he's assigned himself:

the supplier—without, in reality, it ever having been lost since no one noted its absence—of a logical rigor and an exactitude in information that, because of his insistence, makes him annoying to argue with. Actually what Tomatis faults the Mathematician for is his literalness. If, for example, in the middle of a discussion Tomatis cites a German philosopher, by the following week the Mathematician has read all of his work, and he comes back with the intention of returning to the point where the discussion left off the week before. Tomatis has cited this philosopher offhandedly, not because he considers wasting your youth and frying your eyelashes reading his treatises essential, but he is too vain to sidestep the argument. Because of his credulity, the Mathematician is more informed than the rest of them, since all it takes is hearing someone mention an author for him to read their complete works and reappear fifteen days later, refreshed and calm, to have a conversation about them. *To be fair, there isn't much to fault him for*, thinks Leto. Because he isn't even someone who wants to win an argument at any cost; he is kind, modest, and generous. *Except,* thinks Leto, *except when he resorts, without being aware of it, I'm sure, to his magnificent axioms, postulates, and definitions. Then he starts acting like the Werewolf during a full moon, or Jack the Ripper in the company of hookers.*

While they cross, the Mathematician condescends to re-list, without much conviction, the names that come with fixed and simplified expressions and memories glued to the back: Rome, he imagined it differently; Vienna, all the locals seem to believe in terminal analysis; Florence, they also painted what they saw; Avignon, a murderous heat; Geneva, the paved barnyard; London, a problem finding hotel rooms and some manuscripts in the British Museum. They leave behind the intersection, the cable guardrail, the angled sun, and enter the cool shade of the next block. An old man is opening the shutters of a window on the ground floor. The Mathematician who, in an abrupt way, cut off his story a few seconds before, greets him with a tilt of the head and continues walking, pensively. In spite of the difference in height,

Leto and the Mathematician walk at the same pace, neither slow nor fast, so well coordinated that it is impossible to tell if the Mathematician is reducing the length of his strides to match them with Leto's steps or if, on the contrary, Leto's skinnier and shorter legs are accommodating, without visible effort, the step of the rugby-man who's so adept at the *scientia recte judicandi*. For a few meters, they don't seem to know what to talk about. We know what was said above, no?—that the Mathematician, fearing that excessive enthusiasm for his European tour will disqualify him somewhat among those who stayed behind, shares his memories reticently. And yet, in the anxiety of those who have been away and fear that reality has been more intense in their absence, he has been holding, since he met up with Leto, the question he does not dare to formulate, so as not to reveal an excessive interest, just like a jealous person who looks for the opportune moment to begin his interrogation by dissembling with a series of disinterested and banal questions. Meanwhile, Leto is thinking: *I'll need to ask Lopecito if he believed it. Still, he's too meticulous to reject the idea flat out. He has been, for twenty-five years, the ham in the sandwich. And, ever since he died, things have only gotten worse. He could favor mother's argument, though even then she wouldn't be sure to get what she expected without overcommitting herself since they played house, but if she accepts it deep down, the way she does publicly, she risks the supposedly incurable patient laughing at her from the other side.*

Observing him, discreetly and somewhat shyly, the Mathematician detects Leto's withdrawn expression and takes the opportunity to say: *And around here, how was it all this time?* biting the unlit pipe so hard that, instead of speaking, he sputters the question through his clenched teeth and tongue which, inhibited, wraps around the pipe stem and makes it vibrate against the row of teeth. The Mathematician ignores the fact that Leto has more than enough reasons, though he has been around, to feel much more excluded from the bursts of passion that reality might arbitrarily dispense among the circles he frequents: he, to begin with, has only lived in the city a few months and is, therefore, a mere neophyte, a newcomer, and, because he is only twenty-one, is much younger than several of the youngest; he almost never joins a discussion, and if he is invited anywhere it's only as an appendix to Tomatis; he's the only other source of income for a widowed mother, and has to work several account books to support her, and something inside him, surely, like a woodworm in furniture, pre-emptively hollows out any possible passion he may have, which somewhat explains his absences and silences—though he would like it, true enough, if once in a while, something were possible. Leto, allowing a quantity of smoke to spill out through his half-opened lips, from which he has just withdrawn, with careful fingers, the cigarette, responds: he has hardly seen anyone; he rarely goes out; he has almost nothing to report from these past three months.

Imagine a gambler who, for some time, has held the card that will let him win the game but which he cannot play for many rounds because none of the other players have given him an opportunity to do so. Round after round the gambler throws down useless, inconsequential cards that have no influence on the course of the game until, suddenly, the combination he needs appears on the table, allowing him to throw down, euphorically and decisively, the winning card. Leto's timid confession has put the Mathematician in this dominant position.

—What? he says. Weren't you at Washington's birthday party?

Leto shakes his head no, while he thinks: *And even today, this morning, when she says that he suffered so much it's less to remind me of that suffering than to control whether I believe her or not.* And the Mathematician, observing him without looking, instead looking straight ahead at the sidewalk, but observing him nonetheless with the right side of his body, which is to say, the side that is almost grazing, during the walk, the left side of Leto's body, the Mathematician, I was saying, no?, at the same time, although it is always, as I was saying just now, the same, thinks: *He wasn't invited.*

Leto surfaces as though from under water. He has been thinking, remembering his mother, the death of his father, and Lopecito, submerging himself for a few seconds in those thoughts and memories as though into a subterranean canal parallel to the spring air, and in emerging, in surfacing, he finds himself with this good-looking blonde guy, some twenty-seven years old, dressed completely in white, who Tomatis calls the Mathematician, who is just back from Europe and is out to distribute the press release for the Chemical Engineering Students Association to the papers, who has just, also, a few seconds ago, asked him if he was at Washington's birthday party, and as he, with a shake of his head, has responded no, he now fears that the other, who seems to be observing him, is observing him not with contempt, but with disbelief and something like pity. *In the first place, they wouldn't need to invite me. I could have gone if I had wanted, without needing an invitation. But in any case, I wouldn't have wanted an invitation because it would have meant that they don't consider me close enough that it would be a given that I would have to go. But, given that, I have to submit to the facts: I wasn't invited.*

—I couldn't make it either. That day we were visiting factories in Frankfurt. I couldn't hop a jet from Frankfurt because they don't have direct flights to Rincón, says the Mathematician. But I got the full version, a fresh, subtitled, technicolor copy.

Maintaining his lighthearted façade, he squeezes the pipe a bit more with this teeth, compelled by a memory that returns, suddenly, and which still stings him, one of those memories or emotions about which he likes to say, with an ironic wrinkling of his nose, *if they aren't measurable, at least with our current understanding, there doesn't seem to be a reason why they couldn't enter into some general theory or some structure that's subject to mathematical formulae one of these days.*

—You don't say, he hears Leto say.

—Yes, yes, I heard all about it, he hears himself say in turn.

The memory is like a photograph or a shadowy image stamped into the inside of his head, and the emotions and feelings of humiliation and rage form several black-bordered, jagged holes, as if the image had been punctured at many points of its surface with the ember of a cigarette. Three or four years earlier, a poet from Buenos Aires came to the city to give a conference. The Mathematician, who had been corresponding with him for six or seven months regarding a problem of versification, waited anxiously for his arrival, and had annotated a list of discussion points which, after the conference, he hoped to address in order over dinner with the poet. Shortly before the end of the debate that followed the conference, the Mathematician had left to get the car from his father; he hadn't been able to loan it to the Mathematician earlier because he didn't get back from Tostado until 9:00. His father was a little late, and when the Mathematician returned with the car to the lecture hall, it was closed. A guard told him that the lecturer had left with four or five of the organizers to a party, or to eat something— basically he wasn't sure where. The Mathematician felt the first bolt of rage in that moment because, before leaving to get the car, he had taken the precaution of letting several of the organizers know about his momentary absence, asking them to wait for him, but not feeling very secure because he knew that the organizers belonged to the class of people who kidnap celebrities who come from the capital, and since he didn't spend much time with them, because he didn't like to move in semiofficial circles, they wouldn't go out of their way to consider his requests. The Mathematician, when he learned of the poet's visit, had begun working hard, for at least a month and a half, on problems of versification. His thesis was that each meter corresponded to a specific emotion and that you could devise a notational system, if you sufficiently diversified the meters whose combinations were not already too subtle, which only applied to the metric use of pure sounds, for the poem to transmit the desired emotions. The Mathematician was probably only twenty-three at the time; he considered himself a simple theoretician and would have liked the poet, who was twenty years older and had acquired a great reputation, to apply his theories, like the geologist who forms a hypothesis about the composition of the lunar surface and sends an astronaut to the moon to verify it. The Mathematician left the conference hall, already partially blinded by rage, and began looking for the poet. He started crisscrossing the city in his father's car, from one end to the other: he would leave the engine running in front of a restaurant, in front of a bar, would get out to look for them, the poet and the group of organizers, and when he didn't find them would move on to the next bar and repeat the same routine; he tried to disguise his rage behind a calm and mundane façade, passing his indifferent gaze over the lively tables as if he was looking for an empty one or was simply curious. That he was able to maintain his elegance and indifferent façade is admirable because with every passing minute his fury and indignation multiplied. He started to feel like the inside of his head was boiling. After having fruitlessly visited every open restaurant, he went into a bar, asked for a beer, the phone book, and a fistful of coins and began calling the homes of the organizers, hoping that they were at one of their houses or that someone in their family knew where the hell they had gone. But no one knew anything or, if they did know, did not seem inclined to tell him. The Mathematician sensed the unmistakable echoes of some sort of instruction or collusion in their casual responses. Everyone knew, the whole city knew, and, intentionally, concealed it. After all those useless rounds, he started driving the streets at random, hoping to come across the poet and his retinue, and more than once, because of false alarms, he found himself chasing some car that seemed to belong to one of the organizers at full speed or accosting a startled group of people on a dark street. *The Fourteen Points Toward All Future Meter*, which he had taken the trouble to elaborate and type out over the preceding weeks, were just then nothing more than a sheet folded in fourths, lost in one of the compartments of his wallet at the bottom of the interior pocket of his coat. He had lost all subjectivity and had become a purely external being who, no longer reasoning or applying any agency to reality, was instead the passive object of a fixed system that diverted him from his self in the same way that the wind diverts the ping pong ball from its trajectory despite the force and accuracy of the player's shot. Finally, in one of his comings and goings down the dark streets, down the illuminated avenues, after passing the same places for the hundredth time, he remembered that, before the conference, one of the organizers, speaking to another, had mentioned a tennis club where his—the Mathematician's—brother the lawyer was a member, but that he, from disdain for the *bloodlust bourgeoisie*, as he liked, not without reason, to call them, had not joined. A guard stopped him at the entrance and forced him to wait. The Mathematician stood at the gate to the darkened and deserted tennis courts, beyond which he could see, behind a stand of pines, the illuminated windows of the buildings. A yellow rectangle, taller and wider than the windows, formed in the darkness, behind the pines, when the poet, followed by the guard, opened the door to the facilities and approached the entrance gate, crossing the darkness in the pines and the reddish half-light reflected off the clay-covered surface of the tennis courts. He was eating a chicken thigh as he came, and his free hand must have been covered in grease, judging by the way he kept it stiff and far from his body, the fingers straight and separated, so as to not stain his pants. The Mathematician thought he was coming to meet him and bring him to the dinner where, for a while, they could discuss the *Fourteen Points*, and so he waited with an understanding and relieved smile, but in reality the poet was coming to explain that it had been impossible to wait for him, that the dinner was very boring though there was nothing for it but to stay to the end and that maybe later, in some bar, when he had unburdened himself of the group, they might be able to have a drink and, in his words, *bring into the world, together, the highly anticipated definitive text on the theory of versification.* Before the Mathematician could offer an objection, the poet had already disappeared, after offering the name of a bar through a mouth full of chicken, skirting the tennis courts with a sure step, erasing himself for a moment under the black mass of the pines, his silhouette reappearing in the yellow rectangle that formed again for a moment between the illuminated windows and which eventually, after a few seconds, disappeared. The Mathematician stood motionless, with his gaze fixed on some dark point of sky between the entrance gate and the multiplied blackness of the pines, sensing on the back of his neck the satisfied look of the guard, whose instinctive act of blocking his entrance had just been validated by the fleeting visit of the honoree. Then he turned around, walked away without a word, and, taking his car key from his pocket, stopped again after a few meters, holding the key in the air, positioned to enter the lock, shaking his head from time to time, as if debating with himself. In reality, the poet's unexpected attitude had left him incapable of a reaction, as if his internal life ran on electricity and, two or three minutes before, someone had stepped out of the darkness and unplugged him. But really it wasn't more than an obstruction, or a cooling, the kind that happens to certain motors that, as arbitrarily as they have stopped, start up again: when he resumed walking, his steps were no longer distracted but furious; he slammed the car door shut and, after starting the engine, drove away, but not before swerving around the club's entrance with a lot of noise from the motor, brakes, and tires. He drove, deafened by his indignant and tumultuous thoughts, which went in and out, colliding in his head as if, as opposed to a few moments before, the motor was now overheating and about to explode. He went straight to his house and, since at that time he still lived with his family, crossed the entryway almost without stopping and shut himself in his room. Now, that is to say in the now following the now when he had turned on the car and the now when he had driven home, no?, in that now, I mean to say, he tried to stay calm, to find the details in the situation that would allow him to transform his fury into disdain and his disdain into self-satisfaction. But he couldn't pull it off—just the opposite, little by little, and only after getting undressed and throwing himself into bed, he began asking himself if he wasn't misjudging the poet when he'd clearly given him proof of his trust and friendship by coming to the gate to explain the awkward situation he was in and making a date for later, and if he wasn't making a mistake by standing him up instead of waiting for him at the bar like they agreed. The time they'd planned to meet was approaching and, like someone in love, the Mathematician could not figure out what to do, changing his mind every fifteen or twenty seconds, pulled this way and that like a dry leaf in the afternoon wind by those emotions and feelings that, *if they aren't measurable, at least with our current understanding, there doesn't seem to be a reason why they couldn't enter into some general theory or some structure that's subject to mathematical formulae one of these days.* Finally, after having decided with solid arguments that he would not go, he jumped up from the bed, got dressed and left for the meeting at the bar. He arrived fifteen minutes early, glancing quickly and discreetly from the car, before going to park, to see if the poet had already arrived. The Mathematician sat down at the bar to wait. To kill time, he took out the text of the *Fourteen Points* and started editing it here and there so that, when the time came to discuss it, every possible objection would be foreseen and pre-empted. For some twenty minutes, the Mathematician, thanks to his complete concentration on the text of the *Fourteen Points*, kept *those emotions and feelings which, if they aren't etc., etc.*, no?, in the darkness outside the crystalline and well-illuminated cube that occupied the complete space of his mind. But as time passed, the polished and transparent surfaces began to fissure, leaking in, little by little, the indistinct and viscous outside world that, for some twenty minutes, he had seemed to overpower. Since it was now past midnight, the bar filled with people who were leaving the theaters and coming in to drink their last coffee before going to bed, commenting on the movie, discussing hopeless snoops, or making plans for the next day, but around one the bar started to empty again, until at one-thirty the only people left were the Mathematician, a couple fighting in whispers in a corner, and a belligerent drunk at the counter. Finally the drunk was gently driven out by the bartender, and the woman, in a burst of rage, stood up and walked out so that the man with her had no choice but to pay quickly at the register and run after her, and the Mathematician, who was on his second cup of coffee, was left alone in the bar where, discreetly but firmly, they had begun to set the chairs, upside down, on the tables, and to mop the floor. After a while, since it was now two in the morning and the poet had said *eleven forty-five or twelve,* and since the table where he sat was the only narrow islet surrounded by a sea of upside down chairs on tables and the floor where his feet were placed the only fragment, two meters square, where the floor did not shine, ready for the opening the following day, the Mathematician folded the *Fourteen Points* in fourths, picked up his unlit pipe, paid for his two coffees, and went out into the street. A new feeling was mixing with his humiliation and rage: the desperation we feel when we realize that the external world's plans do not bear our desires in mind, no matter their intensity. The moment he left, the lights in the bar went out behind him. If not for the traffic lights and, from time to time, for the fleeting headlights of a passing car, he could have sworn that, in the whole universe, the only illuminated light hung inside his head and that something, in passing, had given it a shake and now lights and shadows shook violently in that too-narrow ring where thoughts, memories, emotions, fast and uncontrollable, exploded and disappeared like flares or grenades. He parked in front of his house. He closed the car door and stood for a moment on the dark sidewalk. For a while now time had been running backward, and just like a traveler, who begins to see an unexpected landscape through the window, in a moment of panic, understands that he's on the wrong train, the Mathematician began to sense the person he'd thought he was being dismantled piece by piece, and replaced by floating loose fragments and splinters of an unknown self, fragments that have their own familiar quality, but seem in their ideas, emotions, and habitual feelings, archaic and excessive. He tiptoed through the dark house, went into his room, and, without turning on the light, undressed and went to bed. Every so often, sparks of tranquility made him say to himself, *Come on, come on, it's not worth getting bent out of shape over a slight or, even, over a series of unfortunate circumstances that no one's to blame for,* but because they were fleeting, they entered the whirlwind and were transformed into the archaic kind, tormenting him, so that, unable to sleep, as the dawn paled the bedroom through the skylight and the blinds, he lost his sense of reality, and the few ties binding him to the known world were loosed. Laying in the dark bed, he understood for the first time in his life, and at his own expense, that with enough pressure, like physical suffering, the spirit can also start to fissure at some unnamable and empty point, practically abstract, and what you could at one time call shame, guilt, humiliation, transforms, multiplied and approaching bottomless, into pins and needles, thumping, agitation, stabbing pain, shudders. For hours he tossed in bed, his eyes wide open, run through by sparking, incessant fragments that burned him from the inside and caused him so much suffering that, much later, when in spite of every effort to suppress them, he recalled them, a singular and recurrent image appeared to him: a human face that someone was slicing to pieces, slowly and deliberately, with glass from a broken bottle. Finally, around 11:00 in the morning, he fell asleep. As he had the habit of spending whole nights studying in his room, no one bothered him during the day, so that around 6:00, little by little, he woke up, thinking that he was surfacing on a different world or that he, in any case, wasn't the same, and for a long time, whenever he ran into one of the conference organizers he tried to hide or, if he couldn't, assumed an attitude of exaggerated jauntiness, without allowing the least bit of reproach to show in his face, to the point that, for some months, his greatest preoccupation was not to fundamentally interrogate himself about what had happened, but to avoid at all cost anyone noticing. And it worked. That burning, which for weeks had transformed his insides into an open wound and that, until it scarred, had been the complete opposite of the clean, tranquil, and well-proportioned external self that proffered smiling, precise statements—that kind of burn, I was saying, no?—which, bearing in mind the insignificance of the spark that started it, seemed to have been generated spontaneously, had gone unnoticed, just like the pain of the memory, to the rest of the world. And he, secretly, to himself, when he measured it from a distance, referred to those days, ironically, and particularly, as The Incident.

—Oh yeah? says Leto. Who did you hear it from?

—Botón, says the Mathematician.

Leto nods. That name, or nickname rather, *Button*, appears every so often in conversation, but to Leto it doesn't evoke any precise image because he's never seen its owner. He seems to be from Entre Ríos, to study law, to have been a reformist leader, to be seen a lot at *vernissages* and conferences, and to be a guitar player. Three or four times he's heard Tomatis say, speaking to a third person, things like, *Last night we ran into Botón falling down at a bar at the arcade*, or once, referring to a painter, *Botón cleans her pipes*. But Leto has never seen him. In fact, when he hears the nickname, the first thing he imagines is an actual button, black with four holes in the center, and only after a quick correction begins to see the image of a person, a guy with straight hair and dark, pockmarked skin, which doesn't correspond to any experience but which makes up, as a stand in, for the absence of experience. *There always has to be something*, thinks Leto. *If there's nothing, you think that there's nothing and that thought is something.*

Yes, Botón indeed, the Mathematician has just repeated. Botón who, as it happened, ran into El Gato Garay at the School of Fine Arts and promised to bring his guitar but, since he hadn't gone back home after the meeting, hadn't actually brought the guitar and, after running some errands downtown, was the first to arrive in Colastiné, where the party was. He had bought three bottles of white wine. *In case they ran out*, says the Mathematician. *He's always afraid they'll run out.* According to Botón—and, afterward, according to the Mathematician, no?—since it couldn't have been later than 5:00 and the sun was still high, and Basso, the owner of the ranch, had just gotten up from his siesta, they had gone behind the house to pick vegetables. According to the Mathematician, Basso has a vegetable garden, raises chickens, and, with some money his maternal grandmother left him, can get by without working. Leto, who doesn't know either Basso or Botón, nor has he ever been to that house, sees two guys picking at black earth, backlit by the falling sun at the end of a mild winter, in the back of a patio whose image comes, without his realizing, from two or three different ranches he's visited, in Colastiné and Rincón, since he moved from Rosario. And the spot where that ranch sits, as the name Colastiné includes a physical area that extends beyond his experience, is an approximate point, more or less imagined, which Leto places, without knowing or even asking himself why, in a border region between his experience and the many purely imaginary fragments associated with the word Colastiné, and which he has never seen.

But soon enough, the Mathematician says, the others began to arrive: the Garay twins, who had wanted to use their house in Rincón but weren't able to at the last minute because their mother had decided to fumigate that week, and Cuello, the writer. *Cuello, like a neck?* says Leto. *Cuello, neck, that's right. The Centaur, Cuello the Centaur,* says the Mathematician. *The Centaur?* repeats Leto, intrigued. The Mathematician starts laughing. *Yeah. The Centaur. Because he's half man, half beast.* Leto laughs too, shaking his head. The laughter, expelled by human throats and which, at the same time, sparks in human eyes, spreads to the morning air outside. A pedestrian, passing them, a man in shirtsleeves carrying a portfolio under his arm, a chubby and all but bald forty-something, laughs too, without their noticing, infected by the burst of sudden laughter he has just heard. And the Mathematician continues: Cuello had come early, according to Botón (who had heard it from El Gato at Fine Arts) in case Noca, a fisherman, who was supposed to bring a load of catfish and perch, failed at the last minute, in which case, since he worked at the Butcher's Co-op, he—Cuello, no?—would be able to get some leftover steaks in a pinch. But Noca did not fail; almost at the same moment as Cuello, but coming from the coast and not the city, he'd arrived with two baskets full of perch and catfish which, after having caught, he'd taken the trouble to clean and gut in the river water. Judging by how the Mathematician tells it, Botón reported Noca's arrival in a manner resembling a Greek chorus. But as he relays it, the Mathematician, applying a rigorous protocol, dismantles his informant's version: Botón, a gringo, assumes a country style whenever he feels like it; he has an excessive taste for the barbarous; the real litmus test is his patent inability to dance a single step of the local folk dances, neither the *rasguido doble* nor the *chamarrita*. He knows Noca: instead of going to fish himself, he spends the day at the disco; he buys his catch from the real fishermen and resells them to the locals. He's going to end up a fruit wholesaler. Still, Botón's version, despite the Mathematician's categorical yet disinterested sociological objections, is the one Leto adopts and retains: the mythic Noca, hunting in the savage river, with timeless skill, for the last perch, prevails despite the collective displacement caused by the social mobility that produces incremental urbanization in the coastal region. But for the Mathematician, were he to notice, Leto's reticence would be neither here nor there: in reality, just as no art critic would think to disparage a portrait by asserting that the pictured model is ugly, or old, or a man or woman, and instead would attack the painter's technique, the Mathematician *couldn't give two shits about the object Noca in its objective objectivity*, he says, speaking poorly and in haste, but not so the description made by Botón, composed, according to the Mathematician, of stereotypical apriorisms and not of real empirical data. *Pure radiotelephonic material*, says the Mathematician.

Leto doesn't laugh now. The word radiotelephonic carries, as though pasted to its reverse side, the image of his father: but sadness isn't what has erased the smile from his face, but rather that somewhat mechanical gravity we assume when, with its insistent call, a thought or memory lures us toward the internal. For a few seconds, the Mathematician's narration, intense and highly detailed, becomes, little by little, loose words, sound without meaning, a distant murmur, as if, despite the identical rhythm of their walk and of their almost grazing arms, they are walking in dissociate spaces, proving how much a memory can separate two people until, finally, the call dissipates, not without leaving a vague pit inside him, like a stain on a white wall whose source you ignore, and eventually Leto smiles and becomes attentive again, and the words of the Mathematician who, as I was saying, no?, is telling

Leto about Washington Noriega's birthday, emerge from the horizon of sound and continue filling his head with not always adequate images. *And the twins* . . . says the Mathematician. They leave the sidewalk; a car stops at the corner, waiting to turn off San Martín; they hesitate, move around it, cross the intersection, which unlike the previous ones is paved and not cobblestone, and reach the opposite corner. They leave behind the sunlit street and continue under the shade of the trees. Since stepping into the street the Mathematician has been quiet, postponing what he was about to say and assuming a vigilant expression at seeing the car approach, an air of ostentatious hesitance when the car, stopping at the corner, blocks their path, and when they leave the car behind his hesitant air gives way to a distracted and reproachful shake of the head, which stops when they reach the opposite sidewalk. *The Garay twins*, Leto goes on thinking. *The twins*, continues the Mathematician when they enter the shade, *had gotten a hose to install a keg of import.* In the hypothetical courtyard, situated in a fantastical place, the human figures, simplified by Leto's imagination, disperse and scatter, active, outlined against the twilight: the Centaur, Basso's wife and their girls, Botón and Basso picking vegetables at the back, the twins installing, at the door to the kitchen, the keg, covering the hose with ice, and Noca's carriage leaving for the coast by a sandy road that Leto and Barco once walked, three months before, on a Sunday morning, to fish. And while the Mathematician dispenses new names, the image, more or less stable, made of assorted memories, is populated by new figures who come to occupy a place and function: Cohen and Silvia, his wife, Tomatis and Beatriz, Barco and La Chichito—the Cohens have come on their own—and Beatriz, Barco, and La Chichito, who had gone to pick up Tomatis at the paper, where he came out with a stack of day-old newspapers, for wrapping up the fish on the grill. According to Basso or Botón, says the Mathematician, Marcos Rosemberg had brought wine the night before, twenty-four bottles, and was in charge of going to find Washington and taking him to Basso's. Finally they arrive, just before nightfall; Marcos Rosemberg's sky-blue car parks in front of the ranch. To be exact, the Mathematician only says, *in Marcos Rosemberg's car,* but since Leto knows it, having gotten in three or four times, he imagines it the proper color, so that he sees, in the twilight, the sky-blue car arrive, undulating and quiet, shimmering slightly in the falling light, in front of the imaginary ranch. *They gave him a prodigious welcome,* says the Mathematician ironically, quoting Botón verbatim. Evidently, the tap to the keg was poorly installed—it came out all foam—so Barco, who is a genius with his hands, dismantled and reinstalled the tap. *Is it working? Is it?* inquired a circle of anxious faces. Finally it started to draw. Because it would cool off that night, they'd prepared a large table, which hadn't been set, under the pavilion, near the grill. Overcoming a moment of confusion, Leto is forced to install the unforeseen pavilion among the trees at the back. Nidia Basso and Tomatis were making a bitter salad in the kitchen. Cohen, the psychologist, who was going to be the cook, was lighting a fire in the grill. Barco was filling glasses with beer, and Basso cut slices of strong cheese and mortadella on a board and passed it around. Beatriz was rolling a cigarette. Washington, who had just relieved himself of his old *Aerolinas Argentinas* bag, which was full of books and papers, held a glass of beer in his hand, without deciding to take the first drink. And Botón? Botón, for hours, seemed to have removed himself from his story, as if the role of observer precluded his intervention in the action. Introducing a subtle variation, the Mathematician comments that, in fact, Botón's version of events demands, with Botón's personality in mind, a continuous revision, aimed at translating the scene *from the province of mythology to that of history,* but Leto, right then, from beneath the persistent image of a courtyard on the coast, on a winter evening, full of familiar and unfamiliar faces that combine vaguely, Leto, I was saying, no?, almost without realizing it, and even though it's always the same, is thinking about another time, about Isabel, the incurable illness, about Lopecito saying next to the closed casket, his eyes full of tears: *Your old man was a television pioneer. He had the inventor's gift. I owe him everything.*

—The idea to celebrate his sixty-fifth birthday was the twins', says the Mathematician. And you have to tip your hat to them for bringing together such a diverse crowd. But as the saying goes: not everyone there was someone nor was everyone who's someone there.

Leto looks at him: Is this a courtesy? But his look bounces off the perfect profile of the Mathematician who, with his gaze fixed on a point of air between the sidewalk and the treetops, somewhat absently, remembers: one night the previous summer when they were talking to Washington, Tomatis, and Silvia Cohen on the Cohen's terrace, and Tomatis, who had been filling his glass of gin on the rocks nonstop, had begun to curse the fate of humanity, purely in jest, raising a threatening fist to the starlit sky, and he, the Mathematician, had started pulling his leg, but Washington, without distracting himself very much from his conversation with Silvia Cohen, had told Tomatis, pretending to answer an honest theoretical question, to let it go, that from a logical point of view the person who purely and simply whimpers under the stars, frightened by the absurdity of the situation, is closer to the truth than someone who, trying to be a hero or a believer in historicity, attempts, in spite of everything, to raise a family or win a book award from the SADE. A quick, distracted and discreet smile flashes in the Mathematician's eyes. But, for some obscure reason, which even he is not conscious of, instead of telling that anecdote about Washington, he tells another, which he hasn't thought about in a long time and which, as he started telling it aloud, was free of its representations.

—I heard that once a fantasy story writer, who was visiting him from Buenos Aires, asked Washington if he ever thought of writing a novel. And Washington puts on a scared face, as if the writer were threatening him. After a moment he answers: I, like Heraclitus of Ephesus and general Mitre in Paraguay, shall leave but fragments.

They laugh, continue on. The Mathematician thinks: *Noca said that, if he came late, it was because one of his horses had stumbled.* And Leto: *He stole the love of his life, turned him into a bachelor, left him in charge of his family, and he says that he owes him everything.*

32

—Supposedly, says the Mathematician, Noca told Basso that he'd be late because one of his horses had stumbled and broken a leg. They stood, Botón had said, five or six around Cohen, chewing cubes of mortadella and drinking beer as an appetizer, and observing Cohen, who was arranging coals and firewood, not without making every kind of grimace and weeping from the heat and smoke from which the spectators remained at a comfortable distance. And when, according to Botón, Basso had related Noca's excuse, Cohen had abruptly interrupted his work and, without stopping from weeping and making painful grimaces, had planted himself, insistently, in front of Basso: *Since when do horses stumble?* he'd said.

—What? They don't stumble? Leto says.

—They stumble, they do, says the Mathematician placatingly. And after a doubtful pause: Actually, it depends.

—Depends on what? Leto says.

—Depends on what you mean by *stumble*.

According to the Mathematician, and always according to Botón, no?, Cohen's argument had been the following: if stumbling is an error, and horses, like every other animal, act purely on instinct, isn't it contradictory to attribute an error to instinct? An instinct would be something that, by definition, does not make mistakes. Instinct, Cohen said before returning triumphant to the flames, is pure necessity. When he turned his back on the spectators to work the fire with exaggerated attention, you could sense, to his satisfaction, a general silence. But a moment later Basso interjected again: He was only relating what Noca had told him, to let everyone know that, if he was late, it was because one of his horses had stumbled and . . . *Yeah, yeah, we get it*, interrupted, with lighthearted impatience, Barco, who had left his post at the keg and reached the pavilion just in time to hear Basso's story and Cohen's objection. What, in his opinion, you had to ask yourself instead, were two things: the first, if it's true that instinct doesn't make mistakes; the second, if stumbling is a mistake. A pensive silence fell over the gathering. Basso interjected again: The problem with Noca was you could never tell when he was mythologizing and when he was telling the truth. And because he didn't provide many details, they were forced to guess whether the horse had stumbled alone or when someone was riding it: Leto evokes, easily, the image of a man on a horse. The Mathematician thinks: *The problem only arises for a horse with a rider. In that case, the error is the rider's and not the horse's.* Just then, though, and always according to Botón, there was a commotion: Tomatis was carrying the fish, which he had just rewashed at the kitchen sink, in an enormous plastic tub (*yellow,* Leto thinks). *You have to wash them again because there's always some sand left behind,* the Mathematician says that Botón told him that Tomatis said. And he adds: *For Tomatis to have washed the greens and rewashed the fish shows how much he admires Washington. He and El Gato are his favorites. Washington, though he isn't one or the other, has a soft spot for cynics and the arrogant.*

But Tomatis isn't cynical and El Gato isn't arrogant, Leto thinks. *Or is it the opposite?* At that point, according to the Mathematician, it's easy to imagine what followed: The fat catfish who offer the fruit of their body year round and the metallic perch who, prudently, only appear in winter, were submitted to the proper treatment for highlighting, perfecting even, their qualities; after filling them with a generous portion of onion and some parsley and bay leaf, they dipped the newspapers in oil and, with a dusting of salt and pepper, wrapped the fish up and arranged them neatly in rows on the grill, where the carefully distributed coals beneath would prevent any of the fragile meat from being lost. *And to think he calls Botón a folklorist,* Leto thinks with a touch of bad faith now that he can detect, in the Mathematician's description, a touch of irony. Because, additionally, the Mathematician insists that whosoever looks to swim unaided in the colorless river of postulates, syllogistic modes, categories, and definitions should accompany his studies with a strict dietary regimen: fed on yogurts and blanched vegetables, the abstract order of everything, in its utmost simplicity, will be revealed, ecstatic and radiant, to the relentless, recently bathed ascetic.

—I'll be right back, the Mathematician says unexpectedly, and taking from his pants pocket several pages folded in quarters, he enters the *La Mañana* building. Leto sees the tall, tanned body, dressed in all white, cross, with elegant strides, the threshold of the morning paper. *After tomorrow, the press release, soaked in oil, will be used to wrap up perch and catfish,* he thinks bitterly. And then: *He left suddenly to force me to stay.* Accepting, passively, the inexplicable need for his company that the Mathematician seems to feel, Leto leans against the trunk of the last tree on the sidewalk. Beyond the bright cross street, at the opposite corner, the street widens abruptly, and trees no longer line the sidewalks. As they have approached the city center, more people have appeared on the streets, and because the commercial district proper starts to concentrate after the next block, the passing cars, slow and humming, are mixed with bicycles, tricycles, and light delivery trucks painted with the names and addresses of businesses. Despite the conversation and the Mathematician's story, Leto is submerged in his own memory, where Lopecito's voice, with his Rosario accent, murmurs, melancholic and stunned. *We built radios in a little workshop on Calle Rueda. And when people started talking about television, during the second World War, your old man started studying English and ordered technical magazines from North America. You were two or three. Don't you remember how, on his own dime, he started putting together a television in the garage you had in Arroyito? You should remember because you were older then. You remember?* He remembers: he slept in the room next door. Every night, Isabel, in a nightgown, would get up three or four times and bang on the locked door to the garage. *Can't you answer? Can't you answer?* she would yell. He listened to the same insistent lament every night. Later, when the house was dark and silent, he would hear the garage door open and close, and breathing and footsteps moving, in the darkness, toward the bedroom. Isabel's whiny, sleepy voice could be heard again, and Leto, holding his breath to hear better, waited for the response that never came: *What can you do, it was a sexual thing*, he thinks, his eyes fixed on the bright intersection. *Or something even worse*. Lopecito, meanwhile, his eyes full of tears, muting his intensity with that whispered register that's reserved for wakes: *Don't you remember before the television came to Rosario we did a demonstration at the Sociedad Rural with a machine he'd built in the garage and there were write ups in* La Capital? *He'd order parts from Buenos Aires, from the U.S., and what he couldn't find he made himself.* Isabel would come in from time to time and hug them, crying. *You'll have to be very good to your mother now,* Lopecito said, and, so that Isabel wouldn't hear, he added in Leto's ear: *While I'm alive and can use my hands you won't want for anything, I give you my word.* And he was making good. But he, Leto, no?, felt like he was on stage, and not that he didn't have anything to say, or that Isabel and Lopecito and everyone else hadn't learned their roles, but they were all acting, on the same stage but in different plays. Once in a while, something they said was so surprising that Leto could only stare, waiting for them to bust out laughing, because he thought they were joking. But the laughter never came. The familiar faces became impenetrable, remote masks, and no matter how much he examined them he got nothing, nothing whatsoever, no?, from anyone. They were like another species, like those invaders in science fiction movies who come from another planet and take on a human form to better facilitate their takeover. His father, for example, whom they had put in a casket, was he really dead, or pretending? And what Isabel and Lopecito said about his person—his father's, I mean, no?—coincided so little with Leto's empirical reality that he heard them as formulaic expressions memorized to further some conspiracy. For that good man, for that inventor who had ended up dedicating himself to the sale of electrical goods, Leto felt neither love nor hate, but rather a neutral anticipation, similar to what we feel when, after smashing a housefly with a shoe, we wonder whether it still has the reflexes to keep twitching a little more over its ruined self. There was something in the man's habits that no one seemed to perceive but which to Leto was the essential and all but singular characteristic that emanated from his person—a kind of sardonic expression that signified something like: *just wait and see, just wait for when I decide to*, or when *that*, rather, *that* which he was on the verge of, and which others seemed to ignore, would be decided. That inner half-smile that, on the contrary, never once escaped Leto, announced to the world an approaching catastrophe whose unmistakable signs its bearer had seen from the beginning. *It couldn't have been only sexual*, Leto thinks, feeling the tree trunk, hard and rough, on his back, through the thin fabric of his shirt. *Even though César Rey argues that, looked at a certain way, even Billiken is a pornographic magazine. No, it was something separate and distinct from the sexual*, he thinks, *a constituent part of himself that stained everything and that poisoned him*. All the afternoons, the mornings, the evenings that made up his life had been corroded by that toxic substance he secreted, and which, whatever he did, whether he was still or tried to stifle it, never stopped pouring out and leaving a pestilent smear on everything. *And*, Lopecito was saying, *your old man was . . . he was a genius with . . . I owe him . . .* etc. Leto remembers that in the garage where his father shut himself up there was a kind of large table, made of pine, bolted to the wall, and a giant heap of casings to radios, full, empty, or with the insides half out and spilling from the back, bulbs, tubes, pins, knobs, loose plugs, colored cables, copper wire, technical books and magazines, pliers, screwdrivers, and even when he didn't take part in the permanent squabble that pitted Isabel against his father, that his father, although somewhat distant, was more or less friendly or indifferent, and that all of those mysterious and colorful things intertwined on the table in the garage never lost their appeal, though he never touched them, not out of fear of his father, who would have no doubt been pleased by his son's interest, but fear of that fluid that, possibly without realizing, his father secreted, and whose signs Leto could detect on everything, the way the earth shows, through indistinct but definitive markers, the clear trail of a snake or scorpion. Leto imagined him bent over the table, under lamp light, working a tiny screwdriver and, for some unknown reason, not responding when Isabel banged on the door each night. *Open the door. I said open it,*

Isabel would say, her tone desperate, until, surrendering, she'd finally go to bed, not without whimpering a while before falling asleep, and, still, the next morning she would wake up radiant, and sing while she made breakfast, straightened up the house, or walked to the market. That sudden change intrigued Leto: Was it faked, or was it the nightly desperation and the whimpering in bed that she faked, or was it all faked, or none of it? *And this morning when, turning from the glowing blue rings on the stove, she said that unexpected, He suffered so much*, Leto thinks, *And I started pointlessly scrutinizing her face, its impenetrability came, precisely, from the absence of artifice. She's not faking when she sings or when she talks or when she shuts up or even when she insists that she's doing one thing when in fact she's doing the opposite. She lives a plain life, in a single dimension*—the dimension of her desire, the desire for nothing, or rather for the contradiction to not exist. And Lopecito, no?, the night of the wake, as soon as they were alone: *Everything came out right for him. When he started in sales he had so much work he called me to offer the whole north part of the province if I wanted it. Nothing would have stopped us from expanding, but he preferred freedom and, more than anything else, shutting himself up in the garage every night to work. He was in love with technology. He was so enthusiastic.* Leto listened, silently, telling himself over and over that even poor Lopecito had been sucked into that masquerade, and with a conviction that exceeded every expectation. That plain universe which, for mysterious reasons, and without their suspecting it, Leto had been excluded from, in a way that made the generalized vacuousness of their actions immediately recognizable, seemed impregnable less because of its solidity than because of its inconsistency—diffuse, irregular, and ubiquitous.

Absorbed, as we're in the habit of saying, by his thoughts or, if you prefer, as always, by his memories, Leto steps away from the tree, walking slowly toward the intersection. He has just forgotten about the Mathematician. Like the stage actor who does a pirouette and then disappears into the darkness off stage or, better yet, like those sea creatures who, ignorant of the sun that makes them flash, reveal, periodically, a glistening spine that sinks and reappears at regular intervals, a few images, sharp and well-formed, approach and move off. Distracted, he crosses the street and arrives at the opposite sidewalk—and his distraction is also what makes him go through with the paradoxical act of stopping on the bright sidewalk and turning back toward the corner he has just left, knowing unconsciously that he is waiting for someone or something, but not knowing exactly who or what, or better yet, and strictly speaking, his body is what turns and stops to wait—Leto's body, no?—that unique and completely external thing that, independent from what, inside, yields control and continuity, now casts, over the gray pavement, a shadow slightly shorter than him—his body, I mean—plump and young, standing in the morning, on the central avenue, giving the world the illusion, or the abusive proof, maybe, of his existence.

In a hurry, the Mathematician walks out of the newspaper office. Seeing him, Leto, for a fraction of a second, thinks, *What a coincidence, the Mathematician*, until he remembers that they have been walking together for several blocks and that he's been waiting for him on the sidewalk for a few minutes now. The Mathematician walks straight to the middle of the sidewalk and, noticing Leto's absence, stops suddenly, disconcerted, but, turning his head, spots him across the street and, resuming a normal stride and smiling apologetically, starts walking toward Leto, who also smiles. And the Mathematician thinks: *Did he decide to leave? Maybe he crossed the street to put some distance between us and now he's smiling back guiltily.* The editor had sat reading the press release on his desk without touching it, as though it were a venomous snake. *They probably have me blacklisted*, the Mathematician thinks. But, like a magician who makes several plates at once dance at the edge of a table, his thoughts are occupied at the same time with Leto, and the Mathematician, to show his good will and that the delay wasn't his fault, hurries a little without managing to get very far, as the traffic on the two-lane cross street is stopped on the corner because of the movement on the central avenue, forcing him to wait a moment at the cable guardrail, smiling at Leto over the cars that are slowly advancing.

From the opposite sidewalk Leto returns his smile with a vague gesture: on the one hand he wants to show that he accepts the Mathematician's forgiving smile, which discharges his responsibility and in any case is already disappearing from the Mathematician's face, but also he doesn't want to exaggerate the display, in order to highlight that, after all, the Mathematician was the one who whistled on the street and who insists on following him on his walk. But the signals his expression sends in the Mathematician's direction are neutralized and his expression is incomprehensible, or at least it doesn't seem to have any effect on the Mathematician's. Leto looks at him: the Mathematician has finally managed to step over the cable into the street, but a car, brushing past, stops him, and when he moves around it the car stops at the corner, but when he gets to the middle of the street another car coming from the opposite direction forces him, again, to stop; the car that paused on the corner starts up again and, just then, the Mathematician's entire body, dressed completely in white, including his moccasins, emerges, as if through the opening made by the panels of an accordion door, from between the trunks of the two cars, the same model but different colors, which are separating in opposite directions. He is present, clearly visible. For some reason he ignores, and that he, of course, is not conscious of, Leto's thoughts and memories are interrupted, and he sees the street, the trees, the newspaper building, the cars, the Mathematician, the sky, the air, and the morning as a clear and animate unity from which he is slightly separated but completely present to, in any case at a fixed and necessary point in space, or in time, or matter, a fluid or nameless, but no doubt optimal, location, where all contradictions, without his having asked or even wanted it, are, benevolently, erased. It's a novel and pleasant state, but its novelty doesn't reside in the appearance of something that didn't exist previously but in a build-up of evidence in the preexistent, and the pleasure, likewise, doesn't reside in a gratified desire but in some unknown source. It's hard to say whether the clarity comes from Leto or from the objects, but suddenly, seeing the Mathematician advance upright and white from between the trunks of two cars that are moving in opposite directions, Leto begins to see the group, the Mathematician included, not as cars or trees or houses or sky or human beings, but as a system of relations whose function is no doubt connected to the combination of disparate movements, the Mathematician forward, the cars each a different way, the motionless things changing aspect and location in relation to the moving things, everything no doubt in perfect and causal proportion so that living it or feeling it or however you'd call his state, but without thinking it, Leto experiences a sudden, blunt joy, in which he can't distinguish the joy from what follows, which sharpens his perception. The car driving away behind the Mathematician is white and the one in front of him, driving in the opposite direction, a pale green—a rare pale green, with shades of gray, as though some white and black had combined in its composition, no?—and the Mathematician, who is emerging from between them, contrasts against the background of trees forming a luminous half-light, over the sidewalk, on the block they just left. What is happening is at the same time fast and very slow. Independent of his physical features, of his dress, even of his social origin or the posture he assumes, nor owing to some affective projection of Leto's, who shares Tomatis's objections and knows him less, the Mathematician, as he crosses the street, is transformed into a beautiful object, with an abstract and absolute beauty that has nothing to do with his preexisting attributes but rather with some cosmic coincidence that joins, for a few seconds, many different elements into an unstable composition which, mysteriously, when the Mathematician reaches the sidewalk and the two cars separate in opposite directions, dissolves, having existed only for Leto.

—They wanted to cut it, says, to apologize for the delay, the Mathematician.

Again he's the Mathematician, a friend of Tomatis, tall, blonde, tan, rich, progressive, dressed completely in white, including his moccasins, carrying a pipe in his hand, just back from a tour of Europe. Leto looks at him quizzically.

—The press release, says the Mathematician.

—Oh, I see. That's a relief, says Leto, laughing, but the distracted seriousness of the Mathematician, who doesn't seem to have heard him, causes him to put on a grave expression. They start walking. Out of the corner of his eye, somewhat awkwardly, Leto observes the Mathematician, who has retaken the inside track. For several meters they walk without speaking. Leto thinks that the Mathematician, offended at having seen that he'd crossed the street and was ready to leave if he took any longer at the newspaper, has shut himself off deliberately to show his disapproval; but what is really happening, what gives him that serious, almost irritated air, is that, burrowing into his information, into his suspicions, into his capacity for psychological projection and the political classification of his associates, putting the pieces together, the Mathematician is all but convinced that the newspaper employee, having catalogued him politically as well, has tried to set up obstacles to the publication of the press release and has even suggested that they might end up cutting it. And Leto thinks, or rather *sees*, no?, Lopecito's face the night of the wake: *He never complained. Nothing ever bothered him. He slept three or four hours a night. He never got tired. He never got sick. He always had great ideas. I never saw him depressed. He always had friends. Not once did he doubt his ability. He always had his sights on the future, always wanted to learn new things.* Lopecito's image is erased. Leto turns slightly toward the Mathematician and is about to tell him something but, shaking his head, as though recovering from a faint, the Mathematician speaks first: *No*, he says, smiling. *I was thinking about those cheap sluts the masses refer to as journalists.*

—Tomatis being a typical example, says Leto.

—Exactly, says the Mathematician. They laugh. According to Botón, Tomatis, when the discussion over the stumbled horse had picked up, had said about Noca: *If a horse walks into a bar and stumbles, it's the horse's fault; if it's walking out, it's Noca's fault.* Everyone laughed, according to Botón, but in reality they didn't know. *In reality,* says the Mathematician, *Noca's horse, and even Noca's story, are irrelevant to the argument. You only need to generalize the problem: Do horses stumble or not? And then, as Barco says, what do you mean by stumble?*

Just back from Europe, the previous Saturday, the Mathematician had boarded the ferry to see a rugby match in Paraná. Leaning on the railing of the upper deck, with his lit pipe clenched tightly between his teeth, watching the big tractor trailers lining up in rows on the lower deck, he sees Botón board at a run, holding a bag in one hand and his guitar case in the other and, judging by the speed and precision with which he climbs the stairs and walks up next to him, without lifting his eyes once, thinks Botón must have seen him from the dock, before getting on the ferry—Botón who, as the Mathematician guessed at seeing him sidestep, clean and freshly combed and shaved, the trucks maneuvering, noisily and almost at a crawl, to board and line up on the ferry—Botón, who the Mathematician, I was saying, no?, has guessed his plans to spend the weekend with his family in Entre Ríos, and who, as soon as they sat down on a wooden bench on the upper deck, at the stern, began telling him, in complete detail, about the birthday party. They've taken the midday ferry for different reasons, the Mathematician because he figures that since the trip takes two hours and the match starts at 3:30, he will have time to walk to the field, and Botón because, as he put it, he should have taken the ten o'clock, since the bus to Diamante leaves at 2:30, but he overslept and now he'll barely have time to get from the docks to the station and jump on the bus. It's cloudy but not cold: both reasons they can stay on deck at midday. Blinded by repetition, they don't see the gradual withdrawal, as the ferry moves away, of the suspension bridge on the southern side, the regatta club, the harbor, Alto Verde on the opposite shore, the inlets, the islands, the canoes and motorboats that, in the opposite direction, are navigating toward the city. The overcast sky is unique: the clouds are small, almost square, stuck to together at the ends, which are a darker gray than at the slightly protuberant centers of each; motionless, they cover the whole sky, to the horizon, almost all the same size, so that the firmament, whose name was never better suited, though the name applies to the starlit sky and not, specifically, to the clouds, gives the impression of being a concave, stone-walled vault. That rocky, stable sky would last all day, until at nightfall, without a sound, it would begin to dissolve, not before passing through a much darker gray, a smooth phase, with an ever-increasing rainfall that would last until the evening the following day. But at midday on Saturday, above the ferry, the river, and the islands, it still conserved that hardness of pavement. Botón, who has left the bag and the guitar on the bench they're sitting on, takes a bar of chocolate from his pocket and undressing it—why not—halfway down its two layers of printed and silvery paper, extends it to the Mathematician who, with distant and pensive courtesy, refuses it. Without formalities, Botón asks, point blank, the inevitable question: How was your trip? And the Mathematician, a few seconds later, with his gaze fixed on the point where the ferry's wake begins to disappear on the surface of the river, hears himself repeat for Botón, not without a certain distaste, the list of cities that bring with them the supposedly empirical images that, ever since his travels, accompany their names: Venice, the real gateway to the East and not Istanbul; Warsaw, there was nothing left; Bruges, they painted what they saw; Madrid, the thing you feel you've lost abroad you rediscover there. Botón observes him a few seconds, without blinking, his head slightly tilted, already thinking about something else, eating his chocolate, and when the Mathematician finishes, without offering any comment, he starts telling his own story, as if their stories, which have nothing to do with each other, were complementary—Botón I was saying, no?, that blonde, curly-haired boy, with a blonde goatee and almost transparent blue eyes, who when he sings along to his guitar does it so softly that you have to lean in with your hand to your ear and turn toward him to hear anything—according to Tomatis, Botón's *only deviance from a rigorous nationalist observance is the excessive consumption of cognac and Paraguayan caña that, while both are national brands, are in fact manufactured beyond our borders.* Botón says that, early in September or late August maybe, he doesn't quite remember, there was a big party at Basso's ranch, in Colastiné Norte, to celebrate the sixty-fifth anniversary of the birth of Jorge Washington Noriega (*the sixty-five years of Washington*, in Botón's words), that he had run into El Gato at Fine Arts and that El Gato had invited him and told him to bring his guitar too, that the guests had arrived slowly—the first of them had gone to the back of the patio to pick vegetables with Basso, who had just gotten up from his siesta. That the thing had lasted til dawn.

—Of course, says Leto. I get it.

—Right, says the Mathematician.

More or less like that, no? What you mean by stumble. Is there just an external hoof and an external hole or a rock in a place of pure externality where, through the intervention of different spacio-temporal factors, an encounter between the end of the hoof and the salient protuberance of a half-buried rock takes place, so that its motive equilibrium is disturbed by the collision, leading to an imbalance of the subject, without notions of error or intention needing to intervene whatsoever in the sequence of events, considering it simply as a physical occurrence in which a specific mass, velocity, force, direction, etc., coincide, or rather, approaching it from an internal or subjective perspective, is this an event whose occurrence is only possible if you admit the existence, among the subject's attributes, of a tendency contrary to what allows it to move quickly on its limbs and navigate obstacles without accident? Neither Barco under Basso's pavilion, nor any of the others present, nor the Mathematician or Leto on the straight and bright street they walk down at a regular pace, have framed the dilemma in these terms, this way, but its outline, irrefutable and stripped bare, floats, identically, despite the occasional frills each of them dresses it with, in each of their heads. *Right*, the Mathematician says again. And Washington, calmly smoking a Gitane Filtre (Caporal) from one of the packs given to him the day before by the director of the Alianza Francesa, wasn't saying anything. He smiled, pensively, but didn't say anything.

Hushed by Noca's symposium, by Noca's horse, by every individual, horse, or human: under Basso's pavilion, on a mild evening at the end of winter, and on a straight and bright street, the hard residue of the event, the outline, the ossified or petrified limit, remains as an obstruction to the problem. Cohen worked the wood and coals. Barco, in a single swallow, emptied his glass of beer and, leaving the pavilion, took his post next to the keg and the tap. Others dispersed as well. Botón and Basso went to the refrigerator to make sure the white wine was chilling properly; Beatriz, Tomatis, Cuello the Centaur, and La Chichito were walking around and smoking, glass in hand, under the mandarins. Silvia Cohen and Marcos Rosemberg were talking inside the house, near the library. Under the pavilion were Nidia Basso, Cohen, Washington, and the twins. Afterward, necessarily, Botón returns, because how else, no?—Botón who at the stern of the ferry tells the Mathematician: Washington always pensive, the twins there, Nidia Basso, and Cohen, satisfied for having, with his objection, etc., etc.—the others dispersed around the patio and the house, on a mild evening, at the ranch in Colastiné, to which Leto, who is listening now to the Mathematician, has had to add an unforeseen pavilion and a grill he can barely picture, since most of the story takes place under the thatched roof of a generic pavilion, more or less the idea of a pavilion, without an overly defined shape, staked in a patio he can't picture with absolute clarity, where familiar and unfamiliar people possessing, as the Mathematician mentions them, distinct gradations of reality, drink a kind of beer that Leto has never seen, smelled, touched, or tasted, but which has been stamped unequivocally inside him, golden, with its head of white foam, probably in circular glasses that, without realizing it, Leto makes coincide with, or deduces rather, from his memories.

God damn it! And me in Frankfurt, thinks the Mathematician suddenly. Residue of The Incident. But he forgets it. Owing, apparently, in the era of Temistocles, to a man named Hippodamus, from Miletus they say, tasked with the so-called urbanization of Piraeus, Leto and the Mathematician, ruled by the chess set form of our cities, arrive at the next corner where the intersecting caesura of the cross street interrupts the straight gray line of the sidewalk. They pass from the sun to the shade, from the sidewalk to the street, from the street to the sidewalk, and from the sun to the shade again without changing the rhythm of their pace and without having to stop once, because, as luck would have it, no cars were passing just then on the cross street. The street is so empty that they can keep talking while they cross or, to be more precise, the Mathematician can continue his story—or rather can keep telling Leto the memory he's been keeping, without having told the outside world a single detail, since the previous Saturday, an opaque and cloudy afternoon on the upper deck of the ferry—the memory, elaborated by Botón's words and proffered between mouthfuls of chocolate, that he, the Mathematician, no?, imagines like this: Barco, the Garay twins, Nidia Basso, and Silvia Cohen start setting the table under the pavilion, the fish continue grilling, the salads sit ready on the stove in the kitchen. *There must have been some general commotion before they settled at the table, coming and going from the kitchen, chairs scraping, clinking of plates, of silverware, hesitations—How many are we? The kids already ate, me and Nidia two, Barco, Tomatis, La Chichito, and Beatriz and the twins eight, Botón and Cuello ten, Washington and Marcos Rosemberg twelve (Cohen: I won't sit, just pick a little from the grill), Silvia thirteen. We're missing Dib, Pirulo with Rosario, and Sadi and Miguel Ángel—a while must have gone by before they started to eat,* thinks the Mathematician.

And he says: It's the most diverse group you can imagine. In sixty-five years Washington had time to make friends in every sector, and for different reasons: Cuello, for example, who is twenty years younger, was born in the same town and calls him his mentor; Sadi and Miguel Ángel Podio, who are members of the left-wing labor union, admire him because in the twenties Washington published an anarchist newspaper; Pirulo and the Cohens discuss the humanities with him; Basso and his wife, Zen Buddhism; Beatriz (Leto imagines her rolling a cigarette) worked with him on a translation of some nineteenth-century French prose poems. Barco, Tomatis, and the twins are part of this entourage, and Marcos Rosemberg is the only one left in the city from Higinio Gómez's generation. Botón considers himself a close friend. *And me in Frankfurt*, thinks the Mathematician. And Leto: *I wasn't invited.*

According to Botón, Dib, who after abandoning philosophy opened a mechanics shop, brought three bottles of whiskey, *Caballito Blanco*, he—Botón, no?—clarified, approvingly, and they started to eat. And Botón says that Barco said (more or less): *If we attribute the stumble to chance, it's obvious a horse can stumble. But if we consider the stumble an accident, that is, deviance from a necessary action, it goes without saying that horses do not stumble. I'm of the chef's opinion, in that case.* And Cohen (also more or less): *I don't have an opinion. I'm only inferring the necessary implications in our notion of instinct.* And Beatriz (also more or less and, to Leto, listening to what the Mathematician tells him, constantly rolling a cigarette): *If we accept the cook's notion of instinct, we would come to the conclusion that horses don't die. Given that instinct is pure necessity, and the first necessity of a living being is its own survival, how can a horse die, given that it's a living being?*

Much more alive than some of us here, says the Mathematician that Botón told him Tomatis said. He can imagine Tomatis saying that from the other end of the table, while he slowly unwraps his fish and scrapes, with his knife blade, the burned skin that may have stuck to the newspaper. Washington, the Mathematician says, wasn't saying anything. Several in the group must have been waiting for him to open his mouth, but Washington confined himself to eating, bent over his plate with a thoughtful smile, pushing down the mouthfuls from time to time with sips of white wine. Botón, on the upper deck of the ferry, says that Washington didn't say anything. *Botón says*, the Mathematician says. Both imagine him: the Mathematician as blonde, curly-haired, with a blonde goatee, eating his chocolate bar to make up for the breakfast he couldn't eat because he got up too late, the almost transparent clear blue of his eyes, recently showered and combed, getting ready to spend the weekend in Diamante, and Leto as dark-haired, imprecise, his skin dark and covered in acne, his hair straight and unruly, of an almost wiry stiffness, without Leto knowing or ever having asked himself, since he's never seen him, why the word Botón, which evokes that string of unknown associations, summed up in the characteristics attributed to their name, makes him look like this.

Washington didn't say anything, no?, sitting there with his eyes lowered, leaning over his plate, where his perch sat unwrapped, open, with its filling of parsley and onions, on the charred newspaper page, and in some places fused, or confused rather, with the fish skin. But, according to the Mathematician, his eyes smiled thoughtfully and, two or three times, he was about to say something, lifting his head and looking at the whole gathering who, except for two or three, Beatriz, maybe, or the Centaur, or one of the two twins, El Gato probably, weren't paying any attention to him. He seemed to be gathering, inside him, the ends of a phrase, of a memory, of something that demands a basic order before it will let itself be spoken—spoken, or rather laid out, articulated, through a sequence of muscular and respiratory combinations, among palpable and impalpable folds of organic material and thought, to the outside world—a familiar music that, even when it comes out in constant and conventional forms, allows itself to be stitched and unstitched in an infinite number of variations.

—Instinct. Set in motion by, the Mathematician says that Beatriz said, and always, and more or less, according to Botón.

—By whom? Or by what? asks Leto.

—What. Probably what. Who, some argue, is already finished, says the Mathematician cryptically.

They've left behind the wide, residential section of the street and are now walking down a narrow, treeless sidewalk where more and more frequently the windows and doors of businesses sit open. Bringing the stem of the unlit pipe to his lips, the Mathematician distractedly starts stroking them with the tip, its bowl hidden in his closed hand. He doesn't say anything now. Above his eyebrows, on his smooth

forehead, his skin wrinkles a little, into horizontal furrows, and between the two little blonde brushes appear two oblique fissures, forming a vertex at the bridge of his nose. Leto, meanwhile, remembers:
Isabel, the past year, Lopecito, the wake, the closed casket, etc.—and
five days before all that, that is, before the wake, Lopecito, etc. no?—as
we were, or rather I, yours truly, no?, was saying: green wheat, already
so tall, from the bus window. He has left Rosario Norte an hour before,
with his mother. They're on their way to Andino, to his maternal
grandparents' house, to spend the weekend. It's a Friday in late spring.
They left Rosario at 1:00. When they leave behind the San Lorenzo
industrial complex, the land fills with tall green wheat, fields of flax,
and, sometimes, yellow sunflowers right up to the shoulders of the
road. Every once in a while they pass a farmhouse, with its windmill
and eucalyptus, which interrupts, as they say, the fields, the same way
stations divide the scant towns in two like a river or a railroad would
in other places in the world. A parallel dirt path separates, in the country, the geometrical grains from the road—and on that path, every
once in a while, a solitary carriage travels, hardworking and unreal,
which the bus, as slow as it is, leaves behind with ease. *He*, helpful and
enthusiastic, went along to the station. That man who, ever since Leto
has had use of his reason, has always been silent, distant, shut away
with his unsuspected chimeras in his radio workshop, for the last
month or so seems to have broken the bell jar that separated him from
the outside world, and has come with them, seeming euphoric, close,
warm, and open. Leto observes him at a distance, incredulous. At first
the change was so sudden that, in his skepticism, he was sure it was
some kind of joke, or a tactical transformation, but his persistence and
his conviction to the role were so intense that Leto's initial incredulity
was replaced with doubt—is he? would he?—all that, no?, telling
himself at the same time, but from then on without concrete ideas or
words and almost without realizing it, though not only his mind but
also his whole body are for some reason saturated with those senses
that more and more resemble the shudder or the silent beating or the

contraction of nerves, temples, veins, muscles, telling himself, he would say, but in that way, no?, that if it was a comedy the intended audience was Leto himself, because for Isabel, Lopecito, and the rest, who were convinced in advance, no persuasion was necessary—he, Leto no?—the only one who suspected that the man had something up his sleeve, that the man had realized—*and decided I was the last obstacle to demolish before his magical circle could finally close, the straggler he had to force in before sealing, hermetically, from the inside, the capsule, and launching it into the interstellar space of his own delirium,* Leto thinks, this time with clear and well-formed thoughts, walking, next to the Mathematician, always to the south, on the shady sidewalk, where, more and more frequently, the windows and doors of businesses are open. On a bright, warm, and calm November afternoon, the bus drives past rectangles of blue flax, of yellow sunflowers and green wheat, leaving behind, slow and regular, the repetitive uprights of the telegraph poles, while Leto, sitting next to the window, candidly observes Isabel who, in the seat ahead of him, calmly and serenely flips through the latest issue of *Ms & Mrs.* The comedy that Leto, after several weeks, has convinced himself is real, produces a tranquilizing and at the same time euphoric effect in Isabel, inasmuch as her old phantasms of marital bliss, upward mobility, sexual satisfaction, economic stability, familial harmony, religious tranquility, and physical well-being have seemed, in recent weeks, to have found their long-awaited substantiation, despite the resistance of a hostile world. Isabel's attention, detached from the intense perfection of the land, is fixed on the page—a weight-loss plan? the horoscope? an interesting recipe? the opinions of a movie star? sentimental correspondence? Leto doesn't wonder anymore, feeling nonetheless, indifferently, definitively perhaps, the abyss that separates them. The magazine, elevated almost to her chest, lets him see the belly which, under a modest skirt, ends at the vertex that the crossing muscles form with the pubis—he was in there, for nine months, and then funneled out, fell into the world. What should he feel? First of all, the ubiquitous mother, the amazing plain, fascinates him just then more than his own; the vast world, so indifferent, nevertheless seems more familiar than the one he was raised in at home. His coldness isn't quite hatred—still, the censure he himself ignores, buried for a long time, feeling now that it's too late to want them to have been different, makes him see his own feelings as though they were controlled remotely by others, an older and distinct species—not hatred, no, but instead a sort of quiet and curious outrage that makes him observe them constantly to see how far they'll go, with the wild hope that, after so much time, with laughter and a shift in pose, they will finally say: *Okay, that's enough, show's over, time to start being our real selves.* He, the kind and helpful man, has gone with them to the bus station, in Rosario Norte, has given the impression, for the last month, of being something else, not his real self, but still very different—his concentrated detachment has become lightheartedness; his distracted indifference, friendly attention; his limp and depressive inertia regarding his family and work, enthusiasm and projects. The day before, he came out of the workshop with his eyes tired from connecting so many thin cables and adjusting so many tiny screws, and while he helped Isabel get dinner ready and set the table, he told Leto that next week, when they came back home, they would go fishing together; they would cross the river on a canoe with Lopecito and camp on the island for a couple of days. He even rang up Lopecito who, of course, sounded excited. And in Rosario Norte, just as they were getting on the bus, he, that man, reminded him: on Wednesday, at the latest, because Lopecito was busy Monday and Tuesday, they would row to the island. In fact, Leto has to put effort into showing that he finds the outing as attractive as Lopecito and his father seem to, but the slightly irked, wary curiosity these altered people inspire allows him to give himself over, to persist, with the same affected detachment one would use to observe the behavior of a colony of laboratory mushrooms, in acting out the different scenes of the comedy, hoping to finally unravel the heart of the plot and its characters. Many years later he will understand, from the overwhelming evidence, that the so-called human soul never had, or will ever have, what they call substance or essence, that what they call character, style, personality, are nothing but senseless replications, and that their own subject—the body where they manifest—is the one most starved of their nature, that what others call life is a series of *a posteriori* recognitions of the places where a blind, incomprehensible, ceaseless drift deposits, in spite of themselves, the eminent individuals who, after having been dragged through it, begin to elaborate systems that pretend to explain it; but for now, having just turned twenty, he still believes that problems have solutions, situations outcomes, individuals personality, and actions logic. Leto observes, with some pleasure, the countryside through the window. Every ten or fifteen kilometers the bus stops at a station for a few minutes to drop off or pick up bags of mail, travelers, the ticket taker, the shopkeepers returning from their restocking trips to Rosario, the packets of newspapers and magazines, the passengers going from one town to another, few compared to those coming from Rosario, as though contact among those towns were prohibited and it was only possible for them to connect by way of the abstract and distant city, those towns on the plains, squared off like the country, regularly and strictly consisting of two rows of houses, most of unplastered brick, four blocks long, one on each side of the highway and separated—each row of houses, no?— from the bus station by a wire fence, a windmill, and a wide dirt street—and on the ends of the four blocks, two lateral streets that close the quadrilateral and rise slightly at the shoulder, towns that are, to put it one way, like a miserly concession from the plains to roughen, at brief and regular intervals, its simplistic, monotonous geometry. To Leto those towns are childhood—that is, in his case, the coming and going by train or by bus, the vacations, in winter or summer, at his grandparents' house, his grandfather's general store with its big, dark shelves, the colored fabrics, patterned with flowers, stripes, polka dots, blocks, or with little black and white flowers, stacked on top of each other and lined up diagonally in the cases, the carefully situated yellow bags of sod, the logo and the letters of the brand repeated on several rows, the pyramids of identical cans of preserves, piled up at the back of the store, the bins of caramels, the rows of cigarette packs organized by brand, the ones with blonde tobacco on the left side of the case, with black tobacco in the middle, toscanos, toscanitos, matches, loose tobacco, and rolling paper on the right, the big bins of sugar, of lentils, of garbanzos, of noodles, the rows of dried cod, stiff and covered with rock salt, the harvesting bags smelling of leather and oil, the bottles of wine, by type, by brand, by size, the glass cases with toiletries, the cooler, the scales, the wood countertop, smooth, dark, and weathered, the calendars and the cardboard advertisements with pictures of movie stars, of soccer teams, funny or artistic drawings, the shoeboxes, the kerosene cans and cooking alcohol in the storeroom, next to rows of detergent, flour, salt, oil, and above all, the boxes of Quaker Oats with the drawing of a man holding a smaller box of Quaker Oats with a smaller man holding an even smaller box of Quaker Oats with an even smaller man holding, no?, an even smaller, no?, to infinity, no?, like . . . no?, childhood, we were saying, or rather yours truly was saying, or rather, that is to say, no?, childhood: internal construction and external wandering, convalescence of nothing, corporeal truth versus social fiction, hope of pleasure versus generalized deception, just like that thing on Sundays, the pursuit, torture, and murder of grasshoppers and frogs between the trees in the back yard, the terrifying nights under the crucifix hanging on the headboard with dried olive branches from the last Palm Sunday, the white nightgowns of his aunts, cousins, grandmother, his uncles drinking cold beer under the trees, the afternoon, the whistles of the express passing through town and filling it with fear, the childhood Leto is already starting to tell himself, without words or concepts—not even with images or representations, no?— *Isn't what I had expected. It's still not what I think it should be like. This can't be all there is.*

Ultimately, as they say, and to say it a second time, though it's always the Same, no?, every thing. He even rang up the man he calls his best friend, Lopecito, to suggest going fishing on the island the following week. And Leto, on the bus, is willing to let himself be carried along, with a somewhat uneasy sense of calm, through those warm and beautiful spring days, to the following Wednesday, on the island near Rosario. That anticipation saturates the entire weekend: arriving in the town, crossing the streets and the bus station, passing the windmill, arriving at his grandparents' house, the dinner, the evening walk through the town, the croaking of the frogs, the intermittent song of the crickets that has always attended, and no doubt preceded, the human night, the intermittent, phosphorescent glow of the fireflies, the smell of the paradise trees, the family gathering on Saturday with the relatives who have been arriving from nearby towns in cars or on the bus, the organized abundance, formed by identical objects repeated over and over in the store, the night spent under the crucifix, the mass, the cookout at noon on Sunday, the women's flower-patterned dresses, the walk around the station with the cousins, and more than anything else, the perfect hour on the plains, the afternoon, and also, every once in a while, in little outbursts to someone in the family, Isabel's foolish declarations of her marital bliss, her upward mobility, her sexual satisfaction, her economic stability, her familial harmony, her religious tranquility, her physical well-being, which he lets run on like background noise whose fictitiousness intrigues him less than its obstinate and emphatic repetition. That insistence betrays her uncertainty, the same way that, on Sunday night when the bus arrives at Rosario Norte, the thing she murmurs, slightly distracted, *Hopefully he hasn't made anything for dinner because I could pop after everything we ate in Andino*, could be translated, Leto thinks, into a way of saying the opposite, because the fact of him waiting with a warm dinner would help dispel the uncertainty that's working on her and which is of such a curious nature—when it manifests itself externally, it always appears to be the opposite.

The man is not at the station, *It's good he didn't come*, murmurs Isabel, after scrutinizing the walkway and the entrance. *It's good he didn't come because anyway we don't have suitcases and the train leaves us a block away.* Leto, who after so many years has become an expert in the art of pretending he hasn't heard anything, or of responding, almost inaudibly, with vague monosyllables, to every irrational, or, as he refers to them privately, false bottom argument laid out by Isabel, turns the conversation to fresh eggs, their bouquet of flowers, the greasy chorizos just made at the farm stand and plied on them in the town.

Slowly they leave the train, walking away from the palm trees lining the avenue to enter the dark, tree-lined block that separates them from their house. Isabel isn't, Leto thinks, in any hurry to get there, as if through some physical inertia her body, contrary to her reason, were trying to express things more truthfully. Twice in a single block she stops for several minutes to talk with neighbors who, sitting in folding chairs on the sidewalk near their front doors, or leaning out a window, have come out to enjoy the cool night, while Leto, keeping a polite distance, with the basket of eggs and chorizo in one hand and an unlit cigarette in the other hand, asks himself if she isn't trying to gain time so that he, who she supposes innocent of machinations and exempted from her intuition, will overtake her and get home first—and all of this in spite of the fact that, to the outside world, they are just a mother and son, a silent twenty-year-old young man, coming back, respectable, straightforward, and a little tired, from a weekend in the country, neighborhood people, apparently the husband is an electrician who works on televisions and doesn't mix much with the neighbors, the boy studies accounting, and she's still pretty even though she's around forty, the men more or less silent and withdrawn, while she sometimes maybe has the habit of talking too much, like she can't stop, or she's trying to hide, to cover up, with words, deep dark fissures which her words, despite her intentions, open at their multiple, secret edges. But she doesn't give up. Leto waits, patiently, or a little callously, rather, at every stop, and when they get to the house, which is dark, silent, and lifeless, and he slides the key in the lock, and turns it, he feels again, coming through the door, the trail of the snake, the indefinite but distinct presence of the scorpion, whose signs, weakened in the previous weeks, have returned, unequivocal and palpable. When he turns on the light, this presence draws him, sucks him, slowly, toward the bedroom, and when he sees the man sprawled on the floor, his skull shattered by the gunshot, the revolver still in his hand, the floor, walls, and furniture splattered with blood, with chunks of brain, hair, bone shards, he says to himself, calmly and coldly, *So that's what this was.* Specifically, *this* meaning the days, the nights, the time, the body, the world, the thick beating life, how the man, in his little electrical workshop, had dismantled them, detaching and separating them into separate pieces, colored cables, copper wires, gold screws, spreading them over the table to inspect them one at a time, neutral and merciless, limiting himself to reaching what he no doubt considered objective conclusions, and later, during uniform and meticulous hours, putting everything back together according to the indisputable logic of his delirium. To achieve his goals he had to construct the comedy, setting a stage, the visible universe, and making all of his so-called loved ones take part, modifying the plot sometimes to convince the most reticent, as had been happening for the previous weeks with Leto, whose mistrust had forced him to make appearances outside his "workshop," transforming his personality slightly and preparing, with Lopecito's unconditional support, when he swallowed whole the supposed week of fishing on the island, for Leto, his reticence becoming hope, to fall, on his return from the country Sunday night, from an even higher rung. Put briefly, and by the man himself, no doubt to himself, and no doubt without words as well, more or less like this: *When I say dance, everyone dances. No excuses.*

Two or three days later the autopsy reveals that he shot himself on Friday at around 2:00 or 3:00 in the afternoon, meaning that he said goodbye with a grin at the station, reminding him before he left that on Wednesday they would cross to the island with Lopecito, then, still grinning, boarded the train back to their neighborhood, walked the block between the train stop and the house at a calm and regular pace, and no doubt without losing his grin entered the house, crossed the hallway, shut himself in the bedroom, and without hesitating or losing the fixed, vindictive grin, blew his brains out.

—I call that an insolent suicide, said César Rey, a few months later, at the bar Montecarlo, in the city, while they watched the sun, through the window, rising into a cold autumn dawn. And Rey can speak with authority because the day before, in fact, he had gotten a hotel room, intending to slit his wrists, but at the decisive moment he had suddenly changed his mind, and after leaving the hotel, he had run into Leto at the arcade's bar, where they proceeded to go on a bender.

—The insolent suicide, says Leto, shaking his head. Isabel and Lopecito were left stupefied by the event—in the director's absence they no longer knew exactly what role they played in the comedy—but Leto himself thinks he has known how to conserve enough cold blood to keep him from the path of the gunshot, though the suspicion of having been the primary target for the last few weeks could be, without his realizing it, proof of the opposite.

The insolent suicide, he thinks, discreetly watching the Mathematician, whose eyebrows indicate a laborious reflection that Leto cannot know, and is not interested in knowing, but which is more or less the following: *Where does instinct come from? Does it belong to the individual or the species? Is there continuity between individuals? Does the latter individual take over the instinct from the point where the former left it or does he reconstruct, from zero, the whole process from the start? Is it substance, energy, reflex? What is our idea of instinct? How was it first formed? By whom? Where? As opposed to what? What, in a living thing, isn't instinct?* And then, forgetting Noca, Noca's horse, instinct, the images he has built up thanks to Botón's story on the ferry, the previous Saturday, on the upper deck, images of Washington's birthday at Basso's ranch, which he didn't attend but will remember for the rest of his life, the other questions, always stirring, underground, and sometimes rising to the surface, suddenly, that follow us, form us, lead us, allow us to be, the old questions first brought up in the African dawn, heard in Babylon and asked again in Thebes, in Asia Minor, on the banks of the Yellow River, which sparkled in the Scandinavian snows, the soliloquy in Arabia, in New Guinea, in Königsberg, in Mato Grosso, and in Tenochtitlán, questions whose response is exaltation, is death, suffering, insanity, and which stir in every blink, every heartbeat, every premonition—who planted the seed of the world? what are the internal and the external? what are birth and death? is there a single object or many? what is the I? what is the general and the particular? what is repetition? what am I doing here?—that is to say, no?—the Mathematician, or someone else, somewhere else or at some other time, again, though there is only one, only one, which is always the same Place, and always, as we were saying, once and for all, the same Time.

For the twenty-seven seconds, give or take, that it took the Mathematician to refocus, silently, on his thoughts, and for Leto to remember, in quick, fragmented and disordered images what, as I was saying, I was saying just now, their bodies advance, in a regular way, down the narrow sidewalk, to the south. Neither of them notices that, without disruption, and without it being possible, with any clarity, to separate the two dimensions, they are advancing in time while doing so in space, as if every step they take moves them in opposite directions, inasmuch as time and space are inseparable and one is inconceivable without the other, and both inconceivable without each other, Leto and the Mathematician, the pedestrians, the street, and the morning form a thick current flowing calmly from the source of the event. Leto thinks (more or less, no?), *For her to come along a year later with the story of an incurable illness just proves her inability to accept the transparency of his message*—and you could add a comparison: with excessive, but for him necessary, means, like the physicists who build a tunnel several kilometers long where they shoot an infinitely small particle because the behavior of that particle will explain all matter and therefore the universe. And the Mathematician, walking alongside him, thinks again, *Set in motion by*, but says:

—Everyone was looking at Washington, who wasn't saying anything.

Always according to Botón. Anyway, he wasn't saying anything, but it seemed, from his pensive and half-smiling expression, his white eyes, the smoke of the Gitane Filtre (Caporal) rising to his face from his hand, which he held more or less at the height of his diaphragm, that he was about to say something. And in fact, he was. Leto imagines him at the head of the table, under the illuminated pavilion, close to the grill, the unforeseen pavilion installed hurriedly among the orange, grapefruit, and mandarin trees, in the dark patio, at the end of winter—Washington, the night of his sixty-fifth birthday, dressed warmly in his thermal undershirt and plaid wool shirt, plus a v-neck sweater with the shirt's collar poking through the top, plus his wool blazer and over his shoulders maybe a poncho or a blanket, his white hair messy and thick, the skin on his face sagging a little but still firm, thick, clean-shaven, and healthy, one of those old men who, maybe because they work a farm, or go fishing, or often ride horses, or sit in the garden to read the paper during the siestas in winter, are tanned year-round, Washington, I was saying, while he forms, with a more and more pronounced smile in his eyes, which he keeps raising to his interlocutors, and a more and more vague smile on his lips, what he is about to say, shaping words, phrases, and gestures, he raises, parsimoniously, his cigarette to his lips and between puffs of smoke exhaled through his nose and mouth, begins to speak.

To Washington, if he has understood correctly, which is somewhat unlikely, as our friend Cohen's subtlety in weighty questions is well-known, and he doesn't even possess the rudiments that the university, spontaneously clearing any number of paths, supplies every student, not to mention the timely remunerations that, at the end of every month, help purge the spirit of material preoccupations that often disturb the progress of the syllogism, in short, if he understood correctly, the horse, having been declared an instinctive being, would be prohibited from stumbling, for the very reasons of instinct, which is considered pure necessity, while all of this is assumed only if you take the stumble, as our friend Barco clarified, in the sense of an error or mistake, not merely an accidental or external occurrence, but rather an internal contradiction in the horse, between the objects in question and the unexpected failure of the execution. Is he on track? Does the absence of an objection authorize him to continue? Yes? Alright, he will continue.

And so on. He, Washington, no?, thought he understood the issue. Here, ostentatiously, almost paternally, the Mathematician grabs Leto by the left arm, to protect him from the aggression of a car that's coming down the cross street, driving threateningly from the previous block, where it had accelerated, after crossing the intersection, according to the habitual system of motor vehicle conduction in rectangular cities: brakes and deceleration before the corner, accelerator after the intersection, reduction of speed midway down the block, and so on successively, which gives the system, bearing in mind that the length of the blocks is more or less constant and despite its contradictory principles, a highly regular nature. Over Leto's head the Mathematician, in one second, analyzes the facts gathered by a glance that scrutinizes the cross street to the west: the cars appear well-adapted to the brakes/ accelerator system, and the three approaching at the crossing with San Martín, one behind the other, judging by the unvarying distance that separates them in spite of the decreasing velocity of the first, appeared set, if they maintained the rate of reduction, to stop and allow the cars arriving perpendicularly down San Martín and the pedestrians crossing the intersection to pass, so that the Mathematician, decisive, drags Leto by the arm, making him stumble when they cross the cable guardrail into the street and forcing him to increase the extension and speed of his steps while they cross, and you could say that the Mathematician, who hasn't for an instant stopped watching, by turns, the cars coming down the cross street, the ones that could turn sharply from San Martín, and the cable guardrail they are walking toward, until he feels released from his responsibility after they cross the guardrail, does not let go of Leto's arm or continue his story before verifying that they can walk safely down the sidewalk. Then he goes on: as Botón has it, Washington, in the first part of his interjection, does not pose a single objection to Cohen or Barco's propositions—furthermore, they seem pertinent to him and he appears to understand the point of view they presuppose. The only thing he finds objectionable, for the clarity of problem, is the selection of the horse as the object of analysis. In his modest opinion, one can handily discard the horse for several reasons. First off, the horse is too close to people (to whom he concedes, without major theoretical obstacles, the ability to stumble), which pollutes the rationale with anthropocentric contaminants, not to mention that the proximity between horses and people has caused every class of symbolic projection to be deposited on the poor animal, to such an extent that, under so many symbolic layers, it is difficult to know where to find the real horse. Likewise, we pretend to know so many things about the horse—we think that it's strong, that it's loyal, that it's noble, that it's tough, that it's nervous, that it loves the *pampa*, and that it's greatest ambition is to win the Carlos Pellegrini prize. We're convinced that if it got into politics it would be nationalist, and that if it talked, it would sound like old Vizcacha. To top it off, says the Mathematician that Botón said that Washington said, because of its more or less pre-eminent position on the zoological ladder, the horse possesses an excessive biological and ontological density: it has too much flesh, too much blood, too many bones, too many nerves, and in spite of its elusive gaze, less indiscreet than the cow's, we can conceive of its presence in this world as not exempt from necessity, in such a way that, through metaphysical negligence, to which not a few thinkers have succumbed, one could even allow an existential category that included both horses and people—in short, if he has understood correctly, what you could say in relation to Noca's horse, which is certainly nothing but a pretext for the discussion, you would have to apply to another being, more differentiated from people than horses, a member of a species of living beings of course, but whose identity, inconsequential but irrefutable, is less disposed to misrepresentation. The mosquito, for example.

Waiting for the effect of his interjection, Washington turns a profile to the gathering and, slowly lifting his head, simulates interest in the crossbeam that supports the pitched roof over the illuminated pavilion. One or two, off guard, also raise their heads and examine the crossbeam, without seeing anything in particular, but the majority of the guests fail to demonstrate, in the seconds following Washington's lecture, the slightest reaction, insofar as an almost ubiquitous silence, disrupted only by the sounds of utensils and plates, settles on the table. Almost ubiquitous: because just as Washington pronounces the last syllable of his interjection, Nidia Basso starts to laugh. Her laughter, suddenly welling up, you could say, under the pavilion, resonates in the surprised ears of the company, reverberates among the tops of the trees cooling in the darkness of the patio, and is finally lost, dispersing into many of the night's different and contradictory directions, the starlit sky in particular—the starlit sky, or rather that thing above our heads, somewhat lost among the horizontal plane, that shines a neutral cover, without omnipotent or capricious or judgmental presences, the starlit sky, no?, which, though no less mortal and likewise prisoner to the incessant solids and gasses, with its apparent firmness, its dimensions and its mystery, expansive and cold, annihilates us.

On the upper deck of the ferry, on the bench at the stern, the previous Saturday, Botón thought it opportune to introduce a quick digression, drawing a sharp caricature of Nidia Basso: according to Botón, whose tone of voice rises, suffused with rancorous qualifiers, Nidia Basso's laughter does not on its own prove that the scene or the words that tie it together are comical, because in any situation, in fact, Nidia seems disposed to laugh at whatever is said, funny or not, insofar as, always according to Botón, her laughter has no connection to the outside world, and even less so with the part of the outside world composed of the words that Washington has just spoken. (*The mosquito, for example.*) What's more, according to Botón, it would be difficult to tell if, in this specific case, it was Washington's words or the silence after that caused it. Even though humorous rhetoric makes frequent appearances in Washington's conversation, Botón argues savagely, the release of tame, easy, high-pitched laughter is a disproportionate response to

Washington's subtle irony, which should probably leave you thoughtful and could, at the most, make you smile, inwardly more than anything, unlike, for example, Tomatis's vulgar, cheap cracks, or El Gato, whose supposed sense of humor consists in mocking the person who's speaking. Listening to him, with his gaze constantly fixed on the spot on the river where the ferry's wake starts to dissipate, the Mathematician suspects that, with the pretext of defining Nidia Basso's peculiar laughter, Botón is exploiting the opportunity, for some unknown reason, to slander El Gato and Tomatis, but while he recounts Botón's distinctions to Leto, in his own words, he omits, though he feels them again, his suspicions. If it were the words, the Mathematician says, then according to Botón it would mean a simple lack of subtlety in perceiving, behind the superficial irony, the gravity always apparent in Washington's words (or vice versa), but if it was caused by the silence, one's hypothesis would have to incline toward nervous laughter, less a sign of the comedy of the world than of neurasthenia in the issuing subject, Botón qualifies with postmodernist taste. Botón thinks that, in fact, if you were to attempt a general classification of distinct types of laughter relative to the circumstances that provoke it, you would realize that the overwhelming majority have little or nothing to do with humor. This is the case with Nidia Basso's laughter. Botón says he never saw her laugh about something that was actually comical, or he didn't notice, or doesn't remember—in any case, laughter caused by something comical wouldn't be, in Nidia Basso's case, anything but a simple exception, a flash of real connection to the world, a fleeting moment of inattention to the incessant and anxious narcissism that suppresses her subjective laughter.

Is Botón capable of this sort of interpretation? The Mathematician asks himself this while he talks, without looking at his companion, and responds without hesitating: In his opinion, no. Among various possibilities for the source of the digression he considers two: either Botón heard a similar explanation from a third party, Tomatis, or Pichón Garay, or Silvia Cohen, or was present for a conversation between them and is appropriating, in a parasitic way, their ideas, or maybe he, the Mathematician, has been framing, to the extent that Botón was relating unadorned scenes in a linear way, the way he presents Leto with Botón's words as if Botón were recalling a riddle in which the Mathematician heard the solution but not the terms that compose it. But there is a third possibility that the Mathematician, as an impartial rationalist, does not discard: flatly rejecting that Botón could be the author of the interpretation, he could concede that Botón, in good faith, has forgotten that it belongs to Silvia Cohen, or to Beatriz, or Pichón Garay and, thinking it his own, repeats it without realizing this, so that when he, the Mathematician, no?, opts for the second possibility, where he claims the interpretation as his own, his situation becomes similar to Botón's, though more acute, because by attributing to himself the interpretation that Botón ignores having taken from Silvia Cohen, let's say, the Mathematician in turn repeats Silvia Cohen's terms, leaving the event in question with so little reality that the value of the interpretation itself is made problematic.

—So, the Mathematician says, to Washington, what is confused in people and horses is clarified by observing the mosquito.

—The mosquito, Leto repeats.

—The mosquito, right, says the Mathematician.

—The mosquito, Leto repeats again, assuming a reflexive intonation.

—The mosquito, the mosquito, the Mathematician says, shaking his head affirmatively.

Their pace, now well-harmonized, is neither slow nor fast, more regular than ever, as if it had taken their legs, their entire bodies, several blocks to find the common rhythm that surrounds them, transforming them into a kind of machine that regulates the differences between their two bodies and calibrates their proportions to obtain a common output. From the outside, the rhythm is so regular it appears deliberate—from the outside, no? And yet you couldn't find two people who were more different than these two: the athletic and rational

65

rugby-man, picture perfect from a physical standpoint, dressed completely in white, including the moccasins he bought that August in Florence, whose father, a liberal *yrigoyenista* lawyer is, nevertheless, the owner of a majority of the farms surrounding Tostado, the Mathematician, as I was saying, no?, fond, for some reason, of swimming in the colorless river of premises, of propositions, of postulates, and to whom Tomatis—who gave him the nickname—claims those same premises, propositions, and postulates give a sick satisfaction, something that Leto, to tell the truth, has never been able to verify, and which could be more about Tomatis's intent, using the Mathematician as a pretext, to slander the exact sciences in general. And the other, Leto, Ángel Leto, no?, skinny, his legs a little crooked, much smaller and younger, slightly myopic, whose shirt and whose pants, of three or four times poorer quality than the other's white outfit, combine less elegantly, Leto, who has lived less than a year in the city, which he came to following Isabel, his mother, who fled the evidence of a suicide like it was a worldwide catastrophe, Leto, who keeps, for a living, several accounts, and who that morning, for reasons as inexplicable as those inclining the Mathematician toward syllogisms and theorems, instead of going to work, decided to get off the bus and start walking down San Martín to the south. Impossible to be more different, although something, in spite of it all, equalizes them—and not just them, no?, the identity that's generic to individuals of the same species, individuals who, after all, speak the same language and, though they come from different cities, were born in the same country and even the same province and therefore possess common fragments of experience—no, nothing like that, which of course is their own and shared with their co-provincials, their so-called compatriots, their countrymen—no, nothing like that, but rather something more particular and at the same time less definite, an impression, a feeling they both carry deep down inside themselves—and never suspecting that the other, or others, also feel it gives it a particular tint and above all reinforces it, the feeling, I mean, of not completely belonging to this world, or, as a result, to anyone else, of never being able to perfectly fit the internal to the external or vice versa, and no matter how hard they try they will always find thin gaps between themselves and everything else, something which, for obscure reasons, they blame themselves for, a feeling so confusing and inconsistently applied that it is confused for thought and for flesh, where the self is the stain, the error, the asymmetry that with its solitary, ridiculous presence clouds the radiant body of the universe. Now, as well, since they began walking down the straight street together, along the shady sidewalk, a new, impalpable tie binds them: the false memories of a place neither of them has seen, of events neither witnessed, and people neither have met, of a day at the end of winter that is not inscribed on their experience but which stands out, intensely, in their memory, the illuminated pavilion, the encounter between El Gato and Botón at the School of Fine Arts, Noca coming from the coast with his baskets of fish, the stumbling horse, Cohen turning the coals, Beatriz constantly rolling a cigarette, the golden beer with a white head of foam, Basso and Botón picking vegetables at the back, shadows moving confusingly as darkness falls, and which, without it being clear how, and above all why, are swallowed by the night.

One almost immediately after the other, the Mathematician perceives, as they reach the corner, two familiar faces: the first belongs to the owner of a newsstand on the beveled corner; as the man is sitting on a bench among his merchandise, situated so as to be shielded from the sun that's striking on the cross street, his head stands out against the low background of weeklies, monthlies, and evening papers, against the color photos of movie stars in bikinis, political and syndical leaders, soccer stars, photos repeated several times, just like the regular, black headlines in the newspapers or the characters in comic strips. From their repetition, the images, which form an oblong background, become almost abstract, transforming into a kind of multicolored guard that seems to decorate the relief portrait of the vendor, whose gaze, lost in the street, the Mathematician does not manage to meet so as to exchange the greeting he has prepared. But, raising his head again, his eyes meet the second familiar face, and this one, passing alongside Leto, smiles back. It's only a familiar face, not actually some-one you could say, to be more precise, he is *familiar* with. A familiar face—or rather, no?—a face that occupies a place between the familiar and the unfamiliar, which he can't match with a name, but which, from having passed so many times across his visual field, has ended up imposing its peculiar characteristics on the Mathematician's memory, just like the Mathematician's face has ended up imprinting itself in the other's memory, so that eventually, when they pass on the street, as proof of their recognition, they say hello. It's true that, in moments of surprise, familiar faces also become suddenly unfamiliar, but there is a gradation that, beginning with these and moving across familiar people first, then across familiar faces, and then across unfamiliar faces and unfamiliar people, the last bulwark of experience, arrives finally at the dark and viscous horizon of the unknown—the unknown, no?, or rather the thing that, beyond the fleeting capacity of the empirical, is background, the persistence we try to force back, unsuccessfully, with those vague signs passing, as though lost, in the day.

Maintaining their identical, regular pace, Leto and the Mathemati-cian step off the sidewalk into the street and start to cross. A slow-moving car intercepts them, and when it slows at the intersection, they move ahead of it, both at the same time, without stopping or varying their pace, without even looking at it, like two robots with a preprogrammed electronic mechanism which makes them automati-cally avoid obstacles, and when they reach the opposite sidewalk both, simultaneously, bend their left leg and lift it over the cable.

The
Next
Seven
Blocks

We were with Leto and the Mathematician who, one
morning, the twenty-third of October in 1961, we had said, just after
10:00, had met on the central avenue, had started walking together to
the south, and the Mathematician, who had heard about it from Botón
on the upper deck of the ferry to Paraná, the previous Saturday, had
started telling Leto about the birthday party for Jorge Washington
Noriega, near the end of August, at Basso's ranch in Colastiné, and
after walking a few blocks together, they crossed the street with an
identical, regular pace and simultaneously bent their left leg, lifting it
over the cable with the intention, more unconscious than calculated,
of planting the bottom of their foot on the sidewalk, no? Alright then:
they plant their feet. And the Mathematician thinks: *If time were like*
this street, it would be easy to go back and retrace it in every sense, stop
where you wanted, like this straight street with a beginning and an end,
and where things would give the impression of being aligned, of being
rough and clean like those well-furnished weekend houses in residential
neighborhoods. But he says:

—Shht! *Il terso conchertino dilestro armónico.*

The unexpected *cocoliche* phrase disorients Leto, especially when the Mathematician stops, grabs him by the arm, and assumes a theatrical pose, which consists of turning his head slightly toward Leto, without making eye contact, while his eyes, gazing in the opposite direction and ceasing to see what's around them, take on an intense expectancy and tender concentration on the index finger of his left hand, which, at the end of his elevated and slightly bent arm, points to a hypothetical point in the space ahead of them where the finger, like the needle on a metal detector, tries to locate the exact source of the music. Almost simultaneously, Leto hears it too, and his several seconds delay in hearing the music seems to be caused less by sensory constituents, specialized or acoustic, than by his submerged distraction in his thoughts. In spite of his delay, both locate the source at the same time: a record store that's advertising itself by hurling music into the street, its doors open to the sidewalk out front. The morning sounds on the central avenue, vehicles, footsteps, voices, seem like cheap resonance, undisciplined and savage, on which the music is neatly mounted, but to the Mathematician's subtle and speculative ear, also seem like both a deliberate and inadvertent contrast, where the juxtaposition of the brute noise and the structured sound creates a richer and more complex sonorous space, a space, I was saying, no?, where pure noise, betraying the real nature of the music by contrast, assumes a moral role, like in those engravings where the mere presence of a skull reveals the maiden's true face. After locating the music's source, the Mathematician's finger clenches, and his hand begins to make rhythmic undulations in the air, which his head, bobbing, accompanies, followed by, the first half-closed, the second stretching into a mesmerized smile, his eyes and mouth. And when they continue walking, the Mathematician's body seems pulled, discreetly of course, by a magnetic attraction to the music, to Leto's surprise, as he can't distinguish, in the sort of moderate bacchant the Mathematician has become, the affect of sincere enthusiasm. The Mathematician's raptures pass, almost as they happen, like a slightly histrionic moment of insanity, and when they approach the source of the music, and therefore hear it with greater clarity, the Mathematician recovers his serene, indolent attitude and once again becomes the measured athlete, blonde, tall, dressed completely in white, including his moccasins, with an unlit pipe in his hand, acting out precise, strict, and elegant gestures, uncalculated by that point in his life, ultimately, the Mathematician, no?, who, completely forgetting the noise and the music, tells him:

—Botón says that Washington presented the mosquito this way: eight millimeters of pulsing life.

Leto imagines it: Botón, Washington, the mosquito. According to the Mathematician, Washington, one night the previous summer, had a casual encounter with three mosquitos, whose behavior, according the Mathematician, and always according to Botón, yielded a series of unexpected results, of a similar order, it seemed (to Washington, no?), to those that the distinguished gathering just now derived in regards to Noca's horse. The previous summer, Washington was working on his four lectures—Location, Lineage, Language, Logic—about the Colastiné Indians, which are only known, for the time being, in their titles: immersed in historical and anthropological treatises, he was forced to work at night because of the heat—unbearable in January and February. Leto, who has gone a couple of times with Tomatis to Washington's place in Rincón Norte, has no difficulty imagining him at his work table, in front of the window that faces the side patio where, protected by shade from eucalyptus and paradise trees, rows of snapdragons, carnations, daisies, and geraniums extend between paths of sandy earth. Leto remembers two or three rose laurels, a wisteria, a *lapacho*, a *timbo* and, at the very back of the garden, like a leftover from the pre-farmed land, five or six yellow mimosa. In the back patio he saw a large, well-tended garden, fruit trees, a corral, and even a rabbit hutch. *During the siege of Athens*, he once heard Washington say, *Epicurus and his friends survived thanks to a self-sufficient economy. I defend myself from the Liberal-Catholic conspiracy by any means necessary.*

So, the summer night, no?, in the middle of the countryside, after a dry and dusty day and the fever of the twilight, the silent but much cooler dawn, and the man on the threshold of old age who, protected from the outside world by the white walls and metal screens, reads, taking quick, abbreviated notes in a journal from time to time. He has spent the day coming and going around the house, avoiding the bright places in the orchard and the garden, alone after his daughter married a doctor and moved to Córdoba—he had separated with his second wife in 1950—accustomed now in his sixty-fourth year to life and death, having left behind periods of impotence, of torpor, and of insanity, but still possessing enough strength to observe, serenely, the summer afternoon from the shade of the paradise trees and wait for nightfall in order to begin to work, which he will do until the next morning. And his story, according to what's left of Botón's story in the Mathematician's, is more or less this: a calm night the previous summer, after midnight. After a light dinner, Washington, with a pitcher of cold water and a dish of plums, has taken up to his study to read, taking notes from time to time, a facsimile edition of Father Quesada's *An account of the adventures of a child lost to the world*, which Marcos Rosemberg had brought back from Madrid for him. Little by little the day's heat diminished, and the internal humming that spans the illuminated section of his mind, monotonously, with its train of apparitions, has been sectioned off by the clear point of his attention that, like the edge of a diamond, has been opening a path that relegates, with successive adjustments, the layers of darkness. Eventually, after several forceful efforts, the layers retract and the faces of the diamond, emerging from the darkness, concentrate on the transparent point that stabilizes and fixes itself, in order to later be perfected at its disappearance, disseminated in its own transparency, so that not only the humming, which is time, flesh, and savagery, but also the book and the reader disappear with it, clearing a place where the eternal and the intangible, no less real than putrefaction and the hours, unfold victoriously. Every so often, his left hand, independent from the rest of the body, slides toward the dish of plums, picks one up and carries it, without possible error, to the half-open mouth that's ready to receive, masticate, and spit out, after a few moments, into his hand, which has come up again, the pit, without a trace of pulp, which his tongue and teeth, on their own accord, have separated with precision and ease, in order to return it to the outside world. The book, resting on others that had been stacked horizontally, oblique, like a bible on a lectern, does not make a sound—except the one from the reader's fingers as they seize, with an index finger previously moistened on the tip of his tongue, the lower right corner of the page in order to turn it—but nevertheless a silent turmoil fills Washington's head. Space and time, swirling around the motionless reader, are powerless to either dissolve or circulate the turmoil and slide around the intangible borders of his body, unable to penetrate the intangible nucleus that is its corollary.

—Washington's legendary four lectures on the Indians in Colastiné, says the Mathematician.

Leto has heard about them—in a fragmentary way, of course, like, in a similar way, everything relating to Washington. He has been working on them—Location, Lineage, Language, Logic—for four or five years, in a fragmentary way, no?, for example, that Washington, who Leto, before moving from Rosario, had never heard of, in fact, that Washington, for example, has been in prison several times, mostly in the twenties and thirties, and that, at the end of the forties, spent time in an asylum, that he was married twice and both times separated, that his daughter married a doctor and has lived in Córdoba for a few years, that the house in Rincón Norte, the land at least, was inherited from his father, a pharmacist in Emilia, with whom he had not spoken from 1912 until his death (his father's, no?), that Washington lives on a disability pension they gave him when he left the asylum and on translations, etc., etc.—and a mess of other things he has happened to fish out of conversations, things he has heard him tell to Tomatis, to Barco, to César Rey, to the twins, *et cetera*.

Assenting without turning to look at the Mathematician, Leto nods his head. They are now even with the record store, on the opposite sidewalk, and when they pass in front they can hear with greater clarity the music that, like them, has been advancing up the straight street, via the melody's more intricate path, to the momentary encounter. But the Mathematician's outward indifference toward it is so complete that Leto feels a rapid irritation, a kind of rebellion, as if, with that subtle indifference, the Mathematician defrauds him—which in a sense is true, because when he saw him absorbed in the music, Leto felt a confused and somewhat problematic admiration for him. Unaware of any external error, the Mathematician continues:

—But that's another story, he says.

The lectures, no? In the calm night in Rincón Norte, in the illuminated, silent study where the smoke of the forgotten cigarette in the notch on the ashtray rises, quiet and regular, toward the lamp, Washington reads, calmly, the book open over the table. And this is when the three mosquitos make their appearance.

Here the Mathematician affects an ostentatious and satisfied pause, jerking his head toward Leto who, to punish him for his flippancy a second ago, decides to not register the effect, abstaining from turning his gaze from the fixed point that he is staring at many meters ahead on the straight sidewalk, and the slightly theatrical smile that had started to stretch across the Mathematician's face is erased, and an indescribable, paled expression, of panic and sadness, appears instead. But just as the decision is made, for lack of resolve or because he disapproved fundamentally of the pettiness in his attitude, Leto gives up and turns his head, assuming an intrigued expression no less theatrical than the Mathematician's satisfied pause. The Mathematician revives. Once more the fog of The Incident, in brief, faint, and successive waves, had overcome him, a fog that the pale expression of panic and sadness, which has just passed, unnoticed by Leto, has been only the most external manifestation, like the lamps in Entre Ríos that, they say, seemed to vibrate the night of the San Juan earthquake. The waves retreat, and in the Mathematician's imagination, Washington, absorbed in his reading, hears the triplicate buzzing much later than when the mosquitos started flying around the room, over his head, somewhere between the table and the ceiling—and this, of course, according to Botón, and according to Botón according to Washington.

Now, almost every door on the street, generally sitting open between two windows, belongs to a business. On the opposite sidewalk, for example, after the record store they've just passed, diminishing the music's intensity, there's a fabric store, a furniture store, a place selling Lux electrical appliances, the women's shoe store Chez Juanita. On the sidewalk where they walk, Leto and the Mathematician successively pass an American diner, dark and dingy in spite of its plastic stools and its multicolor formica counter; a flower shop; one selling fancy pastries; a cigarette store where an older man behind the window is putting on his glasses to study, with painstaking sincerity, his lottery ticket. At every business, from the upper part of the façade, between the first and second floors, the neon signs extend over the street, vertically or horizontally, in different directions and, though they are turned off, form, to put a word to it, a sort of canopy that covers, as far as you can see from a certain height, the central avenue, or like a multitude of rigid standards, in a tight formation that, if they belonged to an army, would intimidate the enemy with their immobility, their quantity, and their variety—each one, like the music from the record store, advertising itself tautologically, repeating, a little higher, emblematically, the message already expressed in a direct and precise form on the windows, in the same way that some religions, as if the presence of a creator were not evident in the creation itself, need to make use, to demonstrate his existence, of some sign of his existence that's separate from the objects he created.

For statistical reasons, more so than actual popularity, the Mathematician is every so often obliged to greet, whether with a quick gesture, a nod of his head, or in some terse, conventional way, the acquaintances he passes—statistics that on the one hand are disadvantageous to Leto since he has only lived in the city a short while and knows considerably fewer people than the Mathematician, a constituent *ab origine*, and that on the other hand, for the last few blocks, considering the gradual and systematic inflation to the number of pedestrians as they approach the city center, increase in the Mathematician's favor the chances of bumping into an acquaintance. In fact, in only purely quantifiable terms is he favored, because in aesthetic, political, emotional, or psychological terms, so to speak, no?, and on moral—as they say, and if you like, and speaking ill and in haste—and existential levels, as I was saying earlier, the Mathematician loathes a good portion of his fellow citizens, especially those of his own class—*the bloodlust bourgeoisie*—for whom he has cultivated, from the age of eight or nine, a concentrated contempt and inexplicable hatred. In spite of their liberal beliefs, his parents are friendly with political bosses and landowners who, likewise, in deference to their aristocratic name and, more than anything, to the expanse of land surrounding Tostado, tolerate their liberal humanism, the way they would the epileptics or pederasts in their class. His brother, Leandro (because . . . no?), several years older than him, for whom, according to the Mathematician, *moral reflexes seem nonexistent and money and social status are the* a priori *principles of his ontology*, has been grooming himself as a landowner since childhood, so much so that even his own parents, despite the genuine affection they feel for him, show a certain prudence when he is around. Leandro, for his part, treats his parents like communists and bohemians. And between the Mathematician and his brother, after several grim altercations, relations are limited, when they're with the family, to an exchange of cold monosyllables thick with innuendo. In spite of this—what a gentleman!—Leandro doesn't miss a single important family event; he never forgets to call his mother every other day, according to custom; and you had to see him on the tennis court, well-groomed and tanned, fairly conceding each of his opponent's points only to steamroll him in the second set. *And, using him as an example, you could never derive a single generalization about human nature, because it's difficult to determine if, apart from his real estate and holdings and evenings at the Jockey Club and the Rotary, he possesses a single genuine human trait suitable to motivating a generalization*—he said once to Tomatis, with the characteristic humor that likes to feign surprise and false neutrality.

Why did he hate them so much? *A psychoanalytic manifestation*, Tomatis diagnosed with flippant disinterest. *When your parents are perfect, you are compelled to project the hatred you should feel for them to every member of their class. Unlike Washington who, it seems, hated his father so much that the quota of love he should have felt for him he transferred to the rest of humanity.*

The Mathematician was shaking his head: *Tsk-tsk-tsk-tsk . . . no.* Accepting that interpretation would oversimplify things. Casually submitting to the subjective hypothesis means ignoring the valid objective reasons for hating them: for example their enthusiasm and acumen for accumulating wealth and the cruelty they demonstrate in defending it; the egocentric ignorance and compulsive narcissism that isolates them from the rest of the world; and the creepy mimesis they have employed in copying foreign style, first the English and French, later the Americans—one of his uncles, the Mathematician's, no?, had proposed in the thirties that the country transfer power to the English crown; they were poor losers, vindictive, they carried genocide in their blood, bigotry in their souls, and vanity in their hearts, and they were prepared at any moment to annihilate everything they considered heterogeneous to their nature and anything that didn't reflect, in its features and gestures, the supposed image of what they pretend to be. *In a word*, the Mathematician always ended up saying after those rhetorical flare-ups, trying to re-establish a balanced and affable tone, *in a word, they are uninteresting.*

The Mathematician's bitter, almost rancid hatred for his own class, excepting its expression in the occasional confidence, was almost never displayed in his words or actions, not because he meant to conceal them, but rather from a kind of fatalism—it wasn't worth wasting time on them, they were not interesting, so why bother spitting in their face when you could spend a lifetime studying Spinoza's *Ethics* or the EPR paradox. Nevertheless, some of that hatred occasionally came to the surface, because the Mathematician, who was attentive, polite, respectful, in some cases to the point of affectation, according to Tomatis, when faced with a patrician, with any sort of tycoon, with the nephew of a bishop, or a minister, or a general's son, could not suppress an ironic genuflection toward what he considered, preemptively and without appeal, the other's ineptitude. If the encounter took place in the presence of a witness, or someone he respected or admired, that irony was not without cruelty, as though by using it he was trying to differentiate himself from his interlocutor as much as possible. The Mathematician, no? How he'd been marked by the very objects of his distaste! Just look at him, on the central avenue, dressed completely in white, including the moccasins he bought in Florence, with an even tan, tall, blonde, insulated from the imperfection and eventuality of those, like Leto, who observe him from the outside, so much so that his mere presence, his exacting and measured expressions, the apparent culmination of his positive traits, further reinforce Leto's feeling of exclusion, of awkwardness, of being, not the whim, but the hopeless mistake of Everything.

But they've reached the corner, that right angle which, in Hippodamus's summary calculations, suddenly interrupting the sidewalk and introducing an evident pause for drivers and pedestrians and facilitating orientation, movement, and visibility—describing, as they say, a space that, in fact, has no shape or name—set a conventional order to the mornings in Peiraeus. Shade, gray pavement, the angled sun, cable, cobblestones, cable, gray pavement, angled sun, shade: there they go, without incident or much modification of rhythm or speed, or trajectory moreover, walking down the next sidewalk. The Mathematician says that Washington lifts his head when he hears the triplicate buzzing, somewhat bewildered, and sees the three mosquitos swirling not far from the lamp. Bewildered because the previous summer it had been too dry for the larvae, and later the nymphs, as they call them, of the so-called diptera, to have increased their offspring, or rather, as they say, proliferate. Mosquitos are in fact not uncommon in the area, and if in winter they hit the proverbial road and disappear, later, in the first weeks of November when the heat gets oppressive, if it has rained enough for the larvae and later the nymphs to flourish, the air turns black in the evening and the warm-blooded animals are forced to go around swatting themselves in the head through tenacious, rapacious, and buzzing clouds. People—man, no?, human beings, who altogether compose what they call humanity, or rather the sum of individuals since the appearance of the species, as they call it, in, it would seem, east Africa, through a qualitative jump across adjoining evolutionary branches, and the specific attributes they attribute to themselves—man, we were saying, or rather yours truly, the author, was saying, has given it that diminutive or pejorative name for *mosca*, or fly in Spanish, no doubt following an anatomic classification by size, imprecise enough in any case, but ultimately, in any case, imprecise or not, there's nothing for it, the naming has to happen. All of this, of course, according to the Mathematician, more or less and always according to Botón, and, according to Botón, I was saying, according to Washington. Thinking about it, no one says *this* mosquito, everyone says *the* mosquito, as if it were always the same one and as if, with that synecdoche, as it's called, we were trying to conceal or, maybe, on the contrary, to suggest, the fundamental problem: one or many? Is it always the same mosquito that attacks every summer night, reincarnated over and over after getting smashed against a white wall, or do new hordes of individuals, pristine and just as transient, avidly sprout up every day, in the swamps, in search of the blood they need, only to, after having been a larva, nymph, an airborne buzzing speck, if they've managed to escape the assassin's hand, propagate, decline, and perish? Is it included among the ones who, definitively, are born and die, or do interchangeable and biodegradable mechanisms successively occupy an eight millimeter entity that bites and buzzes, an invariable essence without contingency or destiny, outside the spatiotemporal melodrama, lacking individual differentiation? Is its function to be someone in life or some anonymous palpitation, absorbed as quickly as it appears by a brilliant, immutable, everlasting, and—even when there are no more little gray bodies to devour—insatiable reality? And prior to that, some say, extrafactually, postemprically, ultramaterially, etc., etc.—ultimately, more or less, according to the Mathematician, definitely not according to Botón, but for sure, he thinks, by way of Botón, according to Washington.

Leto follows the Mathematician's story, told without pedagogical concessions and without preciousness, with some difficulty, as it seems to only gather order and sense as the clear and well-constructed sentences accumulate, not only for the listener but also, and to an even greater extent, for the speaker, more attentive to the story's coherence than the listener, insofar as, concentrating on the formation of his sentences, of his concepts, structuring his memories, his interpretations, his fragments of memories and interpretations, the Mathematician is less vulnerable to sensory interference than Leto, for whom the story the Mathematician seems so submerged in and satisfied with is a heterogeneous composition of vague and opaque words he barely pays attention to, and of transparent passages that allow his imagination, turning on and off intermittently, to construct expressive and fleeting images: there was a feast at the house of someone named Basso, in Colastiné, at the end of August, to celebrate Washington's birthday, and they had started discussing a horse that had stumbled; the Mathematician—it was Tomatis who gave him the nickname—heard about it from Botón the Saturday before on the Paraná ferry, Botón, a guy he has heard about several times but whom he has not had the pleasure of meeting, and then Washington had said that the horse was not an acceptable example for the problem they were discussing—Leto asks himself darkly, without daring to make the case to the Mathematician out of fear that the Mathematician will look down on him a little, what the hell the so-called problem could be—that the mosquito, if Leto understood correctly, would be a more appropriate creature, by reason of its lack of anthropocentric finality, to use as the object of discussion and in fact he, Washington, no?, the summer before, after midnight, while he worked on his four lectures—Location, Lineage, Language, Logic—on the Colastiné Indians, had the opportunity to observe three mosquitos that through their singular behavior acquired paradigmatic value and sufficed, better than the horse, burdened as it is with projections, to clarify the debate, all of this, in Leto's imagination, illustrated with sporadic and fleeting pictures, Basso and Botón picking vegetables at the back of a vague patio on a calm winter afternoon, Beatriz rolling a cigarette, Marcos Rosemberg's sky-blue car, arriving, undulating and quiet, in front of the house Leto has never seen, the perch and catfish wrapped up in day-old pages from *La Región*, dipped in oil, Tomatis and the Garay twins, Barco, someone named Dib, who has a mechanics shop, Silvia Cohen, Cohen, someone named Cuello who they call the Centaur because he is half animal, the slow night under the pavilion, behind the house, the winter night that cools, under the mandarins—they stayed, it seems, until the morning, until dawn even, the last of them, and then they went back, excited and drowsy, to the city, in the first light of the sun and the frozen dew, and he, Leto, no?, could have gone if he wanted, and moreover, if he had known, he was too close to Tomatis to need an invitation, it was strange that Tomatis hadn't said anything, maybe because he considered it impossible that he wouldn't know and that they were so close that it wasn't worth making the invitation explicit, but ultimately, he had to submit to the evidence: they didn't invite him.

Leto raises his arm and points to the next sidewalk, some twenty meters ahead.

—Tomatis, he says.

The Mathematician interrupts himself and looks in the direction Leto just finished pointing, somewhat disoriented at first, as if coming out of a daydream, and when he understands, nods, and a smile starts to appear on his face.

—Indeed. *Pane lucrando*, he says.

Indeed; and, as the Mathematician would say, *pane lucrando*. In shirtsleeves, his head turned to the south, on the upper step of the reconstituted granite stairs that lead to the main entrance of *La Región*, intersecting the door, between the windows that display the two black plush boards where movable white brass letters are arranged into the headlines of the day. Tomatis is lighting a cigarette, with the match cupped between his hands—even though there isn't the slightest breeze and he could just as easily have exposed the flame to the morning air without any danger of it going out. A tall, well-dressed man carrying a portfolio under his arm, and who Tomatis, occupied with lighting his cigarette, is blocking from leaving the newspaper, gives him a little nudge on the shoulder, so that Tomatis, surprised and serious, turns and at the same time moves a few centimeters away, to let him pass, with considerable ill will, stepping down without dignifying the other man's passing, purely cordial, *thank you*, with a response. From the lower step, while he pockets the matches, without taking the cigarette from his lips, he continues to gaze toward the south, indifferent to the turmoil on the street. The cars pass, very slowly, in both directions, intercepting, intermittently, the sidewalk in front of the newspaper, so that Tomatis, standing on the first step of the main entrance, vanishes and reappears, discontinuous and fragmentary, to Leto and the Mathematician. *Seems like he's in a bad mood*, says the Mathematician, less as a result of a genuine observation than as a display, for Leto's benefit, of intimacy with Tomatis; and Leto, for very similar reasons: *Seems like it*.

But it's not exactly that, no—not a bad mood. No. Tomatis, who is facing south, as I was saying, directly toward the city center in fact, and in spite of the passing cars, of the people coming and going, of the morning sun—because it is, as I was saying just now, the morning—of the uneven and shifting excess of the observable, to use just one of its possible names, has been, since he awoke in bed, in a troubled and painful state, externally manifested by a wrinkled shirt, stained pants, and a three-day-old beard, along with an absent and preoccupied expression. Since he woke up, reality has threatened him—reality, no?, another name, and one of the most unfortunate possible for it, and which could imply, because of its obstinate opacity, menace and danger. Once in a while that buildup of danger visits him and covers, darkening without exception, everything. The day before he was fine, in line with himself and the world, and though the day passed without particular incident, he, Tomatis, no?, also spent it without divergence, well-formed to its mold, strictly at pace with his actions and indistinguishable from each of them, waking up, going to work, eating, neutral memories and calm plans, conversations, a walk on the waterfront in the afternoon, taking advantage of the weather, and after dinner some reading by lamplight, on the terrace—a full, consistent spring day, without accident, with its mild tint of permanence, of continuity, of unequivocal and complete existence, one of those days that, with its smooth and monotonous regularity, must have given birth to the idea of eternity. Around midnight, without variation, he had gone to bed, and he, Tomatis, who from time to time, and for weeks, had suffered insomnia, manifested with increasingly desperate tossing in bed until he was, as they say, surprised by the dawn, had, the night before, fallen asleep immediately, without dreaming, sleeping so peacefully that when he woke up the next morning the first thing he noticed was that the bed, with him well-encased between the two sheets, was almost perfectly made, as if he had *just* gone to bed. Nevertheless, at the same moment, unexpectedly, the menace, indefinite and darkening, like in the past, had already installed itself. Right away, things shipwreck against it—or rather, the Thing, the universe, no?, and if you like, another way of referring to it, what there is or what is happening or where it is or where it's happening, or both at once, as if he were passing through zones, through regions, helpless and blind, just a creature, not an individual or a character or a person, troublesome, as they say, and mortal more than anything, wallowing in the empirical until the unimaginable shock of the blackout. And Tomatis, uncertain, indecisive, waits, through the day laced with danger, to receive a blow from he's not sure where, nor of course why, his mind somewhat dirty, like a half-buried glass, covered, you could say, in dried ash and, if you like, full of constituent bubbles and knots that deform what you see. There he is now, sucking the cigarette anxiously, too quickly, absently biting his upper lip, lost to the bright turmoil thickening to the south on the central avenue. From the opposite sidewalk, as they approach, Leto and the Mathematician experience the same tenuous euphoria produced at any unexpected encounter with someone whose company is pleasurable, observing Tomatis's morose posture, his shoulders slumped, his contracted stillness disturbed every so often by awkward and uncoordinated, as they say, movements of his arm or head. When they are even with Tomatis, they stop at the edge of the sidewalk, calling him between the cars, and they have to whistle, click, and shout two or three times before pulling him from his distraction, but when he finally hears them, and sees them shouting and gesturing on the opposite sidewalk after searching various points on the street with a murky and uncertain gaze, a wide smile, without any artificial doubt, where traces of anxiety still persist, spreads across his unhappy face. Tomatis approaches the cable guardrail as well and, laughing and shaking his head, shouts something incomprehensible in the Mathematician's direction.

—Eh? says the Mathematician, leaning a little toward the opposite sidewalk in order to hear him better, and when Tomatis speaks again, raising his voice some, the sound of a scooter accelerating between the two rows of cars drowns out his words again. The Mathematician makes exaggerated faces, trying to hear, shakes his head several times without stopping his laughter, to demonstrate his annoyance, and then, repeating a gesture to Tomatis that indicates he should wait, steps into the street and, quickly moving around the slowly passing cars, starts to cross. More carefully, Leto, whom the Mathematician seems to have forgotten completely, resigns himself to following, lagging a few meters behind and thinking, as he approaches Tomatis and the Mathematician on the opposite sidewalk, amazed at the contrast their external features present: *With the way they dress each makes a fiction out of his body.*

There they are, in fact, hugging, on the sidewalk, patting each other on the shoulders, on their backs, their arms: the Mathematician, dressed completely in white, including the, etc., etc., no?, as I was saying, and Tomatis, his dark messy hair, his three-day-old beard, the shirt and pants he would have changed this morning, after having shaved and taken a warm shower, if the menace, occupying Everything—which could go by another name, no?—had not been ravaging every one of his movements, even the most mundane, needs, tastes, and senses: *If no matter what I'm going to . . . and sooner or later the whole universe is going to . . . what goddamned reason is there to shower and change your pants*, he thinks, with tiny depressed shivers more so than with clear images or words, abandoning himself, with black fingernails and dirty feet, to a foreseen decomposition. Separating himself from the Mathematician, Tomatis aims a severe and at the same time jesting look at Leto.

—You're everywhere these days, he says. And then, to the Mathematician, alluding to the shouts a few moments before, No, I was asking if that tan came from the Costa Azul.

—Partly, responds the Mathematician modestly.

—And so? Tomatis asks. Where do the European girls grow it?

—Some in each armpit, says the Mathematician.

—No way!

—I swear, says the Mathematician. May you drop dead right here.

—Wow, Mathematician! Tomatis says with distracted admiration. Some strange thought crosses his mind and he is silent for a few seconds, looking bleakly at the ember on his cigarette, then turns toward Leto. How's things?

—Things are good. I'm only so-so, Leto says.

Tomatis laughs.

—What subtle humor, he says. And to the Mathematician, Is there such subtle humor in Europe?

—There is, there is, the Mathematician answers, confirming his assertion with a solemn movement of his head.

—A sigh of relief, says Tomatis.

And so on, ultimately, more or less. Leto and the Mathematician have registered, as they say, his abrupt change in attitude, each in his own way and both convinced fundamentally of being the only one to notice, as opposed to Tomatis, who apparently does not seem to have caught on and continues to act in a way that reveals, under his witty euphoria, the depression and murky confusion pasted to the back of his easy laughter and clever turns of phrase. The contrast between the absent and anxious expression they came upon on the opposite sidewalk and his current lightheartedness, so sudden and mechanical, produces a certain discomfort in Leto and the Mathematician, as though there were something obscene and shameful in Tomatis's sudden masquerade, while Tomatis, unaware of those impressions and persisting with his mundane rhetoric, raises his face, darkened by his beard, toward the Mathematician: No, jokes aside, how did it go in Europe? The Mathematician hesitates. A feeling of shame and irritation holds him back a few seconds in the face of Tomatis's compulsive lightheartedness—he would prefer, it's true, for Tomatis, having been surprised in the middle of an internal disturbance, to show less duplicity or more transparency, conforming his behavior to his real state of mind, but at the same time he tells himself—the Mathematician, no?—that maybe there's some pride at work similar to what makes him hide, with meticulous precaution, the evidence of The Incident, and Leto who, without the Mathematician suspecting, is feeling the same things, reaches the same conclusion at practically the same moment: *So much happiness to see us shows more mistrust than love.* All of this of course without words or precise images and, of course, more or less.

After that hesitation which Tomatis, oblivious, does not perceive, and which Leto attributes, with some reason, to the Mathematician's anticipated exhaustion, having already given many recitations, the Mathematician begins, monotonously, to list the cities: Avignon, a murderous heat; Barcelona, the quintessence of the Rosarian soul; Copenhagen, they seemed more proud of Andersen than of Kierkegaard; Naples, felt just like the Abasto Market; Brussels, for *The Census at Bethlehem*;

Fribourg, the Herr Professor must have been on leave; Rome, he imagined it differently; Nantes, a half-meteorological term. Because Tomatis does not seem to be listening, is occupied, severely, in taking the last drag from his cigarette then throwing it to the sidewalk, the Mathematician interrupts himself, but an irritated and somewhat surprised look from Tomatis impels him to continue: Rennes, the streets emptied at seven; Athens, Pergamino plus the Parthenon; Lisbon, you could almost see Entre Ríos from the Plaza of Commerce; Warsaw, there was nothing left; Oxford, a bunch of snobs. Brief, successive, polished and simplified by a fickle memory, the images the Mathematician's words bring out, to the bright morning air, seem to ricochet against Tomatis's disheveled and beard-darkened countenance—Tomatis, no?, pale and unshaven, his hair a mess, his shirt wrinkled and his pants full of stains, who, between Leto and the Mathematician, not only because of his position on the sidewalk but also his height and even his age, has assumed, without looking anywhere in particular but with his head slightly raised toward the Mathematician, such a still posture that the quick and somewhat nervous shudder of his eyelids, to shield them from the sun, looks like an autonomous faculty, a little strange and disconnected from the rest of his body—Tomatis, I was saying, no?—seized, to put it one way, since he woke up, by a menace, the nameless, that will grip him all day, maybe all week, in a darkened zone; and while he listens to the Mathematician talk he thinks: *if I'm going to . . . and the whole universe is going to . . . sooner or later is going . . . is going . . .* while the Mathematician, without breaking his surveillance of Tomatis's ragged expression or the persistent recitation of his thoughts on Europe, thinks: *At least now he's not pretending to listen.* And Leto: *From this version, longer and more ironic, you can tell he admires him more.*

Ultimately, every thing, more or less, no?—and after all, what's the difference. They visited, the Mathematician concludes, several important scientific centers. *Scientific?* Tomatis interrupts, bitterly shaking his head and fixing his stare on the Mathematician's clear and now contented eyes, where Tomatis's subtle rage, more genuine than his lighthearted chattiness, seems to produce considerable satisfaction. *Scientific?* Tomatis repeats, practically shouting. And then, in the same voice, Pushers on the police payroll more like it, pretending to understand what they call reality because they are so sure that what they've decided, without consulting anyone, are plants need to process something they've arbitrarily called photosynthesis in order to do that thing they call growing.

—In a certain sense, I don't disagree, says the Mathematician, unfazed, not ignoring that, in some sense, his engineering studies and maybe his whole person are included in Tomatis's description. And pulling from his pocket a paper folded in fourths, he adds, While we're at it, would it be awkward for you to get the Association's press release into the hands of your colleague correspondent? Thanks.

With the same conviction and goodwill he might demonstrate in receiving a rattlesnake, Tomatis grabs the folded sheet the Mathematician holds out. *With pleasure*, he says, looking away. *If an engineer wrote this, the structure will need to be checked.*

He starts laughing. Leto and the Mathematician laugh. This time, Tomatis's laughter seems sincere, spontaneous, as though, overpowering the depression, not being a coarse engineer who lacks elegance of expression were enough, in the curious machinations taking place inside him, to force the menace, for some unknown reason, to withdraw temporarily. His entire self is clarified by the laughter—the laughter, no?—that sudden euphoria that comes to the face, accompanied by bodily shivers and internal flashes, abstract and present, it's impossible to tell why some images and not others release that instantaneous and brilliant cascade that's let loose for a few moments by the coincidence of things. Letting himself be carried along by the good mood, Tomatis pulls from his own pocket a sheet folded in fourths, almost identical to the one the Mathematician just gave him.

—This morning I wrote a press release too, he says, and, without further clarification, starts reading what is written on the page:

In another man devoured / my own death I don't see / but plagued by geometric flowers / I waste away the hours / and now they keep vigil for me. The Mathematician, who had half closed his eyes and assumed an expression of pleasure in anticipation of the reading, no doubt to demonstrate—and no doubt because of Leto's presence—that he has already enjoyed the privilege of a private reading of Tomatis's poems many times before, the Mathematician, when Tomatis finishes his slow and slightly pitched but altogether monotone reading, turns toward Leto, interrogating him with ecstatic eyes. And Tomatis, falling, as they say, silent, turns to look, with deliberate indifference, at the bright sidewalk, the blue sky, the cars, the people passing on the street. *Brilliant*, the Mathematician hastens to say. And then Leto, after hesitating, *Could you read it again? I missed part of it.*

A faint shadow passes, quickly, over Tomatis's face. Without ever having thought about it, he knows that a request for a rereading is a veiled way of indicating that the effect the reader aimed for has not reached the listener, and that the listener, Leto, that is, no?, to avoid praising what hasn't affected him, uses the request for a rereading as a way to put off commenting, in order to prepare, during the rereading, a formulaic response that will satisfy Tomatis. But in truth Leto was not listening: during the reading, loose, disordered memories, practically without images or content, had plucked him from the October morning, pulling him back several months, to the time when, owing to Lopecito's diligence and as a result of Isabel's compulsion to escape, they had moved to the city. Leto senses, when Tomatis starts reading the poem a second time, his slight humiliation at the unjust judgment, and he senses, above all, while he puts on a much more attentive expression than his natural attention would call for, the gaze fixed on his face, from just above his head, by the Mathematician, who seems to have assumed, in solidarity with Tomatis, severe authority over the aesthetic effect that, peremptorily, the reading should have on him, authority that of course produces the opposite effect, as his excessive pressure on Leto becomes an element of distraction. Tomatis's slow, pitched, monotone voice, slightly different from his natural voice, lays out the syllables, the words, the verses of the poem, constructing, with his artificial intonation, a sonorous fragment of paradoxical quality, as they say, no?, belonging and at the same time not belonging to the physical universe—that's it, physical, no?—which is, also, another name for that thing, the undulating material magma, so outwardly expansive, less apt to ritual than to drift, though the dreamy animal passing briefly through, suspect of his existence, insists on shipwrecking himself against it with blind, classificatory assaults. Austere or lapidary, Tomatis's voice declaims: *In another man devoured / my own death I don't see / but plagued by geometric flowers / I waste away the hours / and now they keep vigil for me.*

—Well-turned, Leto finally remarks.

—Do you have a copy? the Mathematician asks.

Tomatis hesitates a second, and then, aloof and ostentatious, gives the Mathematician the paper.

—Official exchange of press releases between the Chemical Engineering Students Association and Carlos Tomatis, he announces.

—A few more years and this is worth millions, says the Mathematician, dropping a reverent gaze at the typed out verses in the middle of the page, then putting it away after giving it a flamboyant kiss and carefully and easily folding it in fourths, following the folds Tomatis had made. And then he says, Should we walk a little?

—A few blocks, Tomatis agrees, reticently.

They start to walk, following the sun, and take up so much of the sidewalk that Leto, who is on the outside, is practically walking over the cable guardrail and every so often is forced to look over his shoulder to make sure that he isn't about to be grazed by the slowly passing cars. Because Tomatis stayed between them, they form a declining group, from the Mathematician to Leto, not only in terms of their height and weight, but also their age, as Tomatis is a couple of years younger than the Mathematician and three or four older than Leto. But the pressure of the menace, which has surfaced again, distinguishes Tomatis from the other two, in his extremely pale color, his three-day-old beard, his stained and wrinkled clothes, but most of all with his shifty gaze, his ragged expression, the weak shivers of his body, the sudden, rough, and unpredictable movements of his head. Though they pretend not to, Leto and the Mathematician continue to notice it. And after walking a few meters in silence, the Mathematician, in a neutral and indirect way, asks what version he, Tomatis, who was present, can give of Washington's birthday. Because they, Leto and the Mathematician, no?, have Botón's version, plagued with unverifiable interpretations, subjective assertions, and, he suspects, of anachronisms. He met Botón on the ferry the Saturday before and was just now telling Leto what Botón told him. Only when Tomatis doesn't respond, merely shaking his head with restrained scorn, does the Mathematician ask, *Is there a problem?*

The words, *Better that I keep my mouth shut*, spill over the abject rim of Tomatis's nervous lips and, proving the inconstancy of the signifying plane triumphant, continue without transition (and more or less): only more or less, Washington's birthday was a convention of winos, thugs, and showgirls. For example, without going into it too much, Sadi and Miguel Ángel Podio, who present themselves as the vanguard of the working class, eject—at gunpoint—the members of the winning side the moment they lose a syndical election; he, Tomatis, can't understand how they showed up that night without their bodyguards. And Botón, don't start: he tried to rape Chichito at the back of the patio; she escaped thanks to her bourgeois reflexes and the fact that Botón was so drunk that not only could he not get it up but his legs barely kept him upright. And the proof that he was drunk is supplied by the fact of having picked Chichito, who is beyond the reach of anyone who hasn't passed through the National Guard, when there were two or three women present who would gladly have taken a turn around the patio and were frivolous enough that even Botón would have seemed interesting company—they say that Nidia Basso, for example, is a nymphomaniac, and he has heard that Rosario, Pirulo's wife, who works as

93

a nurse in a clinic, likes to bleed herself with a syringe every once in a while. Hadn't they seen how pale she was?

Over Tomatis's head, thrown forward by the force of his disquisitions, Leto and the Mathematician exchange a quick and puzzled look that they use to seal, in that emergency situation, a pact in which their momentary exchange assumes the following precepts as given: 1) this morning, Tomatis seems to be in a special state of mind, 2) their efforts to bring him back to a relatively normalized relational system have up to this point failed, 3) the special state of mind this morning is making Tomatis describe the events surrounding Washington's birthday in a distorted way, flagrantly resorting to caricature and even to slander in his references to the events, and 4) the parties are mutually impelled, via the present pact, to take Tomatis's version with a grain of salt. *Yes*, thinks Leto, who still has some pangs of loyalty to Tomatis, and turns his head: *But where there's smoke there's fire.* The Mathematician, meanwhile: *It's impossible for him not to react.* And Tomatis, under the cascade of malevolent words he would like to stop but which the pressure of the menace forces out: . . . *the universe is going to . . . is going to . . . and I'm going to . . .* Ultimately, in short, and once again, though it's always the Same, as I was saying just now, every thing.

Oblivious to the pact just made over his head and unable to perceive any show of reproach or skepticism or discomfort in the discreet and somewhat embarrassed silence that meets his words, Tomatis continues: to top it off, after dinner, sometime around midnight, Héctor and Elisa, who are constantly brawling, passed out, as did Rita Fonesca, the painter who Botón, among others, makes time with, and who tries to show everyone her tits when she's drunk. And finally, at four in the morning, Gabriel Giménez had come, not having slept for three nights and trying at all cost to get Washington to snort a little packet of coke. The taxi waiting for him at the entrance, according to Tomatis, had been hired the morning before.

The Mathematician has already heard this story from Botón, the previous Saturday, on the bench at the stern, and even from such a dubious source that version had seemed more plausible, or in any case more elegant, than Tomatis's: according to Botón, as we were saying, or rather yours truly was saying, just now, according to Botón, I was saying, no?, Gabriel Giménez had in fact arrived in a taxi at four in the morning, animated no doubt by the little packets of coke, and according to Botón, according to Giménez himself, after three consecutive nights without sleep—a frequent thing in the case of Giménez, of Botón, and above all, in the case of Tomatis and, in Tomatis's case, oftentimes in the company of Giménez himself, who never leaves his side—which means, the Mathematician thinks, that Tomatis should observe some basic rules, for example abstaining from scorning others for something that he treats so indulgently in himself. And, according to Botón, Giménez not only hadn't disturbed the party with his condition, but rather had added, with his innate delicacy and sincere love for Washington, that in normal circumstances Tomatis would be the first to acknowledge, a pinch of salt to the event: to stay with Botón, Gabriel approached Washington and, undertaking a series of slow and genteel genuflections, in which all present could recognize a superior manner, and employing a gesture resembling the offering of the Eucharist, presented Washington with the little packet of coke, a kind of oblong, precious host that Washington, flattered by the distinction that the offer implied, declined with a polite smile and a quick pat on Giménez's cheek, contending to not hold communion with that sect but at the same time declaring himself a supporter of religious tolerance.

—Right, says the Mathematician. Botón told me about it.

Tomatis doesn't seem to hear him. They have reached the corner: a backup of cars and buses cutting each other off fills the intersection, caused by the street becoming pedestrian-only, so that the cars coming from the north are forced to turn at the cross street, and the ones coming up the cross street can only continue straight or turn to the north. Every so often a car horn connotes, through the artificial production of what they call conventional sound waves, someone's impatience and, you could say, the nervous excitement of the drivers, which, added to the authoritarian but inconsequential whistles and arm gestures of a traffic agent standing on a platform, and the general sound of the city, where the nearest and most differentiated noises stand out, add several unforeseen variables to the ideal scheme of periodic intersections as conceived by Hippodamus. Leto, Tomatis, and the Mathematician disperse, adopting independent strategies for crossing, by sizing up, detouring, advancing, and retreating around the motionless cars, and when they reach the other side, almost at the same moment, they resume the initial order, highest to lowest, and continue walking together, this time in the middle of the street, cleared, for several blocks and several hours, of every kind of vehicle—Tomatis in the middle, immune to the circumspect silence of his company, to the somewhat desolate reticence his startling and unpleasant story is generating, and, blinded by the menace's bitter compulsion, continues: No, the truth is it was not a good idea to invite all those people, and many of them, meanwhile, had no right to be there; they should have done something more intimate, with his real friends, the ones who, when Washington turns around, aren't in the habit of punching him in the back of the head: Pirulo, for example, who thinks he has the right to look down on Washington because he's not a member of the superstitious cult of quantitative sociological criteria, or Cuello the Centaur, who now pretends to be one of his closest friends, but in '49 when the Peronists, in order to politically neutralize Washington for demanding that all the power should belong to the people, had him locked up in an asylum, Cuello, who was one of the youth leaders then, had washed his hands of it; and still, he, Tomatis, no?, isn't sure that Cuello wasn't up to his teeth in the machinations. You could say the same of Dib, who, when he was director of the Center for Philosophy Students in Rosario, invented a political pretext for boycotting a conference that the Cohens had organized for Washington that was intended to mitigate his poverty because his pension hadn't been paid for a year—and Dib's true vocation and philosophical rigor can be understood, Tomatis says, when you stop to consider that he, Dib, in whose mouth the word idealist is the worst possible insult, the moment he finished spending the money his father left him, dropped out and went back to the city in order to open a mechanics shop, calculating—while calling himself a Marxist—that the main advantage of a mechanics shop is that it can operate, like the oligarchy's plantations, with very little personnel. In any case, Tomatis says, having been the director of the Center for Philosophy Students is already proof enough of his vocation as a slave trader, because among the habits of those gentlemen is sending the troops to the front during a demonstration while reserving their spots in the hierarchy. No, frankly, there were several too many that night. And several who weren't there who should have been.

Leto gives him a discreet, sidelong, glance, to see whether that last sentence had been intended to make up for not having invited him, but Tomatis's pale profile does not alter when his gaze grazes it. From the other side, the Mathematician, whose attention was also caught by the sentence, concludes fundamentally that, almost certainly, the sentence is directed to his listeners, not because the absence of his listeners at the birthday party seemed a major injustice, but because, in order to mitigate the malevolence of his discourse somewhat, Tomatis strokes—without deliberately meaning to—the vanity of his listeners in order to compensate for the blackness of his descriptions. Tomatis's pause seems to confirm this, and in a discreet but no less peremptory way, exploiting the caesura, the Mathematician ventures to suggest: Aren't you exaggerating a little? Certainly Botón's version isn't altogether trustworthy, especially when he tries, instead of sticking circumspectly to the facts, to season it with his own interpretations, but from what he—the Mathematician, no?—knows about the people present, it seems that, ultimately, Botón's version, leaving aside a few fantasies, probably doesn't stray too far from the truth. And lastly, Tomatis's psychological characterizations—here the Mathematician tries in vain to share a quick look of complicity with Leto over Tomatis's head—if not unjust or incorrect in certain cases, seem to him secondary at best:

You say that Botón is a lush? A gold star for that news! That Pirulo's conceptions are among the most limited and that Cohen is always clouding his with rudimentary psychology? They've already agreed on that twenty times. No; from what Botón told him, the draw of the party wasn't in those banalities, but in the discussion over Noca's horse and Washington's three mosquitos. Ending his circuit, the Mathematician, without even looking at Tomatis, puts his empty pipe in his mouth and, not inclined to making any more concessions, waits for a response.

—Noca's horse, Noca's horse, the three mosquitos . . . Oh right! Now I remember, Tomatis concedes little by little, pretending to have to rummage deep in his memory in order to manifest those insignificant details. And he adds, exaggerating his skepticism, Yes, yes. Possibly.

Although, in his opinion, you have to be careful. If they were to try, for once, to be rigorous, there would be objections to spare: first off, whether or not Noca's horse stumbled is something ultimately unverifiable, given that Noca's fabulations are well-known up and down the coast, from the city all the way to San Javier and even farther north, and his reasons for constructing them—pragmatic or artistic as were the case—but always inspired by wine, are infinite in variety, resulting in a high probability of discussing something that never happened. Furthermore, if he remembers correctly, Noca had offered this explanation to Basso, the owner of the house, to account for his delay with the fish, an explanation that was rooted, as is well-known and beyond discussion, in his total inability to deal with any sort of real criticism, something supposedly caused by his Orientalism—a subject which he barely understands and has hardly read about; and finally, if his memory serves, Cohen was the one who started the argument, while he prepared the fire, and everyone knows that Cohen has a particular tendency to propose problems that appear fundamental only in order to adopt subtle-seeming formulations and supposedly knowing expressions for explaining them; and all of this because Silvia, his wife, is smarter than him, something he endures with considerable pains. *Furthermore*, Tomatis adds before becoming thoughtful for a few seconds, *you would have to decide if instinct, as he assumes, really is pure necessity.*

—Set in motion by, says the Mathematician, taking the pipe from his mouth, waving it in the air, and repositioning it between his teeth. As I was telling Leto just now.

Tomatis doesn't seem to hear him. *You'd have to decide*, he repeats. Furthermore, he continues forcefully, any interjection from Barco, who was very involved in the first part of the discussion, is seriously dubious because he spent it coming and going from the pavilion, where Cohen was preparing the fire, to the keg he had installed at the entrance to the kitchen, and you had to repeat half of what was said while he disappeared to empty foam because he wouldn't let anyone touch the tap, worried that the extremely precarious installation he had fashioned for the hose would fall apart. On the other hand, he asks himself, who among them could have been interested in that kind of discussion? Not counting Cohen who, as I just said, likes to present himself publicly as a dialectician while consumed by the complex his wife's superior intellect caused him; disregarding Basso and his three-by-five irrationality; eliminating El Gato, who during that kind of polemic limits himself to watching the different participants with a sardonic air; Pichón, who isn't someone who likes a lot of saliva in his conversations; Silvia and Beatriz, who were in the kitchen when the thing started, Washington, who didn't say anything until after dinner; Marcos Rosemberg, who doesn't open his mouth since his wife left him for César Rey; and Barco who, as I just said, spent it coming and going from the keg to the pavilion and back. Who else among them could have the slightest idea what they were talking about?

And Tomatis shakes his head, depressed by the number of people at Washington's birthday who couldn't keep up with the discussion. But the alert Mathematician is not convinced: among those who, according to Tomatis, would be capable of sustaining a quality dispute he easily recognizes Tomatis's own best friends, who without the slightest hesitation have been relegated to the mass of humanity in the darkness beyond. And Tomatis? As if guessing the Mathematician's mental interrogation, Tomatis continues, referring to himself: He didn't intervene at all—that useless display of supposed dialectics was liable to give him tremendous gas, so he restricted himself to staying silent at the end of the table, calmly eating his perch and enjoying his white wine—which, if the Mathematician believes Botón's version, is more or less false, given that, according to Botón, Tomatis, whose arteries had already circulated three or four whiskies before he had arrived at the party with Barco and the girls, if in fact he didn't intervene directly in the discussion, then he spent it tormenting this or that person, ridiculing their comments with third-rate word games and reducing to absurdity, out of sheer volubility, the better part of the arguments. Silent at the end of the table, calmly eating his perch and enjoying his white wine, Tomatis insists again, like the second hammer given for good measure so that the nail sinks totally and completely, vaguely suspecting that his credibility with the Mathematician, and even with Leto, who follows the conversation silently, is not far from dropping to zero. But the menace is stronger than his self-respect: With Washington, he insists, it's hard to tell when he's speaking in jest and when he's serious, and the fact that he stayed silent for so long before intervening makes him suspicious. Maybe his delayed interjection was a snide way of saying he was fed up too. That story about the three mosquitos, one that doesn't approach, one that approaches and takes off every time he raises his hand to smash it, and one that on the first try lets itself get smashed on his cheek seems, to him, Tomatis, who is close with Washington, no?, highly unlikely. Even if the thing had really happened and, beyond any doubt, the three mosquitos had existed, appearing in the aforementioned circumstances and behaving the way Washington described, even then you have to ask whether bringing them up could be anything but an indirect way for Washington to tell Cohen, Barco, and company that if they were deliberating over a horse, why not deliberate over three mosquitos while they were at it, so that, since they were already deliberating, they might deliberate in earnest, not at the expense of a poor horse burdened from the word go with the foolish delirium of the human race, but rather, if they could, and since they liked to deliberate so much, over three mosquitos, gray, minute, and neutral—an elegant way of suggesting that the more ridiculous the object the clearer the dimensions of the delirium. And second, if you accept the possibility that Washington was speaking seriously, you have to bear in mind that he isn't infallible. Why don't they analyze a little and see? At this point he, Tomatis, remembers—curiously, it had been almost completely erased: He doesn't know Botón's version, but since he knows Botón, that's more than enough. He therefore discards it. Furthermore he, Tomatis, was present, and though he had not been interested in participating, or maybe for that very reason, he also doesn't consider himself, ultimately, disqualified to reproduce it. Looked at another way, if there's anyone who can boast to knowing Washington well and being able to seize on the multiple intentions that can sometimes be discerned in what he says, it wouldn't be too much of a stretch to suggest that he, Tomatis, would be that person. Alright then, in his point of view—in his, in Tomatis's, no?—if it turned out to not be a huge practical joke—Washington's taste for farce is not as well-known as he is—then Washington's intrusion would have been a meditation, indirect of course, on the concept of destiny, and not an accelerated course on the obscure features of a marginal entomological branch. To him, Tomatis, Washington, who was divorced twice and therefore does not feel obligated, every time he's in public, to demonstrate that he's more intelligent than his wife, is also not so naïve as to believe that when he waxes philosophical about the behavior of three mosquitos, that he is just talking about those three mosquitos and not something else. Because someone who says, about the mosquito, that it's this or that thing, Tomatis says, doesn't in fact say, about the mosquito, anything. It's what he says about himself, Tomatis says, and he repeats this so severely in the bright morning on the central avenue that a woman passing just then raises her head and looks at him in surprise. *About himself! About himself!*, in the tone, not without passion, of someone who, disclosing a conspiracy piece by piece, finally volunteers the fundamental revelation that will end the masquerade, as they say, definitively.

Even Leto looks at him, astonished, rocking his head back slightly to acknowledge the intensity; Leto who, since the Mathematician saw Tomatis standing at the entrance to the newspaper and started gesticulating in his direction from the opposite sidewalk, feels like he has become invisible because of the excessive attention Tomatis and the Mathematician are lavishing on each other, forming a kind of mutual aura, impalpable and bright, that he feels excluded from. And still, on the previous block, the Mathematician looked at him over Tomatis's head to form a sort of complicity aimed at neutralizing the arbitrary and compulsive tirades from Tomatis, who cannot stop himself from speaking, without their knowing it, as a result of the tenacious titillations of the menace. The painful exclusion that makes him invisible incites Leto, paradoxically, to smile constantly, maybe to hide his true feelings, but the muscles in his face, which should obey his intentions and form a smile, resist instead, as though his skin were taut and hard, so much so that, from forcing himself to smile or as a result of his overwhelming sense of transparency, he feels a sharp, sporadic pain in his jaw.

According to Tomatis, therefore, the notorious mosquitos had been, for Washington, a pretext—and Tomatis remembers that Washington nodded when Cohen, as Washington finished his story, offered the following suggestion: If Washington had killed one of the mosquitos, the one among the three that had actually let itself be trapped by the first slap, they shouldn't look for the reason in the mosquito but in Washington. *At that suggestion from Cohen, Washington nodded*, Tomatis says. And also when someone objected that if one of the mosquitos had landed on his cheek to bite him and let itself be slapped to death, it was for the simple reason that it's the females and not the males that bite and you could deduce that the one that had tried to bite him was a female and the two that had kept a distance were male; Washington refuted this saying that first off one of the other two mosquitos had tried to land on his cheek or around there several times, and second, and this was, judging from the emphatic tone he used, his primary argument, that on the level he was referring to, gender was not a principal determinant.

Motherfuckers!, Leto thinks. *They can't shut up about their so-called levels. Whatever. Basically, I don't give a shit.* But this isn't true. In fact, sixteen, seventeen years later he will still remember Washington's three mosquitos.

So will the Mathematician who, one morning in 1979, aboard an airplane coming from Paris and beginning its descent into Stockholm, while he waits patiently for the landing, takes his wallet out and, from among the bills, the credit cards, the identification, withdraws the sheet folded in fourths that Tomatis gave him at the entrance to the newspaper, the sheet whose folds are now more brown than yellow and so worn that, when opening it over the tray table where the remains of his breakfast have just been cleared by the stewardess, the Mathematician is extremely cautious, fearing that the folds, splitting at points, will separate completely. But the Mathematician doesn't even read the five typed verses—only glancing at them, now that the sheet, after so many years and so many transfers out of pure habit from one wallet to another, from one jacket to another, from one continent to another, imperfectly sheltered from the years in the Mathematician's warm pockets, has finally lost its communicative quality and become an object, and, ultimately, a relic, halfway between its material presence and what they call the deep well of memory that sooner or later will notice it; or a fragment, not of Tomatis, actually, who he was discussing just the day before with Pichón Garay as they walked through Saint-Germain-des-Prés, coming from the Assemblée Nationale toward the Place Maubert, no, not of Tomatis, but of the morning when, having just returned from his first trip to Europe, he ran into Leto on the central avenue and they walked south together. The

Mathematician looks at the sheet, shakes his head, then carefully folds it again, and after returning it to his wallet and putting the wallet back into the inside pocket of his sport coat, he puts his empty pipe in his mouth and, folding his hands over the tray table, sits in thought. In fact, he first put it in his wallet when he was changing his pants, the evening of the same day Tomatis gave it to him, and was taking everything from his pockets, his handkerchief, his keys, his empty pipe— he packed and smoked it only every so often—a copy of the press release from the Students Association, and because the sheet folded in fourths was among these things, and he was late to a meeting with the Association, he quickly tucked it into his wallet, and for months it sat forgotten in a little compartment until one day, when the wallet was worn out, even, like the sheet, at the folds, and his mother gave him a new one for his twenty-eighth birthday, in switching the papers from one to the other he found it again. He was about to leave it on his desk, to later file it in a drawer with some other papers, but a superstitious hesitation stopped him, and he felt a premonition, certainly unpleasant since it forced him into a kind of servitude, that if he discarded that sheet of paper something awful would happen. With a shake of the head and a brief and skeptical laugh, characteristic of someone allowing themselves a passing weakness that does not correspond with their personality and which they plan to correct as soon as they have time to get to the bottom of the problem, he tucked the sheet into the new wallet and forgot it again for several months. One day when he was reading in his room, he remembered having it and the hesitation that struck him when he tried to let it go, and because he was in a very good mood and felt inwardly clean, organized, and stable, he decided to take it from his wallet in order to jettison, with a decisive act, the unease that his superstitious reaction had left him with, at which point he opened the wardrobe where his jacket hung, took the wallet from his pocket, the sheet from the wallet, returned the wallet to the jacket pocket, closed the wardrobe door, and, opening a desk drawer, prepared himself to drop the sheet folded in fourths onto some papers that lived, as they say, at the bottom, but at the last second he told himself that doing it that way would be compulsive, and it would be more convenient, instead of hiding it in the desk drawer, to leave it a while, in an ordinary way, on the table, the way he would have done with any other thing. So he left it on the table and sat down to read. Night came. He had been concentrating on his reading a while, stopping only to turn on the lamp, when he realized that it was getting dark, and suddenly he raised his head and saw the rectangle of white paper on the table, shining in the intense lamplight, directed strategically to project a luminous circle over the portion of the table where his hands, the book, and the paper sat, leaving the rest of the room in darkness. But only the paper seemed to be present; seized by another feeling that, as he liked to say, *if they aren't measurable, at least with our current understanding, there doesn't seem to be a reason why they would resist*, etc., etc., no?, seized again by one of those feelings, I was saying, that revealed his frailty, the Mathematician recognized, with the same clarity that he could recognize the energy radiated when combustible material burned, that this paper laying on the table radiated danger, that the sheet folded in fourths had a secret relationship to disparate fragments of the universe, and that if he wanted to protect them from destruction, he should not let go of it for any reason—the Mathematician, no?, who after thinking over the above in a calm and clear way, shook his head like the first time and issued the same short, incredulous laugh. He decided to go out, to stop by the bar at the arcade, eat a sandwich or a pizza near the bus terminal, and come back to work until midnight. But after combing his hair a little, adjusting his tie, putting on his jacket, and preparing to leave his room, an impenetrable obstacle, which in spite of having risen, invisible but corporeal, from inside him, seemed to block the doorway and stopped him suddenly at the entrance. It was the danger that, shining from the table, seemed to radiate from the sheet folded in fourths. The intense hesitation made him turn sideways in the doorway, and he was left standing with half his body in the hallway and the other half in the room, his head turned toward the table where the white rectangle reverberated in the harsh light—the white rectangle holding together fragments of the external world, defenseless and anonymous, but already joined to him by secret connections, people maybe, systems, things, he didn't know, something that he, with such a mundane-seeming decision, might take part in exterminating. He thought that he could not give in and, turning off the light and closing the door behind him, resolved not to give in. He went out into the street resolute, and while he took his first steps on the street—it took him only a few seconds to get there, on account of his speed—he forgot about the paper, but almost immediately he began to slow down until, shaking his head, upset, as they say, more than afraid, he stopped completely. And when he went back for the paper, to neutralize it, and tucked it into his wallet, he told himself he was doing it less out of fear that those fearful connections really existed than because he didn't want his thoughts to ruin the walk. With the world safe in a compartment of his wallet, he was able to think better, and with a cool head it wasn't difficult to realize that neither Tomatis nor his verses had anything to do with that species of nefarious energy that had built up in the sheet, but instead, through some coincidence, an encounter had occurred between the paper, up to that point neutral and inscribed on a different network of relationships, and a moment of personal weakness, owing maybe to exhaustion, to a momentary trans-formation that, in reorganizing the constituent elements of his person-ality, brought them all to the surface without exception, including the most ancillary and most archaic, in order to form a new synthesis that would definitively relegate the useless parts, the same way that, when he was cleaning his desk, he would withdraw and read all the papers stored in the drawers, the ones he would keep and the ones he had decided to throw out. It was a good explanation, and the Mathemati-cian did not place that passing anomaly in the same hierarchy as The Incident but, although he only thought about it from time to time, and always with the same skeptical and brief internal smile, eighteen years later he still carried the sheet folded in fourths in a compartment of his wallet, and though he had memorized the lines, every once in a while he would take it out and look it over, in a mechanical, unpremeditated way, with the gray and somewhat worn gestures of the customary, like that morning on the tray table which the stewardess had just cleaned of his breakfast when the airplane which, as we were saying, or rather yours truly was saying, just now, had left Paris a few hours before and was beginning to descend into Stockholm.

Though it was still February, in Paris, strangely, the weather had been good, a humid and still cold sun, and they had flown at three thousand feet, allowing, every so often, pale sunlight to stream through the windows. Distracted, the Mathematician glanced out, knowing that now, for a few months, until May at least, he would be away in Uppsala, and just as he was looking toward the windows—he was sitting in the opposite aisle, in a middle seat—the airplane flew into a thick, grayish fog, which was the clouds, which seemed, suddenly, to swallow the monotonous and consequently inconspicuous sound of the engines. If Limbo were somewhere among the clouds, certainly at that instant the airplane was starting to cross it. For the moment, before the final landing maneuvers, it seemed motionless more than anything, but because that motionlessness followed the sudden change of dipping into the thick mass of clouds, the impression was of a motionlessness frozen mid-movement, as though time itself and not just the moving machine had stopped. Equally motionless, resting against the back of his chair, his hands deserted on the tray table, the Mathematician, his eyes fixed on a vague spot somewhere in the enormous empty cabin, was so absent from the airplane that, no doubt as a consequence of the illusory and indistinct stillness of the machine, he seemed like a character from one of those fantastical stories, instantly spirited away to a magical world while the real world he comes from remains stopped and as though frozen through the entire duration of his adventures.

He is on the Boulevard Saint-Germain with Pichón Garay; they have been walking from the Assemblée Nationale toward the Place Maubert. Just then they have reached the Rue du Bac; at the entrance to the Assemblée they had split from the delegation—a group of exiles who have just been received by representatives of the socialist bloc, and who promised them, the bloc, no?, to look into the issue, the massacres, the disappearances, the tortures, the assassinations in the middle of the day in the middle of the street, etc., etc., ultimately, as we were saying, from the start, or rather yours truly has been saying—and more or less, no?—every thing. The two forty-somethings, dressed in youthful clothing, have separated from their so-called compatriots and have started walking slowly under the unexpected, cold, and above all humid February sun, as others have written, it's true, many times, although it's always the same—as yours truly has been saying from the start—always, like in the beginning all the way to the end, if there were, as they, the knowing, say, a beginning, and if there will be, as they imagine, an end—I was saying, no?, the same Time, in the same, no?, as I already said several times, in the Same, no matter the city, in Buenos Aires, in Paris, in Uppsala, in Stockholm, and farther away still, still, as I was saying, Place. In a word, essentially, or in two better yet, to be more precise, every thing.

The year before, in May, Washington died of prostate cancer; in June, El Gato and Elisa, who had been living together in Rincón since she and Héctor separated, were kidnapped by the government and had not been heard from since. And around that same time, though it only came out later, Leto, Ángel Leto, no?, who for years had been living in hiding, found himself obligated, because of an ambush set up by the police, to finally bite the suicide pill that, for security reasons, the leaders of his movement distribute to the soldiers so that, if they are surprised, as they say, by the enemy, they will not compromise, during their torture, the entire organization. And Leto had bitten the pill. The Mathematician, for his part, is well-informed of these things, given that, though he was often at odds with her opinion, he and his wife had shared, for several years, until they killed her, in 1974, that singular existence. *The marriage of the Mathematician!* Tomatis, for whom every example of the female sex whose measurements in the chest, waist, and thighs did not correspond to those of Miss Universe is an indistinct and transparent creature, one night in 1970, sitting with Barco on a bench at the waterfront after a long walk, remarked on the marriage in more or less these terms: The Mathematician was one of the most handsome, intelligent, elegant, rich men he had known; more than once he had seen him remain impervious to the advances of the most beautiful girls in the city. Every time that a woman entered a party where the Mathematician was present you could instantly tell that the eyes of said woman were turning, inevitably, in the Mathematician's direction. Tomatis was sure that, for a couple of years, Beatriz, who he had tried and failed to seduce, was secretly in love with the Leibnizian rugby-man. And after years of unflustered, mysterious bachelorhood, the Mathematician had taken up conjugals with Edith. *Incendiary news!* Tomatis says. And just a year later they're married. Tomatis knows Edith: she is fourteen years older than the Mathematician; she's short, fat, ugly, Jewish, a feminist, a Trotskyite and widow of a Trotskyite who, clandestinely militant since 1967, died in a brawl with government thugs, at a bar in the great Buenos Aires. *His parents* (the Mathematician's, no?) *I don't think objected at all, but Leandro, his brother, and the rest of the family, I can see their faces. He crossed the line. Traitor*, said Tomatis, his head shaking with laughter. But he was wrong; consciously at least, as Tomatis himself might say, there had been no premeditation or intention to provoke. The Mathematician felt sincere respect and an egalitarian affection for Edith, and a few years before, when they had been active together in a Trotskyite group, he had been a little in love with her. In any case, they didn't see each other much, and although the Mathematician did not completely approve of an armed rebellion, and they calmly and often discussed these things, they blindly trusted each other and, every once in a while, felt an intense desire to meet again, him to be with someone who deserved the quota of admiration and respect he could not live without and which, as he got older, very few people inspired in him, her because she trusted his intelligence and his loyalty and because he provided her, through his uncompromising critiques, a criteria for reality that action obscured. As soon as they met, despite his being twenty and she a little over thirty, they were like an old couple, connected by a kind of desperate tenacity that made them, because of their differences, marvel at having met, both convinced, for distinct reasons of course, that nothing was possible, but constantly acting as though anything were. They hadn't seen each other for years, the intractable activist and the good son, condemned to join their lives with the common component that luck had granted them, their moral conscience, which, after so much error, insanity, and violence that certainly neither was entirely innocent of, made them react with the same intransigence. They had a shared, official apartment in Buenos Aires and a little house in the Córdoba mountains no one knew about, which they called *the phalanstère* for security reasons, and where in difficult moments they met in secret. She would be at the typewriter constantly and would give him what she called *the material*, reports, political analyses, statements, that the Mathematician read carefully, shaking his head, negatively most of the time, marking the individual themes with different colored pens—he had gone to work in the chemical industry in Buenos Aires and then had become a professor at the university, and he always retained the habit of marking industrial reports, notes, and his students' homework with colored pens or pencils. Finally, in 1974, they killed her. Everything happened quickly, and the Mathematician's initial fear that, because they saw each other sporadically, and she would disappear again and again in an unsystematic way, she would be killed and he would never know it was ultimately unwarranted, because one evening in July an anonymous telephone call informed him that they had killed her that morning and he should disappear because any second the police would be raiding his apartment. Calmly but quickly he packed a suitcase with clothes, books, and papers and caught the bus to Córdoba, hoping that the news was false and that she would be waiting for him at *the phalanstère*, but despite traces of a recent occupation in the house, she never came. He didn't fool himself: the telephone call could have come from one of Edith's fellow soldiers, to whom she had expressed at some point her desire to have her death communicated to him, but it—the call, no?—could have come from the same people who had killed her, given that, although his brother wasn't yet in the government, where he would be in '76, he nevertheless had sufficient influence and intimacy among the security forces to protect him. If the latter was what had really occurred, he still didn't fool himself much: with Leandro more than ten years had passed, since their father's funeral, without their meeting or speaking, and if they passed on the street they ignored each other, so if Leandro had protected him it was to protect the family name, as he might say, and, above all, his own political career—with excellent results, actually, having emerged unscathed from massacres, combat, assassinations, shootings, tortures, concentration camps, bombings, and overthrown governments, he had become a minister in the provincial government in '76, without once losing his tanned, healthy, calm, and elegant appearance, and without having missed a single eleven o'clock Sunday mass or a call to his mother at 8:00 sharp every other day for twenty years. The day after he left for Córdoba, a group of armed men raided his apartment in Buenos Aires and, not before removing every valuable object, tore it to pieces. He had no illusions about this either: if Leandro had been the one to inform him about the raid on his apartment, he must also have been the one responsible for its destruction, in order to teach him a lesson about deviating from the norms that governed the life of his tribe—*the bloodlust bourgeoisie*—like the time when he was undersecretary in another de facto government and had ordered him taken prisoner for several days. He was safe in Córdoba for a few months— only he and Edith knew about the house—but because his sudden appearance in the town, his isolation, and his excessively long stay might awaken the neighbors' suspicions, he returned to Buenos Aires. A Swedish friend put him up in his apartment and found him work at the University of Uppsala. Early in November he landed in Stockholm for the first time. The black and terrible winter waiting ahead disoriented him a little, but in the spring he started walking around, warmly dressed and with his unlit pipe in his mouth, among the houses and gardens of the university, and on Sunday afternoons he would watch televised sports programs. The rest of the time he read his timeless philosophers and the newspaper clippings he received, prepared his courses, and, when the holidays came, traveled south, to Paris, where Pichón Garay lived, to Madrid or Rome, and every once in a while he would stop off in Copenhagen, which he continued to like despite, as he liked to say, its smooth and well-swept streets which seemed to be more influenced by Andersen than Kierkegaard or the Interpretation.

The Mathematician put on his glasses. In the half-empty cabin his sudden and at the same time slow gesture contrasted with the illusory stillness of the airplane, which floated in a bank of the gray clouds like a fragile object wrapped in cotton packaging. To the external equilibrium corresponded, just then, a kind of internal stillness, lacking any moral or emotive primacy and resulting from a chain of events too long, too complex, and too buried to inspire any analytical interest, but paradoxical enough that, with all the bad news, returning to the dark north and his almost complete isolation for three or four months, that unquestionable internal stillness, in the motionless and illuminated limbo of the airplane among the clouds or their coincidence with it, was not much different from well-being. And all because of the walk with Pichón Garay the day before, leaving the Assemblée Nationale and walking down the Boulevard Saint-Germain toward the Place Maubert! After the meeting with the representatives, the other members of the delegation decided to have lunch together, but without having agreed to beforehand, Pichón and the Mathematician declined the invitation. Apart from ideology they had, to tell the truth, nothing in common with the other members of the delegation, who were certainly very earnest, but who lacked the force of experience or memory. And saying goodbye to the others, they had started to walk.

Without knowing how, they began talking about Washington's birthday, maybe because that night had inspired the phrase, *it's like Washington's mosquitos*, meaning something was of dubious reality, which Pichón had employed just then in reference to the promises of possible help for the refugees on the part of the French government. The Mathematician knew the expression well, but the accumulated experiences of the last few years had stifled its memory somewhat, and hearing it again, after a period of forgetting, revived, like the periodic cosmos, and re-substantiated, so to speak, clear and intact, large fragments of his former life, and the Mathematician began to recall, without meaning to, memories of experiences that had never happened. No one knew who had first used the expression, or when, but at the time, after the famous night, it began appearing in conversations, and even once, astonishingly, the Mathematician had heard it used by someone who not only didn't know Washington or any of the guests, but also couldn't have known the story or even imagined it, and if he had heard it, could not have understood it or been interested at all. Pichón had begun to discourse on the expression after having used it, recalling the party without noticing that the Mathematician, who had been visiting factories in Frankfurt when it took place, was nodding along, still, eighteen years later, feeling a sense of shame and humiliation at not having been there, and only through an exercise of will was he able to transform the nod into a negative shake before declaring, and causing a passing confusion in Pichón's memories: *I, unfortunately, was not there.* Pichón couldn't remember well: It was a story with three mosquitos . . . three mosquitos that . . . how did it go? He really wasn't there? Strange, because he clearly remembers seeing him next to the keg, discussing something with Horacio Barco. Wasn't he, the Mathematician, the one who, in the morning, when Pirulo, slightly tipsy, tried to fight with Miguel Ángel Podio over some political story, had tried to separate them? The Mathematician shook his head as Pichón continued assigning him actions that had never taken place, without realizing that Pichón's confusion overwhelmed any disadvantage to the absent and that, after so many years, the events were as distant and inaccessible to those who had participated in them as to those who only knew them as hearsay. And Pichón, who resisted evicting him from his memories, and in truth never would, scratching his chin perplexedly, continued: Really? Wasn't he, the Mathematician, the one who had driven Washington there? Hadn't it been with him that he, Pichón, had gone to pick frozen mandarins to bring to the table and seeing that one of the trees was shaking violently in the darkness had approached, thinking it was an owl when actually it was Barco and La Chichito whispering and laughing quietly, intertwined and hidden in the leaves? And he could have sworn that the Mathematician was among the group who, early in the morning, when almost everyone had gone to sleep or returned home and only six or seven people were left, huddled together drinking *mate* around the fireplace in the house—Basso, Barco, Beatriz, Silvia Cohen, him, Pichón, no?—while Washington, refreshed and calm, started comparing, who knows from what tangent off the conversation, the Hatha Yoga *mudrā* with the Fourierian utopia, arguing that the *mudrā*, which compel the human body into unnatural positions and psychological states that are, *a priori*, considered impossible, refute biological fatalism the same way that the society theorized by Fourier, where everything is deliberately constructed in rational opposition to spontaneous liberal self-regulation, once and for all demolishes the social fatalism that supposedly underlies all oppressive human nature. Pichón barely remembered the mosquitos or Noca's horse, but that conversation, around the fireplace, in the frozen morning, was still with him. And, more than anything, the return to the city. Washington had to do some things before going back to Rincón Norte, cash his pension check or something, Pichón didn't remember anymore, but what he felt sure of was that they returned in two cars, La Chichito's and the Mathematician's, no? And the Mathematician shook his head: *Tsk-tsk-tsk-tsk . . . impossible*; he, just then, was in Frankfurt, he remembers very well. And Pichón was forced, temporarily, with considerable effort and certainly unconvinced, to remove him from his memory, so fresh, clear, and orderly, as if from the previous day; true or false, it was more or less this: excited by the night's drinking, by having stayed awake, by the conversations, they went out into the cold morning to discover that, since the temperature had been falling near sunrise, which had made them at some point move from the pavilion to the house, at many points around the yellowish fields, the dew had been settling in frozen white patches that the already rising sun, shining in a pale sky, had not yet been able to thaw. Pichón remembers the clean, icy air, and that, walking out of the house, Silvia Cohen had gone to inspect the first buds of a tree, asking out loud if the frost would kill them. Everyone had started looking at the sky, the air, the trees, the sandy path, trying to guess, with looks that became suddenly uncertain and solemn, the real severity of the frost, determined to pronounce on the possible survival of the buds, until finally, after a decidedly measured deliberation, they agreed, just as they were getting into the cars, that it was a relatively mild frost and the buds, certainly, would resist it. Pichón had begun to laugh so intensely that the Mathematician, infected, laughed too, and for no other reason, since Pichón's laughter was caused by a memory he had yet to express and would only describe a few seconds later, realizing that if, after inspecting the severity of the frost with their eyes, skin, and lungs, they had agreed on its innocuousness, it wasn't that they had the least capacity for an objective analysis of the weather conditions, but that after the night they had been through, the drinking and the dawn, the momentary carnal exchanges in the darkened margins of the gathering, the excitement of the conversations, they had come out into the icy morning happy and reconciled, and they wanted—because forgetting this realized their desire—for those benevolent waves rocking them to be verified, incontrovertible, in the external.

Like that. Or, if you like, more or less—more or less like that, no? Through his glasses the Mathematician passed his gaze over the illuminated cabin, without paying, as they say, too much attention to the motionless heads protruding over the seats, or to the windows covered by that cottony substance that intercepts the external light and paradoxically emphasizes the artificial clarity in the cabin. Over the years he had gained some weight, but not much, because his conviction that sports was the best way to counterbalance his sedentariness had preserved him—through a methodical but less obsessive practice than the worship of the body that emerged in the West after the death of the gods—from the ravages time inflicts on the body of a forty-year-old, but his blonde hair had dulled and turned somewhat ashen, and extremely fine wrinkles, closer to those of an infant than an old man, creased his face in clusters of more or less parallel lines whose orientation reproduced on his skin the hidden location of his facial muscles. The sudden burst of laughter on the Boulevard Saint-Germain, the day before, resonated inside him with the singular quality of sonorous recollections that, while they return silently to memory, do not lose their timbre, color, or intensity. The well-being came less from the implicit but ultimately restrained joy of the conversation itself and the context that produced it, than from the effect of certain words, of certain associations that, in an unexpected way, allowed him to unbind, or unglue rather, sections of his life that had become superimposed and stuck together, the way those posters on city walls, under successive layers of paste and printed paper, form a kind of crust whose tattered and distressed edges can barely be made out, though you know that on each covered page persists, invisible, an image. Since the day before, many of those covered images had reappeared thanks, not to his own memories, but to Pichón's—Pichón, no?—who despite the privilege of experience was just as lost in a deceptive uncertainty, while at the time he, the Mathematician, had criticized himself for having been in Frankfurt, depriving himself of the means of capturing, at a fixed point in reality, the approximate sequence of events with the network of his five senses.

Suddenly the Mathematician remembered a dream, or rather, a nightmare. He had been passing a somewhat vacuous gaze over the

116

cabin, produced by the emotional neutrality transformed, as the laughter dissipated in his memory, from the well-being of a few moments earlier—and if, as they say, pleasure is nothing but the absence of pain, his internal vacuousness, without a doubt painless, could be considered a consequence of that well-being. The airplane's illusory, slightly oblique detention in the cottony Limbo persisted, blocking the windows, and the Mathematician, sitting at the outside end of a row of seats halfway to the back, could see the cabin floor declining almost imperceptibly down, toward the front of the plane, and he thought again, somewhat amazed, of that elemental mechanical paradox that demonstrates that motionlessness is what creates motion, that motion is simply a reference to motionlessness, and just then the machine, which had swallowed him in Paris and would spit him out in Stockholm a few minutes from now, as if it had been aware of his thoughts, correcting its position, its speed maybe, or its direction, he couldn't tell, produced, benevolently, a series of vibrations that caused it to tremble a little, along with everything it carried inside, as though it had wanted to confirm for the Mathematician that the Limbo was transitory, a variant lull, and that each of those vibrations was reactivating time, space, matter, thought, until, after those two or three shivers that reintroduced the swarm of distinction into the heart of the singular, it returned to complete stillness. The Mathematician's nightmare was as follows: Walking through an indistinct and deserted city, he found a piece of paper lying on the sidewalk, a kind of rigid strip four or five centimeters long and one centimeter wide; for several moments he stood observing it, without mistrust but without hurry, trying to understand its significance, its use, the likely circumstances that had brought it there—almost, almost its mystery. Bent toward it, but without deciding to pick it up, intrigued, he observed it, until finally he took it up into the palm of his hand to study it closer, realizing that it actually wasn't a rigid strip but a sheet folded like an accordion, whose external band, seen from above, had looked like a flat strip. Now that he had it close, he noticed that he had missed the primary feature: what he had thought was a stain in the middle of the strip was actually his own portrait, printed vertically, his head and shoulders, not clearly either a drawing or a photograph, his own portrait, no?, with an expression that seemed naïve, youthful, somewhat tender. Fascinated by his discovery, his fingers shaking a little, he turned the strip to the opposite face, in the literal sense of the word, and another portrait was printed in the middle of the strip, at the same height as on the obverse side; only the expression had changed, so much so that, for an instant, he thought it was someone else—but it wasn't, it was him, himself. On the reverse side, the expression was furrowed, solemn, and seemed to be trying to display a strength of character that because of its ostentation was ultimately unconvincing. All of this inspired a certain levity and heightened his curiosity, and taking the ends of the object between the tips of his index finger and thumb, he began to unfold the accordion very slowly, confirming what he had predicted, that on each face of the folds on the paper, at the same height as the previous, there was his portrait, not clearly either a drawing or a photograph; on each of the portraits the expression was so different that, although he knew it was the same person, for an instant he suffered the brief delusion, passing a moment later, that it wasn't him. Separating his symmetrically facing thumbs and index fingers toward the edges of the paper, he unfolded the accordion a little more, knowing that he would be increasing the variety of miniature portraits, printed vertically at the same height, beginning now to form a small multitude of, to him, amusingly conventional expressions. A second-rate actor in the broadest downmarket television series wouldn't have employed more vulgar gestures to effect innocence, pain, guilelessness, intelligence, avarice, resolution, disdain, cunning, desire, emotions, and traces of a personality which appeared so domesticated, so pliant to conventions, that they stank of servitude but nevertheless revealed, through hidden details, a compassionate attitude toward the spectator. *Of course*, he thought. *This is a dream. It signifies that we don't have one personality but many. In addition, all the expressions we assume are insincere, incomplete, and conventional. My dreams are so transparent*, and he continued unfolding the strip. By now he had unfolded it so much that he stood in the middle of the sidewalk with his arms stretched apart, and the sheet, which started off straight and rigid, seemed to have softened somewhat, because of the increasing width, and curved down. His first moment of unease, abruptly effacing his amusement, was a physical one, because he realized that, no matter how far he stretched his arms, he wouldn't be able to unfold the accordion completely, but at the same time he figured out that he could let go of the ends, grab the sheet with both hands and open it from the middle in order to complete the operation without needing to stretch his arms and instead sliding the paper strip apart with his hands, letting the already unfolded ends accumulate on the ground. He did this. But as he slid it open, it continued unfolding. At his feet, on the indistinct and blurry sidewalk, the accordion folded strip accumulated in two symmetrical piles, without his being able to reach the center. He quickened the sliding but the only thing he accomplished was to instill them, on account of the diversity of effigies printed on the folds, with caricaturish life as the stereotypical expressions were juxtaposed and, through a phenomenon similar to retinal persistence, created a contradictory and unknown face: then the expression was distorted and lost its conventional aspect, taking on vertiginous and demented features, so that, sensing that his unease was becoming anguish, he decided to slow down. Now, as they passed slowly, the effigies were increasingly decayed and indistinct and the whiteness of the page darkened, taking on an exhausted and yellowed tint. His anguish grew when he sensed that the texture, consistency, and temperature of the paper had changed, resembling a material that was familiar but which he resisted examining directly; he continued slowly unfolding the infinite strip with this head turned away and his eyes closed tight. Shaking his hands he tried to release the strip, but it was useless. He turned his head and opened his eyes. He was naked on the sidewalk, and the strip he was sliding open between his fingers was the skin coming off his own body in a continuous and even ribbon, like a bandage being unwound. It was a single, infinite length of skin unwinding. And when he screamed, sitting up in the hotel bed, in the dark, without realizing at first that it was a nightmare, it was because he had started to realize before waking up that when the strip finished unfolding, where he was, where he had been, nothing would be left, not a speck, not a sign, not anything that his purely external body was carrying inside it—nothing, no?—but a hole, a transparency, the invisible and once again homogenous space, the passive receptor of the light he had considered his kingdom and yet where not one of his false features would be imprinted.

—On top of that, Tomatis says, do not forget that by then the beer and the white wine were beginning to take effect.

Not in Washington, of course, he clarifies, but Beatriz and Silvia are not ones to shy from the bottle. And Cuello, forget it—unfortunately his congenital populism blooms once he's put back a few glasses, and it ends up being impossible to dissuade him from his fixed idea that the best way to fill the silence at a party is with folklore. Pirulo, on the other hand, is an evil drunk and likes to get in fights—he, Tomatis, can understand the resentment of someone who has nothing but American sociology to help him deal with reality. Early in the morning, he doesn't remember why anymore, Pirulo had started exchanging blows with Dib, and he and Pichón had to go and separate them—Dib and Pirulo, who had been such good friends in school and claimed to have mobilized between them the entire Rosarian student body in '59. You can see, Tomatis suggests, why living with Pirulo makes Rosario look for comfort at the end of a needle. What happened was they found them punching each other at the back of the patio— Dib had blood running from nose and bloody stains on his sweater. As soon as he, Tomatis, no?, and Pichón looked away, they had started again: Dib had Pirulo by the hair and was dragging him across the patio, between the mandarins. Finally Barco, who's like two meters tall, had to separate them. Between the three of them they pushed Dib and Pirulo to the bathroom and made them wash their faces, all of this in low voices, whispering so that the people under the pavilion wouldn't notice. Which failed, of course, and two minutes later he, Tomatis, no?, Pichón, Pirulo, Dib, Barco, Basso, Nidia Basso, Rosario, and Botón were all in the bathroom, yelling at each other in what they imagined were low voices. Basso wanted to kick them out, but Nidia intervened on their behalf; Rosario was shaking her head and not saying anything, staring at Pirulo with a look that more or less said, *You had to make a scene again*; and Botón, who only an hour before had tried to rape La Chichito, was acting like Dib and Pirulo's behavior was a personal insult to Washington. *Don't let Washington find out, please*, he was saying melodramatically, when a minute earlier La Chichito, all disheveled, had come crying under the pavilion, holding up her skirt because Botón had broken its zipper. He had gotten the idea, Tomatis recalls, that Dib and Pirulo had to give each other a conciliatory hug, an idea thoroughly in Botón's style, and if you needed further proof that Botón and reality were entities of a contradictory nature, he insisted on volunteering this genteel exhortation while everyone else, divided into two groups, was making a superhuman effort to hold back Dib and Pirulo, who had been glaring at each other during the reconciliation and at the slightest distraction started hitting each other again. Finally the whole thing ended when . . .

Abruptly, Tomatis cuts off his story and stops so unexpectedly that Leto and the Mathematician take two or three more steps before stopping too, noticing when they turn around that Tomatis, in the middle of the street, is surveying, with a worried look, the trajectory they have just traveled together, as though he were measuring the distance. In fact, since they left the entrance to the newspaper, they have covered three blocks, and after crossing, with some difficulty, the cause of the bottleneck at the first intersection and continuing easily in the middle of the street thanks to the absence of cars, they've crossed two more intersections without paying any attention at all, Tomatis concentrating on his story, and the Mathematician and Leto on the somewhat awkward reproach the story causes them to feel. Guessing the distance, a more and more scornful expression takes over Tomatis, whose gaze, which has become sullen and evasive, deliberately avoids meeting Leto's and the Mathematician's. A bitter, humiliating thought, unexpected and scattered, overwhelms him when he realizes that, absorbed in the details of his story, he has let himself be dragged three blocks, something along the lines of, *as if they didn't know that everything is going to, that I'm going to, that sooner or later the whole universe is going*—no?—*as if they didn't know, and worse still if they don't know it, coming along and asking me to sign up for this senseless adventure, walking three blocks with them and telling them about Washington's birthday*, a thought painted so clearly on his face that the Mathematician who, out of respect for what you might call Tomatis's hypothetical strength of character, has been trying to intercept his gaze, gives up and, just the opposite, admitting defeat, tries to give him an opportunity to excuse himself.

—Maybe we're taking you too far from the paper, he offers.

Not taking part, somewhat indifferently, in such a delicate situation, Leto has started thinking, *It could be that he had an incurable illness, like she insists, but the most important symptom isn't the cellular degeneration but the act of lifting the revolver in his hand and pressing the barrel to his temple.*

—Everyone at the paper, says Tomatis, from the editor down to the very last sports reporter, and most of all the editor, and most of all the very last sports reporter, can suck my ass—which translates, the Mathematician imagines, if he has understood correctly, into more or less the following: *the paper doesn't have anything to do with this, and it's out of delicacy and so I don't get twisted up in neutered discussions that I don't point out the ones actually responsible.* And all because of the scattered and nameless pressure of the menace, of the turbulences in the neutral, which in a single stroke, through unexpected coincidences of flesh and scent, unhinges and tears apart! For a few seconds they remain motionless—motionless, why not, no?—if you leave aside, and it's worth asking why, the cohesion, to put a word to it, of what are apparently called atoms, the, if there are no objections, cellular activity

122

or the so-called circulation of blood, the supposed muscular effort, the magnetic disturbances surrounding them, the continuous flow of light, the imperceptible drift of the continents, the so-called terrestrial revolution and rotation, the general gravitational force, as the papers have it, and including, if you bear in mind the latest issues of the specialized journals, the expansion or, depending on how you look at it, collapse of what they call the universe, motionless, ultimately, if we accept, having come this far, the word, unsatisfactory of course the more you keep at it, when, on second thought, the motionless would be, rather, a whirlwind or a stationary stampede—motionless, then, as yours truly, no?, or better yet—in a word, or in two better yet, to be more precise: every thing.

And like that they separate. Shaking his head a little next to two bent fingers along his temple as though he were taking a mental note, with a look that said, *if I don't make you pay for this it's because I'm not begrudging*, Tomatis, without conceding any other sign of farewell, turns around and starts walking toward the newspaper. Corpulent and dark, somewhat strange in the morning sun, he seems to be reconstructing, while he moves away with an uneven keel, a kind of imaginary dignity that the encounter with Leto and the Mathematician had displaced. Leto observes him, more distracted than relieved, asking himself, without realizing it, now that Tomatis has shaken them loose, how he, Leto, can likewise shake off the Mathematician. His indifference toward Tomatis's abrupt and humiliating departure is nothing but a modest revenge for the fleeting complicity between Tomatis and the Mathematician who, a few moments earlier, had kept him on the periphery of the aura they radiated. The Mathematician, after shaking his head lightly for a few seconds, turning resolutely toward him, seems to consider the incident finished.

—They can cut one of my nuts off if I know what's bugging him, he says, exaggerating his annoyance.

And both of mine if I have to keep at it with these clowns, Leto thinks, but while he resumes his walk next to the Mathematician, who with a single stride has reached him and continues without stopping, instead of showing his irritation, he assumes an impartial attitude and says:

—You can tell a mile off that he's not well.

The Mathematician does not answer, wrestling, somewhat exultant, his head held upright, with the quick bind of his own disquisitions, and Leto abandons him to his silence. In any case, for several minutes, he has been withdrawing from the bright street, from the October morning, immersed, as they say, in a single object, the damned revolver that the man—his father, that is—insolently according to Rey, and no doubt resolute, had raised to his temple the year before, taking care not to fail as regards the results—a discreet but familiar object that he, even as a child, would from time to time withdraw from the wardrobe, where it was stored in a wooden box with other knickknacks, so he could play gunslinger. Once, in the middle of a fight, Isabel ran to the bedroom melodramatically and took from the wardrobe, and from the box, the revolver that he, Leto, no?, knew wasn't loaded, while his aunt Charo, who had arrived in the middle of the fight, struggled to pry it from her hands. They cried and argued while the man, without saying a word, had locked himself in the garage to clean up the tools that Isabel, a few minutes before, in the fury of the argument, had thrown to the ground, cables, screws, parts, radio bulbs smashed to pieces, against the man's unfazed silence, his father, no?, who didn't even assume a stoic or resigned expression—nothing like that, no, nothing, not a single theatrical gesture, no intemperance, a creature made from material that, in contrast to the appliances he assembled and dismantled, built of countless small parts and interdependent fragments to make them work, seemed solid, without internal turmoil, lacking external signals to betray any contradiction, absorbed in preparation for the single act he would carry out years later, intending to obliterate, the way someone might flick a fuzzball from their shoulder, the vulgar error that the indistinct shades clattering around him called the outside world. He must have been eight or nine at the time—Leto and the Mathematician cross, oblivious, just like many other pedestrians, who move around them in every direction, down the street and the sidewalk, from south to north, from north to south, from east to west, from west to east, tracing straight, oblique, parallel or diagonal trajectories, the intersection where a row of cars waits, you could say, patiently and resigned. Eight or nine, only, because, and this he remembers well, the garage was the one in Arroyito. It must have been three or four in the afternoon on a summer day, a silent siesta whose brightness was dimmed by the dark screens on the doors and windows, protecting the house, clean and cool thanks to Isabel's persistent work, which in spite of the nightly weeping she cleaned, swept, and polished, without missing a single corner, humming, no?, every morning. The man was in the workshop, in the garage; Isabel, dressed to go out, was waiting for Charo somewhere in the house; he, Leto, stretched out face up across his bed, his head hanging a little over the edge, held his arm up and, with the back of his hand fifty centimeters from his head, was wiggling his fingers without stopping, not closing them and keeping them well-separated, fascinated by their shape and by the movement they were capable of, personifying each of them a little, while at the same time, his mouth open, he amused himself by making his vocal chords vibrate, emitting a string of gut-tural and somewhat fractured sounds, changing the sound every so often, going from an *a* to an *e*, to an *i*, going back to the first one, or vocalizing all of the vowels one after the other and modulating, like a virtuoso, the intensity of the vibrations. With a strange curiosity, he seemed to touch certain regions of his own body the same way that, he might say, now that he's older, he would have tried out a new suit the night before a wedding. His fascination was so intense that, when the shouting started, a long moment elapsed before he heard it, and when he got up and walked slowly toward the workshop, where the shouts seemed to be coming from, his alarm did not efface the curios-ity, but rather made it change direction. Both of them were in the workshop; Isabel, crying and gesticulating, was hitting the man on the chest and face, not with her hands or her fists, but with her forearms, while the man, rigid and leaning back somewhat, received this without moving or reacting, his eyes wide open, more questioning and patient than surprised, so unfazed that Isabel, humiliated and enraged by this new disillusion being inflicted on her, after looking around a moment, distractedly, for something to discharge herself against, found the long, pine work table and, again with her forearms, keeping her fists shut tight like two stumps, started sweeping the surface of the table, throwing everything on it to the floor. She only opened her fists when some object resisted and she was forced to grab it in order to smash it against the concrete floor. Calm, unfazed, not even pale or with his lips pressed together, the man followed her, gathering up the falling objects and calculating with a professional objectivity, before returning it to its place, the damage it might have suffered. The scene lasted a few minutes until Isabel, realizing that everything in existence, independent, outside herself, was intractable and would not bend, took on an extremely intense expression—of resolve, possibly—and started running toward the bedroom. He followed her, knowing that the man, behind him, as though he were alone in the house, would continue piecing together, slowly and meticulously, his working materials. Leto saw his aunt Charo, who has coming in from the street just then, look once at Isabel and take off running after her toward the bedroom. He saw them struggle, fighting for the unloaded revolver, and when Isabel finally gave up, Charo took hold of the revolver, put it in the box, and replaced the box in the wardrobe, and when she closed the wardrobe door Leto could see, reflected in the mirror, an image of Isabel, standing near the wardrobe, the image of Isabel perfectly reversed, the image that, when the door closed completely, disappeared from sight. Finally, Isabel let herself fall, sitting on the edge of the bed, and for several minutes aunt Charo, crying a little as well, tried to console her. He, Leto, no?, observed this from the doorway, expecting, hoping almost, maybe without realizing it, that they would not notice his presence but, as though she had read his thoughts, maybe *because* she had read them, Isabel, who had now calmed down somewhat, locked eyes with him, and assuming a fatigued and commiserative expression, made a gesture that, as he was perceiving it, he tried to exorcize with all his strength so that it wouldn't be produced, knowing that she would hold out her hands in his direction, encouraging him to curl up with them, and when he saw the soft and round arms calling him, he took off running and shut himself in his room. He stayed there until dark, not thinking that he was shutting himself in, unworried and without remorse—no, he stayed there playing and hearing, every so often, the sounds of the house, the man from time to time leaving the workshop to go to the bathroom or the kitchen, the return of Isabel, humming, seeming contented again and a little self-absorbed, and starting to make dinner. When he realized it was time to eat, he went out to the kitchen and helped set the table. She seemed refreshed and calm, careful and nimble in her domestic chores, satisfied almost, and at eight or nine years old, those inexplicable but seemingly authentic changes in mood mesmerized him. When everything was ready, she told him to go call the man to the table, so Leto, unhurried, crossed the house and, through the half-open door, peeked in to the workshop installed in the garage.

The man, maybe because the smell of the food had reached him, or because the usual time for dinner was approaching, or because hearing Isabel humming in the kitchen he understood that the routine of the house was operational again after their fight that afternoon, was standing in front of the table, organizing his tools, the way he would whenever he left the workshop, even if it was only to eat and go right back half an hour later. One glance was enough for Leto to see that everything was in its right place again and that not the slightest trace of what had happened remained. Serious and pleasant, the man, hearing him come in, offered a quick look of consent, but during the momentary distraction that the look caused him, his fingers, searching the surface of the table near where it met the wall, touched something so unexpected, intense, and brutal that the arm drew back and his whole body, contracted and rigid, jumped or was sucked backward, while the man, with a pained look, rubbed the hand and arm that had just retracted. Leto was too familiar with the man's occupation to not realize that he'd received an electrical jolt, *shock therapy*, they called it, but the surprise of witnessing the manifestation of something they had terrorized him with ever since he could toddle gave way to astonishment, to panic almost, before the unexpected reaction from the man who, after recovering from the surprise, took on a strange, malevolent smile and, still rubbing his arm, started to speak, to talk to the invisible force that had shaken him, to converse almost, in a tender but at the same time ironic and defiant tone, not without malice, the way he might have talked to a living thing, a puppy or a person whose intimacy was problematic. Ironic, with hate-laced affection, the man chatted, reproachfully, with the unseen. Leto approached the table and leaned toward the wall where, standing on his toes, he was able to see the end of a cable, made of naked threads of twisted copper wire that the man started to push back, to duel almost, like an excited dog, with the end of his index finger, which he drew near and withdrew from carefully but daringly, to test its intensity, the limits of its force, of its territory—invisible and vigilant—you could almost say, and several times he was forced to pull back quickly, but not needing to stop smiling or talking to it, in a constant and playful whisper, intense and familiar, an exclusive and morbidly authentic treatment that—and Leto was sure about this—the man did not provide anyone else in the world.

The Mathematician, meanwhile, seems to have calmed down. As they continued down the middle of the street, incrementally weaker traces of his agitated silence were reaching Leto. Tomatis's attitude, after generating skepticism and even a kind of confused and agitated brooding in him—in the Mathematician, no?—as they separated, when Tomatis showed what they call an open display of hostility, has instead transformed, in fact, into a somewhat charitable psychological evaluation, a resignation that induces him to minimize the arbitrary in Tomatis's behavior and attribute it to a passing moral failure of which

Tomatis is more victim than perpetrator. In fact, he had to suppress the momentary waves of The Incident which, rising from the darkness, appeared several times during the debate he has been having with himself. He has had to suppress them, it's true, but they were suppressed. And so, breathing deeply, and noticing that Leto, who is walking next to him in silence, apparently overwhelmed by Tomatis's insolence, also seems to emerge from his thoughts prepared to continue the conversation, the Mathematician lifts his head, contented, and straightening himself a little, looks with euphoria or resolve at the straight and bright street extending before him. He sees it sharp, clear, living—he wonders if, submerged in psychological trifles, he has been missing the best things. His attenuated enthusiasm, modifying even the rhythm of his stride, reaches as far as Leto who, almost simultaneously, comes out of his self-absorption and senses that the fact of being there, in the present and not in the swamp of memory—though he does not ignore that the extinct endures in the material, in the bones and the blood—of being there, in the morning sun, produces a shiver of pleasure and a startling sense of liberation. *Not such clowns ultimately*, he thinks and lifts his gaze, meeting, for a prolonged moment, the Mathematician's eyes, which are open and radiant. The incidental Tomatis, a soft and dark mass that polluted the morning with its sticky splatters, disintegrates into the past—both time and place, matter interlaced with breath or fluid or whatever—which the translucent but harsh succession of experience, unfathomably ineluctable, deals out and discards—discards, no?—or drops, into an abyss, out there, into what is, by definition, inaccessible, and about which Leto and the Mathematician, in unison—if you'll allow the expression—and without any kind of words, think, *it's not worth worrying, just now at least, when a whim of chance, a setback becoming a boon, a stringing of the disperse globs of the visible and the invisible, of the ambiguous clumps of the solid, the liquid, and the gaseous, of the organic and the inorganic, of waves and particles, have come together to deposit in us, in the translucent center of this morning and no other, a reconciled deliverance.*

More or less. The Mathematician brings his arm up, grabbing the horn of the pipe in his hand so that the pipe stem sticks out between his middle and ring fingers, and, tracing a semicircle in the air, designates the present, which is to say the sidewalks, the street, the rows of shops, the illuminated signs, the people standing on the sidewalks or walking in different directions, the various perspective planes that stretch down the straight street, made linear by optical illusion as they extend toward the horizon, the morning light, the sound of voices, footsteps, laughter, motors, horns, the familiar smells of the city, of the heat, of the spring, the clear and incessant multiplicity which could also be, and why not, a new expression for that.

—Occurrence, he says.

Touched by a sudden loquacity, Leto responds, *The philosophers' straight flush. It was this street. This moment. So many burned or made to burn.*

—To hell with them, says the Mathematician, afraid that Leto, so circumspect a few moments earlier, would fall, disappointing him, into grandiloquence. But immediately he repents: *And what of it, when all's said and done? The manner in which a truth manifests is secondary. What matters is that the truth is clear,* he thinks, more or less. And then, incorrigible: *Manner, exactly—it would takes years to come to terms with the terminology.*

They cross the street. Without realizing it, they have accelerated a little, and looking at them you would say that they are hurrying somewhere in particular, so as to arrive on time; their rhythm and expressions translate as dexterity, facility, and ease. But they are going nowhere, in fact, and unburdened, you could say, of duties or destination, they walk inside an integral, palpable actuality that spreads through them and that they likewise disperse, a delicate and transient organization of the physical—delimiting and containing, during an unforeseen lapse, the dismaying and destructive blind drift of things. The Mathematician observes that the clarity of things sharpens and persists, not only in the whole but also in the individual details, and that the notorious *reality* he has heard discussed so often is ultimately nothing but this, the thing just now surrounding them, and which at the same time is, and of which he at the same time is, object and surrounding—always at the same time, as we were saying, or rather yours truly was saying, and at the Same, no?, which could be called something else—place, I was saying, no?—and the Mathematician, stimulated by the persistence of his vision, thinks that he is beginning to understand everything, from the start, comprehending, in a single look transforming into thought, the shape and form of what moves, vibrates, and congeals in this translucent medium, relating each of his perceptions with such quick and strong nexuses of so much precise and universal evidence that, almost bothered by his simultaneous enjoyment and comprehension, he imparts, austere and decisive, a command: *Substitute an equation for the ekstasis.*

This could be, according to the Mathematician, no?, R = (R, naturally, for reality). Reality equals—and this capital R, the Mathematician reasons, should correspond to an expression describing it so exhaustively and rigorously that whenever the word is used all of the perfectly identified terms of the equation would be automatically implied. The first term is him—the Mathematician, no?—not a given as an individual, but as a constant in the equation, a subject S, a structured and transitory but at the same time invariable moment of possibility for conceiving the equation; and to resist the interpretation of a plurality of equivalent moments to the cognitive act, he decides to add a lowercase s so that the plurality of the subject—which could be the Mathematician or anyone else on the street right then or anywhere else or at any other time—is a constant included in the term. You would have, therefore, the Mathematician tells himself, $R = Ss$, for starters. But wouldn't it be too naïve to put Ss before an object O, as though they were antagonistic and the juxtaposition an overly simple operation that destroys the unity that exists between them? Ultimately, yes, bearing in mind that Ss, as a subject of the equation, is already implied in O, the object he intends to formalize. In that case $Ss\ O$ constitutes an entity. This entity can be referred to as x, which gives $R = x (SsO)$. *Elegant*, thinks the Mathematician. But his entity immediately falls apart: if there is a distinction in Ss, the lowercase specifying the transindividual order of the S, the capital O on the contrary does not distinguish among its different components, of which S and Ss are not the least important—in O you have to include Ss not as the subject of the equation, but as an objective component of O, where all of the contingent objects that are not O are also included in the universal and all-inclusive objects S, Ss, and O, if a lowercase o designates the multiplicity of contingent objects that compose it. This gives $R = x SsO (S Ss O)$ . . . On the other hand, the heterogeneous and contingent designation of the lowercase o, that is to say the concrete moments of O, also present several complications, given that its number, function, nature, etc., can be determinant or indeterminate—the Mathematician continues, no?—meaning you would have to designate its determination and indetermination at the same time, since if they are designated by their determinant, an indefinite number of its attributes would not be included in its definition. But since S and Ss, as objects, are not free of indetermination, instead of writing o^n it would be more exact, the Mathematician tells himself, to formulate it the following way: $R = x SsO (S Ss o)^n$—and so on, or rather, to be more precise, more or less.

Leto observes that the Mathematician is walking with his eyes half closed and wearing a pensive smile that he attributes to some kind of rhythmic test he set for himself, or for Leto maybe, as if, concentrating, he was preparing to adapt himself to any change in rhythm, velocity or even trajectory that Leto, unexpectedly, might decide to employ. In any case, this is what Leto interprets in his expression, and accepting the challenge he imagines in the Mathematician's face, he accelerates a little more, so unexpectedly that that Mathematician, whose modest person is trying to formulate an equation—valid forever, anywhere, in any language—to once and for all substitute the word *reality* with a more manageable tool for thought, reciprocates the acceleration without turning his head and, changing his stride, as though marching, adapts to Leto's pace. Unfortunately, the *ekstasis*, more akin to animal pleasures than complex abstractions, vacates once again from the equation, and his whole body prepares for possible approaching changes, while above, inside his head, the fragile distinctions that as pure diversion he has been trying to sort through, are demolished by the muscular effort and silently fall apart.

Thanks to years of training on rugby fields, the Mathematician could easily, if he wanted, with a few vigorous strides, overtake Leto who, because of his shorter and less prepared legs, would need to supply extra effort to follow him, but, actually, he doesn't want to, and he allows Leto to lead, forcing him into a contradictory effort intended to mitigate rather than impel the force of his stride, and so each of his steps is measured and careful—fruit, as they say, of a controlled energy that produces more aesthetic and, you could say, moral satisfaction in him than a continuous acceleration, taking him to the limit of his strength, would produce, in a race, for example, and after a few seconds he adapts so well to the effort, matching the imperceptible but constant increase in velocity that Leto adds to the walk, that the idea of an equation to stand, in any language, time, or place, for the word *reality* appears again obstinately but in the form of euphoric convictions or visions that follow one after another in the lucid part of his mind: *It's the visible plus the invisible. In every state. Me plus everything that's not me. This street plus everything that's not this street. Everything in all its states*, thinks the Mathematician, somewhat self-exultant, and in order to see the street in a different state from the one he is seeing, he turns his head, without modulating the rhythm of his stride at all, and starts to look, over his left shoulder, at the street they have been leaving behind. Leto, tense and vigilant, observes all of these gestures out of what they call the corner of his eye, puts on a rigid grin when he perceives the head turn and, very slowly, as though it were something millimetric and ritual, copies the movement. The Mathematician, who likewise notices, waits a few seconds while they take two or three steps and, to take Leto by surprise and make him hesitate, continues, with the rest of his body, the turn he had just made with his head only, without interrupting his walk, so that now his whole body is facing the part of the street they have already traveled and the Mathematician continues as before, but walking backward. Leto carries out the same movement with a fraction of a second's difference, satisfied by his quick adaptation to the Mathematician's inexplicable whim. Upright and even more tense because of the unnaturalness of their movement, rhythmically and cautiously in reverse, they arrive, without realizing, at the intersection, underestimating the disturbance that their singular attitude is causing in the people passing them. Two or three have to step aside to avoid a collision. From the sidewalks, others look at them with surprise, with indignation, or with an incredulous and condescending smile. An old man stops and looks after them, shaking his head reprovingly. But they ignore them, less so out of insensitivity than because of the extreme concentration their walk demands, and most of all because, whether or not they think it in words, the straight street they are leaving behind is made of themselves, of their lives, is inconceivable without them, without their lives, and as they walk it forms along with the movement—it's the empirical edge of the occurrence, ubiquitous and mobile, which they take with them wherever they go, the shape the world takes when it gives in to the finite, the street, morning, color, matter, and movement—all of that, let us be clear so it's well understood, more or less, and if you like, while it's always the Same, no?, and in the Same always, as I was saying, but after all, and above all, what's the difference!

The
Last
Seven
Blocks

To be clear: the soul, as they call it, is not translucent,
it seems, but murky. The motives compelling it to be carried away,
on this block, by what they call play and elation, just as arbitrarily,
and in a no less unforeseen way, submerge it—to use the expression
once more—in an intense melancholy on the following block. Or so it
seems, in any case, no?

In fact, Leto and the Mathematician, after walking backward
through the intersection, have slowed down suddenly, and instead of
continuing down the middle of the street have returned to the sidewalk and to a regular walk, not slow or fast or somber or blissful, just
slightly below the midway point between pain and pleasure maybe, on
the same side of the street where the shade line, because the sun is now
closer to 11:00 than 10:00, approaches the wall. The Mathematician,
for example, after his exultant equation—or so he thinks to himself—
is absorbed, for a few seconds, by the ancient murmur, so ingrained in
the species that even when it is ignored completely, no one, no matter

how shallow, when their mind clears, or even on the dark reverse side of their other thoughts, ever stops mulling over: *Where did the world come from? Is there a single object or many? What is . . . ? no? etc., etc.*—and after a few seconds of wandering and brooding, noticing that Leto, while he walks, is gazing distractedly at the illuminated signs extending above them down the street, decides to refute Tomatis's assertions point by point in order to put things back where they belong. He also suspects that Leto, without daring to acknowledge it, agrees with most if not all of those assertions. His withdrawn attitude could be a form of mistrust, a reticence that, out of discretion or maybe even out of hypocrisy, is not manifested. He is about to open his mouth when Leto beats him to it.

—Tomatis's dementia is out of control, he says. That kind of sequential slander doesn't do him credit. It was coming out his ass. Why does he have to attack Rosemberg? And what did the twins do to him? Not even Washington got off.

—I know. Not even Washington.

And, you have to admit, in a completely underhanded way, adds the Mathematician. *But Carlitos is like that. There's nothing you can do about it. Capable of the monstrous and the sublime. How a guy like him can slump so low is beyond me. Some days you can't control him. And I think stress affects him too much, and instead of trying to resolve a problem like every other mother's son, he can't think of anything better than to take a shit on the people around him*, the Mathematician explains insistently, stimulated by Leto's unforeseen confederacy, having thought him on Tomatis's side, and the discovery of their relative correspondence in certain moral assessments seems to allow him to objectify, you might say, his own critique. He, the Mathematician, no?, he, for example, knows the story about Washington in '49, when the government locked him in an asylum because he wanted, as he said, *to dissolve the Duma and the party and organize the country into soviets.* He knows what happened because it's well established among the left-wing groups he has belonged to for a long time. Washington came from the anarchist, socialist, and communist sets, and in 1946, a break with his group lead him to a passing, reactionary association with the Peronists. The left wing had filled the city with leaflets with his mug shot, his full name, and the words *FASCIST TRAITOR* in large red letters. The Mathematician had the chance to see one of those leaflets—an old Trotskyite militant, who had been collecting documents for a history of the working class in the province, showed it to him. According to the old man, at that time Washington thought that the working class would be represented by the Peronists and that the men on the left should move toward them and not farther off, and that Peronism, as it was a new movement, could be open to any change. The Peronists gave him a provincial seat. Just a few months into the new government, Washington represented the leftist opposition in the party. And knowing him, you can imagine what this meant: two-thirds of the parliamentary sessions ended in fistfights. Ultimately, Washington, who was receiving death threats every day, carried a gun to the capitol. The left wing treated him like a fascist and the Peronists were saying that he was on Moscow's payroll—*him*, who since 1915 *at least* had more than once exchanged gunfire with the nationalist groups and who had declared war on revisionism ever since Trotsky's expulsion from the Soviet Union. The fact is that between '47 and '49—on this he, the Mathematician, has a first-hand account—things deteriorated so much that Washington, fearing an assassination, didn't sleep two consecutive nights in the same house, and every time he went to the capitol he was surrounded by a group of armed men, all members of his faction, whom he trusted completely. One night they put a bomb in his house; later, when he was coming out of a pizzeria, they machine-gunned him from a car—he came out unharmed, but one of his bodyguards died in the shooting and another took a bullet in his spine and ended up paralyzed. The more others tried to silence him, the more enraged he became. And according to two or three people who were close to him at the time, the Mathematician says, Washington, as stubborn as he was, ended up coming slightly unhinged. He must have known that what he was trying was impossible, and if he didn't realize that it wasn't possible, so much the worse. The fact is he was constantly agitated—he barely slept and was always on street corners gesticulating with two or three of his comrades, interrupting official meetings with savage outbursts, distributing leaflets on the streets and to unions, organizing demonstrations with small groups of dissident factions from the worker class. If they tried to arrest him, he used his legislative immunity. The truth is, most of the workers in the party looked at him like a strange bird when he told them they needed to take power, and once he was even shitcanned from a union hall because they thought he was a communist. Maybe his desperation had made him lose his sense of reality, and the proof that he had hit bottom this time was that shortly thereafter, after a period of depression when he was released from the asylum, he, who had been in the fray every day for thirty-five years, abandoned politics forever. Finally, in '49, even the people in his own faction distanced themselves from him—some abandoned the party, others, their principles; he was the only one, out of pride or blindness maybe, who still wanted to make the two coincide. He didn't carry a weapon to the capitol anymore, and he slept in the same place every night. Meanwhile, the others, the ones who had bombed his house and machine-gunned him outside the pizzeria, were in no hurry to subdue him; it was such an easy job that, letting themselves get carried away by an artistic impulse, and to show off and prove themselves professionals, they were looking for an opportunity that would present a real challenge. And just then, enter Cuello the Centaur.

No, according to the Mathematician, Tomatis does not have the right to suggest that Cuello plotted against Washington in '49—in fact it was just the opposite. Cuello comes from the same town as Washington, and even though Washington is twenty years older, they've known each other for decades. Since, meanwhile, a general consensus credits Cuello with only moderate intelligence, the Mathematician thinks that you have to look for the source of their friendship on a

140

different plane. And, according to the Mathematician, that level would be the gratitude Washington feels toward Cuello, owing, precisely, to Cuello's actions in '49, which were, the Mathematician says, more or less the following: Cuello, who belonged to the party youth, did not completely disapprove of Washington's positions, and agreed with him in a vague and confused way, as his political consciousness was decidedly precarious—nonexistent, actually—apart from a generalized sympathy for populism based on his affection for folklore. If his consciousness improved somewhat in the fifties it was no doubt through the influence of Washington who, for reasons that were difficult to untangle, he admired to the point of idolatry. Washington has been a guru to many variously loyal and renegade people, but none of his disciples (naturally, he did not consider them disciples, and they would not have dared to proclaim themselves as such) had been more devoted. Ever since Washington joined the party, Cuello had gotten close to him and never left his side again. Whenever you bumped into Cuello, wherever you were, you knew that Washington was somewhere nearby. And, inversely, you could be sure that anywhere Washington was the center of attention, Cuello would be hanging around, attentive and silent, on the periphery. No one noticed him, but everyone took his presence for granted. It was mystifying, if you considered everything that separated them—what was holy to Cuello was hateful to Washington, though of course he never pointed this out. It was hard to tell if Cuello ignored people's bewilderment at his intimacy with Washington or if, perfectly aware, and stoically intensifying his devotion for that reason, he withstood it. Of course, if anyone might tactlessly call him the Centaur to his face, no one would have dared to use the name in front of Washington. It was normal to get to Washington's place in the afternoon and find them both under a tree, sitting in low chairs drinking *mate* and sporadically exchanging laconic phrases so full of allusion that it was hard to tell what they were talking about. Maybe, since they came from the same town, mutual and purely material experiences—things, people, places—facilitated their conversation, but, according to the Mathematician, there must have been something else, since more often than not the opposite happens with people who come from the same place—they actually avoid one another when they meet outside of their place of origin, as though the fact of knowing each other before made them lose some of their consistency. No, according to the Mathematician, that loyalty comes from the end of the forties, when Washington was locked in the asylum. And it was based, reveals the Mathematician, raising his voice to a lightly conceited and defiant pitch, incited by Tomatis's unjustified innuendo, that loyalty was based (he knows from a reliable source) in the fact that Cuello, leader of the youth movement at the time, arranged for Washington to get locked in the asylum and receive a disability pension, in this way averting his assassination. According to the Mathematician's sources, Washington's disappearance was imminent, and Cuello's people, citing his overly erratic recent behavior and a few of his peculiarities, had convinced the parties to Washington's forthcoming execution that he was insane and that they would take responsibility for removing him from circulation. Naturally, a few of Washington's old friends accused Cuello of hatching a conspiracy, as they say, and two or three times covered him with red paint and tar outside his house, threatening to kill him, but when Washington began receiving visitors to the asylum—at first they had him in a straitjacket and everything—the only person in the party who he allowed to visit was Cuello. In any case, Cuello visited every week, bringing him food, clothes, books—he even, the Mathematician insists, had tact enough to stop the party from publicly accusing the left wing of having pushed Washington to insanity. According to the Mathematician, Tomatis's insinuations signified a lack of respect not only for Cuello but, above all, for Washington, who in those hard times probably relied on Cuello not just as political or emotional support, but as a measure of reality when not only the others but also his own reason seemed to be deserting him. Cuello became his last reference point, his last bridge to the outside world, and a year later, when he left the asylum and fell into a depression that lasted until the end of '51, Cuello was the only person who was willing to see him. Cuello would spend whole days in Rincón Norte sitting with Washington, who didn't say a word and would shake his head every so often, releasing a long sigh. Several months passed before the terrible, stupefying silence, little by little, was replaced with the laconic, allusive, and sporadic exchanges that made up their conversation, exchanges whose meaning was for the most part difficult to guess because, when a third person arrived, without masquerade or haste, but rather in a plain and natural way, they stopped. Around other people, Cuello ceased to exist and Washington himself only spoke to him every so often, as though taking note of his presence or giving him life for a few moments with his words—interrogative, respectful, and not without a remote and ironic complicity: *Would you agree, Cuello?*—Washington never used the familiar form with anyone and no one with him, except his daughter—*There you are, Cuello, just like I said, isn't it?* to which Cuello would not even respond, restricting himself to existing, to gathering density and volume from the external world, the same way a sorcerer conjures, in empty space, to the senses of the audience, a being that until that moment had been invisible, and whose presence lasts only as long as the incantation. Since he worked as a secretary in the Butcher's Co-op—his wife was a music teacher at the normal school—he never showed up at Rincón Norte without a strip steak, which Washington would cook after they had talked a while, and which they ate standing next to the grill, without plates or anything, cutting bites from the same steak on a little board. According to the Mathematician, Washington had stashed Cuello at his house for a while because the Comandos Civiles were looking for him, until the hardest months passed and he was able to come out of hiding. It was strange to see them, so different and so close at once. Every so often Cuello would publish a collection of folk stories in papers and magazines that Washington considered the height of absurdity and even of shame, but it was normal to see one of Cuello's books on his desk, with its corresponding dedication and a bookmark sticking out among the pages, proving that Washington read them. Sometimes the Mathematician thought that, when lots of people were around, Washington's expression sharpened if he sensed any irony toward Cuello among the company—so much so that even the slightest irony was immediately repressed because of the tension that began to settle on the group—and only when that shadow disappeared completely would Washington's expression soften again. It had been said that, more conscious of the other's weaknesses than of their own, steadfast and alert to those only, they watched over one another tacitly. If anything refuted Tomatis's insinuations, according to the Mathematician, it was Washington's consideration for Cuello—according to the Mathematician, no?, who, in addition to dismantling Tomatis's assertions in regards to Cuello, took advantage of the opportunity to refute the ones that, in his opinion, Tomatis was gallant enough to smear on La Chichito: *He would prefer it if she were a virgin. That would ease the rejection. The only girls he wouldn't take to his room are either hysterical or bourgeois.*

But the Mathematician shuts up, and for two reasons: the first is that he considers himself, and without a doubt is, what they call a gentleman, or rather, considering that, according to the exact phrase that crosses his mind, *he couldn't give two shits about La Chichito's virginity or virginity in general,* he doesn't want the attentively listening Leto to think that he is suggesting that La Chichito isn't a virgin, and the second—actually more important than the first—is that if he goes on too long with the problem, Leto could assume that virginity in general, that non-issue *par excellence,* might occupy a space in his thoughts, no matter how small. But a third reason contributes to his silence: they have reached the corner, and because at this intersection the road opens to traffic again, the same bottleneck as several blocks back, when they started walking down the middle of the street with Tomatis, is repeated in the opposite direction. Crossing is going to be, the Mathematician's face seems to say when they stop at the cable and take in the so-called panorama, a problem, but in any case we will try to solve it, Leto reads in the expression of the Mathematician, whose concentration on the task at hand is so intense that, shaking his head thoughtfully and rubbing his chin in a mechanical way, softly and distractedly—and to Leto's unmistakable disbelief—he starts singing to himself.

The situation really is complicated: the cars coming from the west down the cross street, since to the north the central avenue is set aside for pedestrians, are forced to continue east, or turn south on the central avenue, while the ones traveling south to north on the central avenue are forced, for the same reason, to turn east on the cross street—or they will be, rather, because for the time being the rows of cars meeting at the intersection are jammed up and not moving, no exaggeration, even a millimeter, motionless and scattered chaotically on the street despite the theoretical efforts and arm waving of the traffic agent, who has abandoned his platform and who, added through historical experience to the mechanism of Hippodamus's excessively abstract project, justifies *a posteriori*, with his impotence, the invention of the traffic light—in truth no less abstract in its mechanical periodicity, inadequate for the non-periodicity of phenomena, than Hippodamus's invention, whose imperfections it pretends to correct. Leto, meanwhile, sustains his disbelief and—why not—his vague disillusion: first off, the Mathematician's singing, his preoccupied automatism, do not coincide with the ferrous self-control he attributes to him, maybe because of his scientific grooming and social origin, and second because the tango lyric, on the Mathematician's tongue, sounds anachronistic, giving him an impression similar to what he might feel hearing a soprano voice coming from the mouth of a boxer. Furthermore, the Mathematician's reaction seems disproportionate relative to the obstacle they have to overcome, as they say—there is, now, something monstrous in his expression, not unlike panic, which the even European tan, functioning, unintentionally of course, as a mask, allows through. And to this is added the singing, which instead of developing the melody in a way that will impel the song's lyric, continuously repeats the same phrase over the same melodic fragment, but with a constantly accelerating tempo, in an increasingly softer voice and more and more slurred diction, making the words incomprehensible as his panicked look ricochets around the motionless cars, whose bumpers, which almost touch, demand extreme skill from the person who wishes to cross. The Mathematician's gaze pauses anxiously on the thin spaces between the bumpers and then turns toward his own pants. *His pants*, Leto thinks, following each phase of the Mathematician's desolation, *The risk of staining his pants.* The soul, as they call it, which just now yours truly said was not translucent but murky, *the Mathematician's soul*, Leto thinks, without using, naturally, the word *soul*, nor without, for the most part, anything resembling words, *the Mathematician's soul, which with ease distinguishes the real from the counterfeit, the right from the wrong, and which possesses enough integrity to return things to their right place when Tomatis unleashes his slander up and down the street, disintegrates and falls apart at the possibility of staining his pants.*

Taking control of the situation, and pretending not to have noticed any change in the Mathematician, who, although his attitude is no less anxious, has finally stopped singing, something he notices with relief, Leto starts looking, among the bumpers that are too close together, for some that will allow them to pass to the opposite sidewalk. There are at least three rows jammed up at the intersection, although in fact the actual idea of a row is less than adequate, owing to the irregular positions of the cars, boxed in to the spaces left open as though they had appeared simply in order to be filled—but now, down the entire cross street, there are no spaces open and you would have to stand on your toes and look west at least a block and a half to see the last of the cars still moving, prudently supplementing themselves, if the expression fits, to the ones that can't move any more. Resolved, Leto inspects the bumpers in complete detail, then looks up and sees five or six people on the opposite sidewalk looking for a way through in the opposite direction, but when he finds a space a few centimeters wide, he turns to the Mathematician—paralyzed by the ineluctability of the stain, concentrating on his dazzling white pants—and making an almost imperceptible gesture, prompts him to follow. An internal battle manifests on the Mathematician's face, a battle whose outcome, uncertain at first, ends up confirming, in a provisional way of course, the thesis, to pick an expression, humanistic they call it, and as they have it, that in the creature called man, the so-called rational faculties—currently God, country, home, technology, class consciousness—always end up overcoming the irrational—excrement, suction or mastication, sperm, blood, self-destruction—in a constant way along an indefinite, rising curve, so that after a quick and ill-disguised hesitation, imitating Leto, in whose hands he has blindly and helplessly deposited all of the decision-making power, the Mathematician leaves the sidewalk and ventures, slowly, into the street.

Leto makes a nervous, superfluous gesture, removing and then immediately replacing his glasses, and, turned slightly at an angle, after gauging his chances of success in one glance, begins to cross, slowly, between two bumpers, followed, at a half meter's distance, more or less—always more or less, no?—by the Mathematician, whose proportioned and muscular figure, so necessary for carrying, while evading his opponents, the prolate spheroid ball from one end of the pitch to the other isn't, in the present circumstance, of any use whatsoever—just the opposite, in fact. The wide, loose cut of his white pants, in deliberate opposition to the arbitrary tightness currently in fashion, also contributes to making his progress more difficult, unlike Leto, whose relative slightness and lack of fetishistic interest in his cheap pants facilitate, as they say, the task. But out of discretion, in order not to humiliate the Mathematician too much, Leto magnifies his own difficulties: he only had to glimpse the fissures in what they call his soul, and, conscious of the ineluctability of our disillusions, accepts, shrouding himself a little from the inside, that myths always give way to the so-called reality principle. Nevertheless, trying not to get caught, he keeps an eye on the white pants while they cross, turning his head discreetly, likewise not wanting the stain to happen, not out of sympathy, but rather out of fear that the stain would cinch his misery, complete it, and in front of him the Mathematician, who in spite of Tomatis's insinuations seems to be someone who deserves love and a certain admiration, would shipwreck on the dark and indistinct shore to which the clear morning air is the fragile, momentary counterpart. But with patience, luck, and skill, they manage to cross. One stage, at least, has been left behind, to put it one way, but actually, if before stepping into the street they were obstructed but able to retrace their steps, as they say, now retreating is impossible, and the passage between the bumpers confronts them, not with another passage, but with the red chassis of a car blocking the way. Leto investigates, over the red car, the possibilities of continuing forward offered by the disposition of the cars stopped on the street and notices that, from the opposite sidewalk, the group has likewise been examining a possible itinerary and has also ventured into the street, diverging a few meters to the east, and is now crossing, single file, between two cars, impelling him to likewise turn east. Sidestepping the red car and making sure to check that the submissive Mathematician is following, he confirms, dejectedly, that the red car's front bumper is almost touching the rear bumper of the next car, and when he lifts his head to check on the progress of the group from the opposite sidewalk, he notices that after turning east to cross the first open space between the bumpers they have now reversed course in search of a second passage through the next line of cars. Swiftly—the word seems appropriate here—Leto sizes up—that's how it's said—the two possibilities, west or east, aware of the need to make a decision in the forthcoming fraction of a second, facing the dilemma of either throwing himself, blindly, into unexplored territory, or trusting the accumulated experience of the others who are coming in the opposite direction, confirming—only in a certain sense, no?—and to put it one way, the reversible nature of space and, choosing the second option, turns suddenly, bumping into the Mathematician who has been obediently following right behind him, anxiously studying—the Mathematician, no?—over his head, the chances of success offered by the territory. Confused, they try to step aside for each other several times, blocking the other's path each time, now that, clearly, the Mathematician resists leading the way but refuses to step aside, afraid that if he leans against a car, the pants, whose hems and legs he is trying to preserve, will suffer the much-feared stain on the backside. Leto recognizes this and, leaning back against the red car, lets the Mathematician past and slides against the chassis, cleaning it off with his own pants and, brushing them inconspicuously in order to not make the Mathematician feel guilty, or maybe fearing that even if the Mathematician notices his sacrifice, inhibited in his moral reactions by the excessive attachment to his own pants, he won't feel any guilt, begins to retrace his path and move west. One last twitch—you might say—of responsibility makes him glance back quickly to make sure that the Mathematician is following.

Now then: the moment they stepped into the street, as though the contact between the soles of their shoes and the asphalt had triggered a complex mechanism of sonorant activation, the numerous motionless cars, relatively silent up until then, in protest of some signal from the attendant, or in gregarious imitation, or for the plain voluptuousness of existing in a slightly more intense manner through the repetitive, musical declaration of the so-called self, have begun, almost in unison, to fill the innocent, bright morning with the sound of their horns. The surrounding space breaks down into sonorant planes whose different tones and intensities mark the limits, perimeter, distance, and location relative to Leto and the Mathematician who, at the center of the horizon of artificial sounds seem to move in a medium more resistant than the air, judging by the undertones, you might say, of effort and displeasure that accompany them, like the same sauce on different dishes at a banquet or a passing contingency as subspecies of eternity, the sequence of emotions that the crossing's misadventures cause them. At last they find a space between two bumpers wide enough to cross, but they are forced to stop and wait because the group from the opposite sidewalk—led by a grey-haired man in shirt-sleeves carrying a briefcase, almost certainly a lawyer coming from Tribunales or a high-ranking government official on his way to do business at a bank downtown—found the path before them and has started crossing it single file. The grey-haired man passes between the bumpers with his head down, lost in thought, with a solid lead on the procession, but the woman behind him, a housekeeper who has gone out to run errands and holds the family wallet, with a piece of currency sticking out, to her chest, gives them a look that Leto, unlike the Mathematician, cut off from any social commerce, takes up with a knowing gesture, to calm her, because he thinks he has noticed in the look from the woman, fifty-something and plump, of very modest origin, as they say, a kind of excessive culpability for the fact that she, a simple *señora de barrio*, was presumptuous enough to cross before two educated-looking, well-bred young men. Leto's look attempts to express, to no effect because the woman would never admit it, the common origin of humanity, starting from the so-called collateral branch of certain primates, as they call them, in west Africa, some seventy million years ago, give or take, on top of the idea espoused by more than a few religions, according to which all people are equal before God, added to his personal conviction that the best form of social organization would be an egalitarian order, with a rotation of roles, minimal government, and a socialization of the means of production, but only a fraction of a second after their eyes meet, the requisite lapse to express her culpability to the two young scholars, the woman lowers her eyes, somewhat ashamed for having dared to look, confused by the knowing look returned by one of them, full of intimations that she cannot nor does she care to unravel. The third in line the Mathematician cannot ignore: it's someone he knows, the engineer Gamarra, an Organic Chemistry adjunct, who he liked to play ping-pong with at the student center. Sixty-something and well-dressed, he passes while stroking the end of his tie, which is striped with oblique, wide, yellow and green lines, and greets him with an inclination of the head and a short monosyllable that Leto, observing impartially nearby, attributes to the embarrassment of the situation. And finally a young woman, dressed in a little flowery outfit, whose crocodile skin wallet hangs from her arm and rubs against the hood of a car as she passes without even looking at them. The passage itself, more narrow than the first, and which forced the people crossing in the opposite direction to turn their body slightly and continue sideways, presents a greater obstacle, as having to cross sideways puts both pant legs in danger at the same time, and when they set off, the car horns whose sound you could say they've been swimming through, go silent all at once. Only one protests, one more time, somewhere along the central avenue, but doesn't start up again. After they cross the bumpers, Leto, without stopping, turns east and without much trouble locates the passage found by the people coming in the opposite direction—wide, flat, open, with the cable guardrail at the other end, so easy to cross that, without turning, Leto knows that the Mathematician, behind him, is already recovering his personality, and that when they step onto the next sidewalk and start walking side-by-side, he will once again be the tall, elegant, tanned young man, dressed completely in white, including his moccasins, worn without socks and which unbeknownst to him were bought the month before in Florence—the Mathematician, a perfect, poster boy specimen who speaks slowly and clearly and who has gone out this morning to distribute the press release from the Chemical Engineering Students Association, about the trip to Europe recently taken by its recent and imminent graduates, to the newspapers.

But he's wrong. When they reach the sidewalk the Mathematician is still struggling with himself—or so it seems to Leto who, when he comes up alongside him, on the side closest to the wall, continues to notice his dumb bewilderment while he processes the humiliation of having been, for several moments, hostage to his own pants, and Leto, relieved, senses the surfacing, in the Mathematician's silence, of a sincere remorse, a resolve to be better in the future, a sense of certainty that he won't ever again be swallowed up by the penumbra he just now escaped, and the conviction that those weaknesses are just momentary, knee-jerk reactions that a sensible person discards with the help of a liberating intellect, or so Leto assumes the Mathematician is thinking, in his ascendant evolution. They reach the corner. They turn. And when they have resumed their path on the central avenue, to the south—as I was saying just now, no?—the Mathematician, having reconstructed himself after his compulsive eclipse, clearing his throat two or three times, reemerges into the morning sun. But Leto is thinking: *They would give humanity everything, just not their pants. They can accept anything but a stain on their pants. They're gentle as lambs except when their pants are in danger. They are not to be trusted, even when they've given up everything and claim that they've kept only their pants.* Using the plural he assigns the Mathematician to a vast, enemy horde, to the legion that, entrenched in a blind, vain defense of its own pants, constitutes a perpetual threat to the rest of the world. But the Mathematician's voice, slightly pitched at first because of his contrite throat clearing, recovers its impartial tone, its calculated preciousness and—Leto has to admit—its pleasant sound.

—On several points, Botón is more credible than Tomatis, he says, resuming the conversation as though nothing had happened. *Maybe*, Leto thinks malevolently, inclined to listen but also to controlling, severely, at every step, to put it one way, and in a literal sense as well in the present case, his credibility. But like every other time his rigorist projects give away almost simultaneously to their formation, plowed under by what you might call an organic relativism that comes from his insecurity maybe, or from a negatively charged rigorism that he directs against himself—to tell the truth, he wouldn't mind being like the Mathematician, to be able to separate the authentic or at least the probable from the problematic, and at the same time be so enmeshed in historicity to know that he should avoid, at whatever cost, a stain on his pants. On the other hand, their coincidental, negative judgment of Tomatis equalizes them not only through their similar vision of things, but also through their intimacy with Tomatis himself, an intimacy that, paradoxically, the negative judgment intensifies rather than diminishes. And finally, Washington's notorious mosquitos have intrigued him: in the coming and going of thoughts, memories, associations, of false images that from this moment, and for the rest of his life, he will retain as though they were real memories, the mosquitos swirl, gray and clear, pass over and over across the visible part of his mind where, like in a variety show, a parade of images are called up, as they say, by the Mathematician's detailed commentary. The Mathematician, passing egocentrically from a pathological preservation of his pants to an impartial and effortless refutation of the Tomatian maledictions, continues thus: Does Rita Fonesca, when she's got some drinks in her, try to show everyone her tits? He, the Mathematician, doesn't deny this. It's likely. But does she not in fact have a right to? And making a wide and theatrical gesture after stopping abruptly, like the magician who suddenly manifests his beautiful assistant in a sequin leotard at a spot on stage that had been completely empty up until that moment, he stretches his arm toward a shop window, pointing it out with an open hand and a broad, satisfied smile.

Tamely, stopping likewise, Leto looks toward the window indicated by the Mathematician's open hand. Behind it, the building, still closed, is in semidarkness despite the white walls that emit, in that darkness, a kind of glow. At the back, the only furniture, a desk and a couple of armchairs, are somewhat obscured by the semidarkness that dissipates near the windows flanking the door to the street, screened behind a sheet metal curtain. Hung from the white walls are several unframed paintings of a distinct form, generally very large and on which they can see, from the street, various abstract lines. But, well-exposed to the window indicated by the Mathematician, also without a frame and leaning against a white, wooden easel, one of the paintings is displayed in order to be seen from outside the building, through the window. Next to the painting is a white card that reads: GALERÍA DE ARTE – RITA FONESCA – DRIPPINGS – 1959/1960.

—She has a right to, no?, insists the Mathematician proudly and enthusiastically, pointing to the canvas displayed in the window, which Leto has begun to look at. And since, bothered by his insistence, Leto doesn't respond, the Mathematician falls silent, as they say, without being able to stop himself from observing, as he did during Tomatis's reading, Leto's aesthetic reaction. But this time Leto forgets his presence and penetrates, to put it one way, the surface covered to the edges with paint, withdrawing so much and so suddenly, from the outside world, that he doesn't even hear the car horns starting, for a few seconds, to honk again and then stopping because the lines of cars that were stuck at the intersection have started, at a walking pace, to move again. Leto has never seen a painting like this: it's a rectangle about a meter tall and some eighty centimeters wide, without representation of any kind, no figure or silhouette, not even a vague or distorted shape, but rather an accumulation of drops, smears, splashes, and splatters of fluid paint in various colors that superimpose, contrast, are neutralized, blend, and combine, and, together, harmonize miraculously despite the irregular, frenzied, and dizzying randomness with which the paint was dripped onto the canvas. *She can show the whole world her tits if she paints this well,* he thinks, mesmerized, tempering with this crude parody—coincidentally allowing him to express his admiration—the unmistakably violent emotion produced by the painting. No color dominates, notwithstanding the flashes—not periodic because their combined distribution doesn't conform to any regularity—with which they stand out every so often, and always in close relation, as they say, to the others, at different points on the surface. The splatters, thin for the most part, sometimes thicken into whirlpools, into smears superimposed several times, into variously sized drops, which, upon hitting the canvas, falling from different heights, thrown with varied force, or consisting of mixed quantities of more or less diluted paints, therefore color in a distinct way each time, not only because of their size, but more so because of their perfectly individuated scattering across the canvas. Meanwhile, the smears and tortuous splatters extend to the edges, the four corners nailed to the frame, in a way that makes the area behind the frame into a continuation of the visible surface; the viewer can easily intuit that the visible area is just a fragment, and the

154

eye, reaching the edges where the surface folds, senses the indefinite extension of the intricate apparition continuing, with its unexpected combination of colors, of densities, of speeds, of jumps and accumulations, of abrupt turns and temperatures, beyond the tormented canvas. They're not forms but formations—temporarily fixed traces of a ceaseless flux, no?—a sensible cluster, you might say, at a precise, tense point in time, tenuously juxtaposing, without annihilating, intent and accident, and adding, to the present, unbinding thrill and radiance. Leto shakes his head several times while tucking his upper inside his lower lip to express his admiring perplexity. The Mathematician, who has been looking at the painting and at him simultaneously, constantly examining his reactions, follows willingly and gratefully when he turns and continues walking.

A sort of manifold pride fills the Mathematician, first for having introduced Leto to a talented artist, since it's always pleasant and calming to have been first in anything, second because he interprets Leto's admiration to be sincere, which in a certain sense confirms his own artistic taste, no?, and finally with the refutation, without wasted words but instead a simple presentation of proof, of another of Tomatis's slanders, or in any case of his slanted view, as they say, of the facts. Because in fact, the Mathematician says with an easy smile that's aimed at demonstrating his complete lack of interest in moralizing about the issue, it's a patent fallacy to claim that when Rita's drunk she tries to show everyone her tits because she's actually always drunk and most of the time her torso is completely covered. No, if she does that every so often, according to the Mathematician, it's not from alcoholism or exhibitionism, but out of shyness: what to do, what to say, how to act in society? Should you fake interest in mundane conversations and behave pretentiously, attempt refutations of impervious yet completely false arguments, rationalize a preference for quince over yam candies or Miró over Dalí? Ugh, no! Better to sit quietly in a corner drinking gin after gin after gin and smoking cigarettes without saying a word until suddenly, at a given point in the evening, in order to finally take action after an intolerable paralysis, not knowing the right way to behave or the right thing to say, just to discharge her anguish, *pow*, tits unleashed. This of course without any forethought, in a more or less compulsive way, when, not only everyone else, but she herself least expects it. He, the Mathematician, has several times had the fortune of seeing her at work in her studio: she paints without an easel, puts a rectangle of canvas straight on the floor and all around the canvas arranges cans of paint in which she dips sticks of different widths— pieces of broom handles, rods, tree or shrub branches she peels with a knife, brush handles—and then drips over the canvas; other times she pours paint into a colander and lets it drip over the canvas, or she pierces holes directly into the paint cans and runs them over the canvas. Nearby, on a little table, she has a bottle of gin, glasses, a dented aluminum bowl filled with ice, and a bunch of packs of Colmenas and Gaviláns. Sometimes, if the canvas is too wide, she moves around the corners with her sticks and paint cans and colanders, but if the width permits she stands over it, her legs spread wide apart so as not to step on the canvas, bent over toward the floor all day—one of her favorite jokes, she has always the same two or three, which only she laughs at, is that to be a painter you have to have *a trucker's kidneys* and that actually the gin isn't for inspiration but to ease the pain in her hips. Once in a while, says the Mathematician, she stands up, takes a good drink, and then goes back to work with her cigarette hanging miraculously between half-open lips, holding her head rigid to keep the ash from falling onto the canvas; every so often she stands up to tap out the ash and consider her progress. It seems strange to him, the Mathematician, no?, that she's such good friends with Héctor, the other painter, because it's hard to imagine two more dissimilar modes of practicing or understanding the work—this on top of having such different personalities. Héctor takes weeks, months, to finish a painting; she, on occasion, paints three or four a day. When he has an idea, Héctor puts it into practice exactingly, patiently, making calculations, theories, and all his paintings, even all his sketches, have a theoretical foundation, not counting the fact that his paintings are sometimes monochrome, or they have one or two colors, or different tones of the same color, and are almost always geometrical. Héctor finds what he's looking for before starting to paint; she paints constantly and stops when she finds something. He, the Mathematician, once heard her say that being a good painter consists of knowing when the painting's done, when to stop; and in fact, the paintings that don't come out, because she's actually gone too far—which happens most of the time—she crumples and throws in the garbage. Several times a day she has to throw out the results of hours of work—several times a day—because her hand, which had been passing ceaselessly over the canvas, dripping highly diluted paint, has not performed the exact movement needed to impress the final colors in a way that makes their combination—incidental and chaotic up till that moment—begin to radiate an exalting inevitability and grace, says the Mathematician, more or less. But, bent over the canvas, swaying a little because of the gin, absently tapping out her cigarette, she must be the first to notice, in the apparent disorder, the magical proof. Not just in that way is she different from Héctor—and what's curious is that they feel a sincere and reciprocal admiration, and two or three times a week they'll spend all night getting drunk together at a hotel bar. Héctor talks constantly, and she doesn't speak a word except when she's had a whole bottle of gin, then she talks nonstop, unless its to unbutton her blouse, and she shouts and laughs at whatever until—no one knows why and least of all her—she ends up insulting whomever she's talking to. They're both around thirty, and they studied a while together at the Fine Arts school, but while Héctor spent time in Europe visiting museums and carrying on theoretical discussions with the cream of the European avant-garde, she has never once left the city. Héctor buys his sweaters in Buenos Aires, and sometimes even orders them from Rome or Paris; she's always walking around in the same skirt and the same blazer, paint-stained just like her hands and sometimes even her hair, with big, worn-out men's shoes on her feet and no makeup on her face, a

Gavilán or a Colmena always hanging from her lips, a mismatched manicure most often trimmed with black grime, constantly looking for someone—a man or woman, it doesn't matter—to bring home with her for the night because she can't stand to be alone; it's rare for her to go to sleep before dawn, she's endlessly coming and going to fill her glass with gin and get ice from the dented bowl. And in fact Botón, who the wicked tongues don't know what else to whisper about, because he has an official girlfriend in Diamante, that wasted bullet known as Botón, says the Mathematician (more or less), thick as he is, happens to be—along with Héctor, of course—one of the few people who knows how to handle her. It's the hidden side of Botón, which he himself is careful to hide, preferring instead, who knows for what obscure reason, to present himself to the world as an alcoholic woman-izer. What's clear is that Botón would abandon anything, at any time of day or night, if she called him. He, the Mathematician, thinks that if some sort of sexual relationship existed between them, it must have been only early on, and if they apparently get drunk together most of the time, it's only with her that Botón is careful because he knows that in the morning he'll have to take care of her, and if at the party he got as drunk as Tomatis claims it's because he couldn't prevent her coming with Héctor and Elisa in order to stay until the morning—the morning, no?—when after a whole day of disappointment waiting for the night's deliverance you finally understand, as the vain blackness fades at the first dismal light, that the day, that dreadful and endless film, is starting again.

The Mathematician strikes a balance, as they say, between Botón's virtues and defects, to the considerable annoyance of Leto, who has to correct the rather summary image he has been putting together. To Leto he was a pimple-faced, dark-skinned kid from Entre Ríos, a law student with more affection for wine and guitars than for the Civil code, a rape enthusiast in his free time, with a more or less conven-tional taste in books, and a somewhat obtuse intelligence, but now it turns out that he's an exemplary young man, protector of the avant-garde, a kind of saint who's capable of the greatest sacrifice (staying sober) if a higher end—this is the expression used in these cases—demands it. A doubt starts to take hold, as they say, of Leto, and he wonders if the Mathematician, in setting himself in radical opposition to Tomatis, has lost his critical faculty and is overstating the case, or worse still, Leto's sensitive intuition tells him—though with nothing resembling words—or worse still, I was saying, if the Mathematician, having tasted the bitterness of human misery, life reduced to trying to keep a pair of pants from getting stained, only to rediscover, you could say, the ambrosia of life, the good in all things, sees virtues even in Botón. But these thoughts pass quickly, like silent sparks or dark flashes in the back of his mind, which is concentrating instead on the unforeseen lunge his body has to make, alongside the Mathematician's, to step into the street, and a driver, seeing them, brakes slowly, and leaning toward them slightly to look at them through the windshield, makes a friendly gesture indicating that they can cross, which they do then and there, as they say, hurrying with an ostentation that, actually, doesn't speed things up but instead lets them respond to the driver's friendliness with their entire bodies, an ostentatious hurrying that more or less signifies, *we're hurrying as much as we can, so much that we don't have the luxury of responding to your friendly gesture, but in fact our own friendliness consists in hurrying* and which, ultimately, though it doesn't speed things up very much since what has increased is their ostentation and not their velocity, still transfers them, like it or not, to the opposite sidewalk.

Curiously: Botón had actually, the previous Saturday, on the upper deck of the etc., etc., no?, related to the Mathematician the arrival of Rita, Héctor, and Elisa at Washington's birthday—at around 2:00 in the morning, apparently—Rita and Héctor already tipsy, to use Botón's eloquent diminutive, and Elisa serious and detached as usual, acting like she was there involuntarily, declining to sit on the pretext that she was only there with Héctor and Rita, who were just stopping by to say hi. Of course they would be the last to leave—Rita because she can't go to sleep before sunrise; Héctor because of the never-ending conversations he gets tangled up in with this or that person, about anything whatsoever; and Elisa standing near the grill at first then later near the door when the morning cold forced them inside, her purse pressed to her stomach, not drinking anything or talking to anyone, just to make it clear that she was being held there involuntarily by Héctor and Rita. He, the Mathematician, knows all of these details through Botón. Leto nods again, to show that he has understood, encouraging the Mathematician to continue: at that hour, 2:00 in the morning, things were going well—a short laugh escapes from the Mathematician, which Leto interprets as amusement at the recognition of the typical behavior of the group, most of whom the Mathematician knows well, and the recognition of the typical in each of them and the typical in the whole group produces a pleasant sense of familiarity with the world, and something like nostalgia, too—in Leto's interpretation, at least—for the irrevocability of not having been there, of having been, on that same day and at that same hour, visiting factories in Frankfurt, victimized by humanity's maladjustment—if the expression fits—to time and to space, as they call them, a two- or three-second laugh that, translated into words, might more or less say: *How easily I can imagine them! How easily I can picture them now! How easily my senses can reconstruct that night without having captured it before! What sad luck to be in Frankfurt! What sad luck that the trip to Europe overlapped with Washington's birthday! What sad luck that human beings, all living beings in general, prisoners of sequence, are forced to exist at a single physical point in space at a time, and that it's impossible to abstract the successive transitions required to move from one point in space to another!* the same way that Leto, who wasn't there either, as we were saying, or rather yours truly, etc., etc., doesn't stop thinking something or feeling something somewhere inside him, and not with anything resembling, etc., etc., which, converted into a verbal approximation, could more or less be the following: *Two or three allusions from Tomatis imply that not inviting me was a premeditated decision, but they could also imply the opposite, if in fact they didn't invite me because of some involuntary lapse, although on second thought the allusions were probably just a probe to find out why, given that they thought it unnecessary to invite me, I didn't go, which would imply that they themselves were offended, but even allowing this possibility, that they consider me so close to Barco, the twins, and Tomatis that they didn't need to invite me, any way you look at the thing, the facts force a submission to the evidence, they didn't invite me.*

And so on. In actuality—actually an expression, no?—Botón, on the deck of the ferry, almost from the moment he began, had started talking about that, about the arrival of Rita, Elisa, and Héctor, referencing the painters' advanced stage of intoxication, as they say, because, having failed to catch the ten o'clock ferry due, it was obvious, to the all-night session he'd just ended, he was making what they call a subconscious effort to downplay his own behavior by exaggerating the others'. And, according to the Mathematician and always, and until further notice, according to Botón, the moment Héctor got wind of the earlier conversation—about Noca and Noca's horse and Washington's mosquitos—he started asking everyone there how it had been; what Noca had said about the horse and why; how credible his assertions were; how Cohen, Barco, and Beatriz had interpreted them and how they responded; and above all—and during this section of the interrogation Washington remained impassive and smiling as though he weren't listening—and more than anything, the Mathematician said that Botón said, how exactly had Washington's interjection happened and in what way was it connected to Noca's horse, if it connected at all, and also wanting them—Héctor, no?—to tell it step by step, in complete detail, since he was starting to make sense of what had happened and could possibly clarify the murkier points of the problem somewhat, something which, given his state of tipsiness, as Botón would say, naturally inspired an intense skepticism among the gathering. To all of this Washington offered no response. Here the Mathematician felt obligated to clarify this impassivity for Leto, saying it's a classic joke of Washington's, consisting, when an explanation is demanded, of pretending not to have heard anything, a joke he only plays on those who are already familiar with it, in any case, since the opposite could come off as pride or hostility, two attitudes completely foreign to Washington, an innocent joke, besides, since those who are already familiar with it know well enough that he enjoys staying silent and smiling for a long time and that, moreover, the joke always precedes one of his interjections. *Another of Washington's classic jokes*, the Mathematician annotates, satisfied that the joke conforms to his inclinations, *consists of describing Omar Khayyam as the author of a treatise on cubic equations, pretending to not know that he also wrote the Rubaiyat.* What's clear is that Washington's silence goes almost unnoticed amid the uproar and laughter that Héctor's insistence generates. *Let's put you to bed, my love!* Dib was shouting from the other end of the table while inserting a cigarette into the gold-plated mouthpiece that matched his gold-plated cigarette case, gold ring, and gold wristwatch, all glowing against his matte complexion, his rail-thin body topped off by a somewhat equine face divided into two mismatched halves—the top longer than the bottom—behind a large nose that supported gold-rimmed glasses above a black, well-trimmed beard.

But Héctor isn't easily intimidated: smart, occasionally pedantic, with prize-winning paintings in San Pablo and Venice and five or six hanging in the international avant-garde sections of European museums, always with the vague suspicion, most often suppressed around other people, that everything occurring in his absence forms or could form part of a vast conspiracy against his person. According to El Gato, the possibility of a dialectical contest with Washington is particularly exciting to him, a mania that, out of delicacy, Washington pretends not to notice, which, since it provokes Héctor even more, actually generates the opposite of the desired effect. Cohen describes him as ambivalent and, in reference to him, once employed the following jest: *He'd like them to like him and no one else like him, but not like liking anyone but him; he likes those who like him to not like each other; it's not unlike him to not like it when those he likes like him, and to not like that he likes*

them; he'd like to stop liking people's liking and make people not like him.
But he, the Mathematician, in spite of everything, recognizes Héctor's
genuine interest not only for the *quadrivium* (arithmetic, geometry,
astronomy, music) but for the *trivium* (grammar, logic, rhetoric), with
which he means, Leto assumes, that Héctor, aside from his talent for
painting, is not undeserving of invitation to any circle that's discussing
certain universal questions, however small.

Leto nods, his expression more or less abstracted, to show that he
has understood not only that Héctor is well-versed in certain questions
but also—and especially—what those questions are. But the Mathematician doesn't even see him, occupied as he is in specifying and
organizing the details of the memories he obtained, through Botón,
the previous Saturday, on the bench at the stern, on the upper deck
of the ferry, and which will accompany him the rest of his life. You
could say the memories parasitize other experiences, but they don't,
for this reason, lose force, sense, or cohesion. In fact most of the details
are familiar and, because of this, it's not difficult for him to piece
them together, in contrast to Leto who, new to the city, or relatively
new at least, has to patch them up—with assorted memories that are
unconnected to the objects being evoked or with vague images that
aren't traceable to any experience related to the events—alongside the
fragmentary, scattered, and sometimes confused image the story produces in him and which, paradoxically, because of its fragmentation
and hypothetical nature, just like a fairy tale, leaves profound and vivid
traces in his memory: Basso's ranch, Silvia Cohen, smarter than her
husband, the table under the pavilion, the conversation, Beatriz rolling
a cigarette, the ferry to Paraná, Washington's ironic silences, Pirulo's
wife bleeding herself with the syringe, Washington's three mosquitos,
tiny and gray, swirling around the summer night, buzzing clearly, in
the illuminated studio in Rincón Norte, Noca's horse stumbling in a
field along a coastline partly made up of coastlines previously visited
and transferred to the above—all of that, no?—also mixed, but not
carefully measured, with the contradictory assertions made by Tomatis

and the Mathematician, who continues, clear and distilled, as they say: *Until Washington gives in and says*—Washington, no?—*no, I was saying that last summer*, etc., etc., to Héctor, whose attentive but somewhat severe, hostile silence and pre-emptive expression more or less signify: *Yes, yes, I'm listening, but in any case, say what you will, I already have a refutation prepared.* Washington's expression, meanwhile—a singular masterpiece of highly controlled art that in no way betrays an awareness of Héctor's threatening severity—Washington's expression, I was saying, along with his words and the intonation used to pronounce them, compose something that, in what they call an organized or discursive form could be formulated more or less like this: *I don't know what the others have led you to believe, but if I were you I'd ignore them. Don't waste time on my meandering trivia, there's nothing to refute. Everyone here is a little overexcited by the alcohol and the party. No one can hold them back. I'm an old man—sixty-five Aprils today exactly—living in Rincón Norte, retired, occupied exclusively with his little cottage. Watching that my chicory doesn't go to seed and watering a lot during the hot months doesn't leave me time for much else. Our friends here exaggerate, don't believe them. As you seem even at a distance to be an intelligent man, you can't help but see how scatterbrained they are. But since you are so kind as to let me take up your time and insist on the pleasure of hearing me prattle, I'll tell you that last summer, after dinner, I sat down to read something, I don't remember what, Mitre's* Rimas, *maybe, or a novel by Cambaceres, when out of the silence appeared three mosquitos that started buzzing and swirling around me, until eventually they distracted me from my reading. And that's it. As you can see, our friends here get worked up when they drink.* Héctor, according to the Mathematician, and always according to Botón, aware of having been stalled by Washington's rhetorical tricks, which, fundamentally, he is forced to recognize as effective, because by avoiding any affirmative discourse, as it has been called, Washington has compelled him to renew his request for information, disarming his killer refutation—Héctor, we were saying, or rather yours truly was saying, feigning a disinterested curiosity over certain fragmentary reports he would prefer not to amplify, specifically because of the limited faith owed to their friends in their current state, to which Washington does not seem to have succumbed, he starts over: But hadn't they said something about Noca, the fisherman? Had he misheard or had they mentioned Noca's horse? Hadn't there been some talk during dinner over whether horses can or cannot stumble, and hadn't this been the actual reason why Washington had brought up the mosquitos? Washington spends a considerable length of time trying to remove a tobacco strand from his lower lip, with particularly inept fingers, after having listened to Héctor's questions with complete attention while—according to the Mathematician, and according to the Mathematician always according to Botón—looking fleetingly into Héctor's eyes and then fixing his gaze on the dark patio beyond the pavilion, the dark patio now beginning to chill in the morning air, then responding slowly, and if his words can be summarized, and because in any event a summary is always required, they might be summarized like this: *That's right, that's right, I don't deny it: our friend Noca said something about his horse. He said that if he was late with the fish it was because his horse had stumbled that afternoon along the coast, as per my eminently unverifiable assertion. Noca, who is of my same generation, like me isn't a top seed. And when our friends Cohen and Barco started discussing whether or not a horse could stumble I offered my modest reticence— it's not that I wanted to deny the stumbling of horses, it wasn't anything like that. Noca just happens to be a walking threat to the principle of sufficient reason, and if you want to discuss something it's better to ignore his assertions. That's why, with utmost caution and not intending to draw any conclusion, I told the story of the three mosquitos. Basso, you've got the bottle handy; be a gentleman and pour me a finger of whiskey? Thank you.* And according to the Mathematician, without saying another word Washington started sipping his drink and, fixing an extremely deferential look on Beatriz, who was watching him with a furrowed brow and a kind of malevolent smile, said: *Did you know, Beatriz, that velvet dress looks very pretty on you? Thank you, Washington,* says the

Mathematician that Botón said that Beatriz responded, suggesting that she followed his meaning, but with a somewhat exaggerated intonation meant to show that she was aware of his evasive maneuvers.

And so on. According to Botón—according to the Mathematician, no?—Héctor, hearing the response from Beatriz, hesitated a moment (though it continues to be always the same), panicking briefly, possibly thinking, and with some reason this time, that the vast conspiracy, implicating even his most precious possessions, so to speak, even Paolo Ucello and the cosmos, was just then reaching a decisive juncture, and if he hoped to dismantle the organization that had finished off his master Malevich and whose cloaked schemes had succeeded in keeping several women from falling in love with him and sometimes wore holes in the elbows of his Pierre Cardin sweaters, he needed to put all his faculties to use, including his intelligence which, and why not admit it, says the Mathematician, *is of superior quality*, capable of swimming effortlessly in the waters of the *trivium* as well as the *quadrivium*. The best thing would be to demonstrate that in spite of the conspiracy he had understood everything, and since the active members of the organization refused to confess, he would explain things to them step by step and in complete detail. Like so: Noca had nothing to do with it. You had to consider the assertion and forget about the subject. If Washington had brought up the mosquitos it was because he wanted to improve the proposition included in Noca's assertion, and the fact of bringing up the mosquitos seemed to grant Noca some credibility, assuming he had correctly interpreted the evidence gathered from this or that person, although, frankly, the present company wasn't at its most loquacious. One of the mosquitos never approached Washington, another approached repeatedly and when Washington tried to swat it, it took off and flew away, and the third one had let itself get swatted immediately. That was it, right? He wasn't mistaken? In his opinion, given that Washington had made the comparison, to Washington the mosquito that lets itself get swatted is in the same situation as the riderless horse that stumbles. Washington was the one who suggested this.

All he was doing was clarifying what Washington had said. He wasn't for or against either Washington's assertion or Washington himself. If there were objections they should be directed to Washington. And if he had stated things poorly he hoped Washington would offer some corresponding clarification.

According to Botón, Washington rearranged the blanket, which was already sitting well on his shoulders, and directing himself to Héctor's somewhat anxious expectation, which stood out among the general expectation, shook his head, saying, no, Héctor hadn't stated things poorly, but rather just the opposite, almost perfectly, that no one, least of all him, Washington, could have done better, and for that reason, naturally, not the slightest clarification was necessary. Some might consider the horse/mosquito identification excessive, somewhat abbreviated maybe, and he ran the risk of the yellow press publishing essays to that effect, but he, Washington, wasn't going to split hairs, realizing that, out of necessity to the exposition, and given the lack of useful information in such a thorny subject, simplifications were inevitable, and it was up to the insightful listener to introduce the necessary qualifications.

—I understand, I do, Leto says. But watch the guardrail.

The Mathematician, wrapped up in the Héctor-Washington controversy, does not seem to realize that they have reached the bright corner, and that two steps from now they will reach the edge of the sidewalk, so wrapped up in fact, even now, and twice over, so to speak, that Leto, who has assumed a protective attitude toward the Mathematician after the incident with the pants, is afraid that in his abstracted walk with his gaze fixed on the future, that is, on the end of the street, the Mathematician will fail to perceive the drop-off of several centimeters between the sidewalk and the street and will fall to the ground. He fears this for several reasons, among which the Mathematician's so-called physical integrity enjoys a significant place—if the expression fits—but not, though not far behind, the primary, belonging to his apprehension that an error in translation, just a common motional

167

accident, a false step, might completely demolish the harmonious image of the Mathematician which, after forty-five minutes of walking, give or take, he has begun to appreciate, and whose recent fissures, occasioned by the incident with the pants, are at the point of healing. An accident after such an event could dramatically transform a situation which, in general, falls into the category of comedy—comedy, no?—which is, if you think about it, just a delaying of the inevitable, a merciful silence toward the brutal progression of the neutral and its nauseating confusion, the passing, gentle delusion of celebrating the error rather than wasting one's voice and impotent fury cursing it.

Leto's fear also has an external justification: the corner is practically deserted and they have now left behind what is referred to— certainly out of convenience—as the city center, where the somewhat more crowded cluster of shops, vehicles, unlit billboards, and people produced a particular turmoil which they crossed with certain indifference, owing to the internal effort required by their verbal exchanges and the subversion of moral energy, you might say, that it cost them to oppose Tomatis's insistent and blind maledictions. And because, paradoxical as it may seem, the decrease in danger in a certain sense increases the risks as their vigilance relaxes—or so it seems to Leto, in any case—he has the impression that the Mathematician, impassioned again after the bad moments they went through a couple of blocks ago, having forgotten them, is now more vulnerable. But he is wrong: in full control of his so-called physical and intellectual faculties, the Mathematician adapts to the transition across the cable and crosses over without losing the thread of the story—so to speak—which, because of his unnecessary circumspection, Leto himself forgets. Leto's distraction has other causes: as they cross the street, now that most of the shops have disappeared, you could say, they give way once again, if you like, to the suites, waiting rooms, and offices of various professionals, the old, single-story houses with ornate façades and iron balconies that evoke the persistent comparison with a mausoleum whose tombstones would one day be decorated with the bronze plaques announcing the name of the owner and the nature of his trade. At the same time, that accumulation of professions, by class, whose so-called economic and social logic he is not ignorant of, makes him conceive of the city not as though it were divided into neighborhoods or sections, but rather into territories in the animal sense, an archaic and violent demarcation of ritual, bloody defense. And he is so absorbed in this depressive sensation that, without realizing that they have reached the opposite sidewalk, he is the one who trips over the guardrail. *And to think I worried for him because of the excessive love he has for his pants*, he thinks with a certain childishness, while everything spins around inside his head as he stumbles onto the sidewalk. And as he thinks this, practically falling, a pleasant and unexpected sensation surprises him: the Mathematician's strong arms, which have made his tackles feared and admired in every university campus along the coast, and including in Buenos Aires, in Córdoba, in La Plata, and even in Montevideo, prevent his fall and support him fraternally thanks to his quick, precise reflexes and the unique opportunity that destiny presents him to demonstrate to the world, and above all himself, that he is capable of an awareness of external objects and phenomena besides his pants. For a few seconds Leto finds himself tilting forward, his feet barely touching the ground, wrapped in the Mathematician's thick arms, feeling the contact of the white, immaculate shirt against his cheek, his half-displaced glasses pressed against his ear by the Mathematician's chest to keep them from falling, the cigarettes and matches, which he carried in his shirt pocket, scattered on the sidewalk because of the violence of the jolt that projected them forward.

—Saved, he hears from the calm and somewhat ironic voice of the Mathematician somewhere above his head, which is pitched toward the sidewalk pavement.

—Thanks, Leto says, straightening up and releasing himself a little from the arms that have not decided to let go. He adjusts his glasses after checking to see that they haven't been damaged and goes to gather his cigarettes and matches, but the Mathematician, pre-empting him, already has them in hand, and having finished reinserting—with some difficulty—the cigarettes that had come out of the packet, hands them to him.

—Thanks, Leto repeats, somewhat humiliated by all of that solicitude because, overwhelmed by the speed of the accident, he is unable to discern the discrete way in which the Mathematician conceals his authentic concern.

—Alright then, where were we? Leto asks, removing a bent cigarette from the packet and returning the packet to his shirt pocket. Hurrying somewhat, to overcome the situation, as they say, but with his hands still trembling, he lights the cigarette and puts away the matches. His shadow, slightly shorter, projects over the gray pavement next to the Mathematician's.

They continue. While they try to appear indifferent and outwardly calm, in the depths of their so-called souls—apparently not translucent but murky, as we were saying, or rather yours truly, the author, was saying just now—they struggle with emotions that anger them and that they would rather not see expressed inside themselves, humiliated by the thought that the other, because of his apparent indifference, is too noble to feel them. In Leto's case it's a belief—tenuous, it's true, but very present—that what just took place has ruined any pretense of superiority toward the Mathematician, accompanied by the shameful suspicion of being excluded from any other sphere in which he might feel equal or superior to him, while the Mathematician, beginning to sense that the happiness he feels at having saved Leto from falling is growing into a kind of euphoria in which he senses certain non-altruistic elements, is filled with guilt. But let's be clear: assuming that we agree that—as we have been saying from the start—all of this is just more or less, that what seems clear and precise belongs to the order of conjecture, practically of invention, that most of the time the evidence is only briefly ignited then extinguished beyond, or behind (if you prefer), what they call words, assuming that from the start we have agreed about everything, to be clear let's say it for the last time, though it's always the same: all of this is just more or less and as they say—and after all, what's the difference!

Saved, the Mathematician could have said again. The character—it's the exact word that corresponds to him in the present circumstances—walking a few meters ahead of them turns at hearing their voices and stops to wait. At an age when most others are sure to feel lost in a dark jungle, he possesses an overabundant self-satisfaction, and his pale brown checked suit, lightweight and tailor-made, the perfectly adjusted knot in his tie, the imperceptible rose-colored dots on his suit, his long, waxed hair, the matching colors of his suit and his tan—slightly clearer than the Mathematician's, which inspires, as they say, his admiration—testify to his self-satisfaction—they proclaim it even. Standing in the middle of the sidewalk, he waits for them with a wide smile directed exclusively toward the Mathematician, who, Leto senses, reticently returns it. But when they reach him, the Mathematician softly extends an indifferent hand that the other grabs and shakes tenaciously, even going so far as to cover it with his left while doing so. And Leto is on the verge of feeling invisible again, as he was in Tomatis's presence when, in an unexpected and peremptory way, the Mathematician introduces them: *Do you know each other? My friend Leto. The doctor Méndez Mantaras.* And then, as though to apologize to Leto, he adds: *He's a distant relative.* The distant relative extends the tips of his fingers, barely allowing Leto's hand to graze them, and then fixes a disapproving look on the Mathematician, which more or less signifies: *As though the family didn't have it bad enough with your parents' eccentricities and your quirks, you had to come along and introduce me to one of your communist friends in the middle of San Martín just to burn me.* But the Mathematician, without hesitating, responds with a severe and penetrating look: *Is something wrong? If so then get going right now and if not then drop it*—more or less like that, no?—his eyelashes slightly pinched, as they say, looking down at him so much that Leto wonders if the Mathematician, magically, like the superheroes in comics, has grown subtly taller. The distant relative, apparently no less

171

muscular than the Mathematician, or only slightly less so, as though the difference in size were of a category distinct from the physical, notices the peremptory warning immediately and, to Leto's surprise— expecting a reaction proportional to the unequivocal severity of the Mathematician's look—puts on an elusive and conventional smile and starts throwing out pleasantries: *How's the family? Beautiful day, no? Let's walk together to the corner since we're going in the same direction,* etc., etc., to which the Mathematician, as they begin to walk, starts responding in a condescending and even disdainful way that the other, unfazed, pretends not to notice, or that maybe he only half-listens to, occupied as he is in digging through his cache of pleasantries in order to toss them one by one—with his fake cheerful and fake familiar tone—into the morning air. *How's Tostado? Did you go to the Saturday rugby match in Paraná? And come to think of it, how was Europe?* To this last question, after a contrary hesitation, as though he couldn't decide how to take it, the Mathematician starts to deliver—this is the word that sounds best here—a mechanical, fast summary, and like-wise abundant response in which the string of cities and accompanying images—evoked for those he admires at the even and gentle rhythm of a carousel—have, in the present case, the same force, frequency, and effect on the other as a series of hammerings: Warsaw, there was noth-ing left; La Rochelle, sparkling white; Paris, an unexpected rainstorm; Brussels, for *The Census at Bethlehem*; Bruges, they painted what they saw; Vienna, all the locals seem to believe in terminal analysis; Biar-ritz, our oligarchs would have loved it; Palermo, the gods passed through before disappearing; Venice, the real gateway to the East, not Istanbul; Segovia, arduous in the yellow wheat, etc., etc., in a rapid, precise way, pretending to believe that the distant relative understands what his allusions denote, but formulating them, Leto thinks, in the most condensed and cryptic way possible, so that the relative, who seems to be attempting an intense concentration of effort so as not to miss anything, won't understand them. Moreover, Leto senses that the Mathematician, although simulating a conversation with his distant relative, is actually talking to him—to Leto, no?—as though he were performing a practical demonstration of the other's absolute ineptitude, insofar as every one of his words and gestures seems not to say what it normally would, but instead rehearses a categorical formula corroborated over and over by the accumulating evidence: *See? See? Don't bother wasting time on him, he's not interesting.* Even the memories of Europe, fleeting, fragmentary, radically condensed and simplified now that they are somewhat distant, he presents with an exaggerated vividness and a false spontaneity, intending to amplify their familiarity, which in a way diminishes the complicity because Leto, as much or possibly more than the distant relative, believes in the authentic possession of those memories and in the aura they confer on their possessor. Further, no doubt: what to Leto represents a place to project his imaginary energy—so to speak, and if the expression fits—to the distant relative is nothing more than another quirk of a member of the most extravagant branch of the family. Then again, the Mathematician's phrases don't seem to have any effect on him, since in the seconds of silence that follow them, the distant relative has time to find a new topic of conversation, or of monologue rather, and obliterating any response in advance, begins to speak: The night before he had gone to the city center with his wife—who in fact is second cousins with the Mathematician—to see the premier of *The Wind in Florida*, and the movie seems to have made what they call an indelible impression on him, and strenuously recommending it, as they say—to the Mathematician, no?, given that Leto's presence continues to be problematic to him—and inspired by the renewed empathy remembering it produces, he begins to tell him the plot. According to him, it's the story of a family of pioneers on the Florida panhandle—apparently that's how it's referred to there—who, after fighting for years against the Indians, build a ranch that little by little is transformed into a huge plantation. The movie tracks three generations, the pioneer grandfather, the landowner father, and his two sons, one good and one bad, who fall in love with the same woman—the widow of a neighboring farmer who was killed in a brawl with the landowner over an argument about property rights. The widow first falls in love with the bad one, but when she realizes her mistake, she falls in love with the good one, and at the climax a hurricane engulfs them and the plantation house is destroyed in a blaze. Instead of yielding to his distant relative's hope—after being shaken by pathos—of sympathy from the others, the Mathematician, having received the story with deliberately ostentatious skepticism and insulting silence, forces him instead to hear a counter explication of the same in the following terms, more or less: As far as he can tell it's a piece of garbage intended to justify the slaughter of the Indians, the brutal seizure of Mexican territory (though it takes place in Florida the story is clearly a metaphor for all of Latin America), and the absorption of small business by big monopolies, with the president of the Lions Club dressed up as a landowner, a showgirl passed off as a Methodist widow, and two stock actors playing the roles of the brothers, the good blonde one, neat and clean-shaven, and the black-haired bad one, with a curly beard, to implicitly suggest that Anglo-Saxons are the morally and physically superior race. And at the climax—what a coincidence, no?—the hurricane and the fire happen. All this had to happen at once and he—the Mathematician, no?—wonders if the fire starts at the same time as the hurricane just so that the rain can put out the flames and, after an inconsequential scare in which all the evil darkies are exterminated, the blonde gallant and the showgirl can rebuild the mansion as though nothing happened and continue exploiting their neighbors like before so that their grandchildren can drop their atomic bombs on Hiroshima and Nagasaki with a clean conscience. And the Mathematician finishes his interpretation with a short, satisfied, and somewhat exaggerated laugh that serves, though Leto is unaware of this, as supplementary evidence to a kind of indictment concentrated in the counter-explication: *They are not interesting. They are ignorant and ambitious and their worldview is rooted in a murderous solipsism. They hate what they don't understand and despise what doesn't resemble them. Although through mysterious aspects of my temperament and my own personal efforts I've managed to differentiate myself as much as possible, the tragedy of my life until the day I die will consist of having been born among them. To maintain or expand their privilege they are capable of humiliating their parents, of sending their own brother to prison if they detect even the shadow of opposition in him. To perpetuate their caste they would lay waste to the universe. To treat them differently from the way I do would be a dangerous mistake. Anything you can do to dismay or neutralize them is useful as a form of self-preservation, but apart from that, for the things that really matter, it's not worth wasting time on them, they are not interesting.*

And so on. That tenuous and somewhat feverish, passing cruelty, a kind of violent courtesy directed toward Leto and intended to demonstrate his absolute difference from the character—the word could not be more apt—walking with them, does not attain its objective, strictly speaking, as they say, or at least does not attain it completely, because although Leto does not fail to notice, in the Mathematician's contemptuous hostility, an instinctive response to the other's pretensions, the response seems disproportionate, and the distant relative's efforts to simulate that they are walking along in a normal conversation produces less malevolent pleasure than it does a certain compassion. To the Mathematician's short and poorly concealed laugh, the distant relative responds with another, of similar style but less effective because of its defensiveness, intended to more or less signify: *To us normal people that kind of twisted interpretation of a beautiful movie goes in one ear and out the other*, but his avoidance of the Mathematician's eyes prove that he is not what they call a well-matched adversary, and the renewed pleasantries he starts sputtering confirm this: He could swear that the Mathematician's white moccasins are Italian. Is it true? Has he heard that his boy was champion in the youth division of the interclub tennis league? The strawberries from Coronda this year were tasteless, but the asparagus came out first rate, etc., etc. His sentences, spoken carefully and with a certain insistence on an obligatory response—like a letter certified with return receipt, you could say—seem to dissolve in the air before reaching the Mathematician, who not only doesn't register them but, with his head turned toward Leto, actually ignores even the physical presence that speaks them. Moreover, while the other talks the Mathematician busies himself in formulating more completely, and in more explicit terms not worth squandering on his distant relative, the narrative mechanics of *The Wind in Florida*—thinking that there always needs to be a climax at the end, he says, more or less, is equivalent to ignoring that objectivity is incomprehensible enough for its catastrophes to occur unnoticed and end up being nothing but statistics, anonymous blips in some distribution index; besides, the coincidence between the climax and the fire belongs, it seems to him, the Mathematician, to the category of comparisons so obvious that they border on tautologies. The monologues interlace and Leto, who out of courtesy and curiosity tries to listen to both at once, does not manage to concentrate on either until, aware of the competitive nature, as they say, of the situation—who will demonstrate most definitively the ineptitude of the other—grows disinterested in both. Moreover—and Leto asks himself if the distraction isn't deliberate—the hulk of the Mathematician absorbed in his explications keeps the distant relative so far away as he walks that he, the distant relative, is only left with a thin strip of sidewalk to use, forcing him to execute a continuous slalom around the cable guardrail. And when they reach the beveled corner—or so it's called—that widens the sidewalk, the distant relative stops talking, and taking advantage of the space, slides behind Leto and the Mathematician and, hurrying a little, beats them, as they say, to the bright section of the sidewalk, waiting for them, three meters ahead, with a triumphant expression that, far from affecting the Mathematician, on the contrary, becomes the definitive substantiation, as they say, of his proof: because just as Leto, owing to an instinctive politeness that nevertheless does not suppress the vaguely demented and, you could say, exclusively intrafamilial nature of the tacit altercation in which he doesn't feel implicated whatsoever—like the foreign tourists indifferent to the so-called domestic struggles of the countries

176

they visit—just as Leto, owing to an instinctive politeness, as we were saying, or rather yours truly was saying, is about to move toward the distant relative who's waiting for them with a satisfied look in the middle of the sidewalk, the Mathematician, grabbing him by the arm with a hand whose years of rugby and crew have endowed it with what they call above average strength, detains and forces him to continue straight while the right hand lifts and drops quickly for a brief goodbye accompanied by an inaudible grunt that—Leto guesses without seeing, or just barely seeing—rearranges the distant relative's triumphant smile into a stupefied, outraged grimace as they step over the guardrail into the street and begin to cross the bright and all but empty intersection.

—He's a venomous snake, the Mathematician whispers as they cross, without letting go of his arm. He's a regular at the intelligence services and the eleven o'clock mass.

Leto discharges a thick mouthful of smoke and starts to laugh, thankful. He, until the year before, went to mass every so often and more and more infrequently, and though he has stopped going without much reservation, for someone to place the eleven o'clock mass among the fundamental credentials of human iniquity serves to confirm, *a posteriori*, the just nature of his defection. But also, and above all, he feels thankful because he has sensed, in the Mathematician's somewhat brutal contempt for his distant relative, a gesture of seduction toward himself, which, being unexpected and fleeting, is therefore all the more intense. The dispersed and scattered elements suddenly come together as they cross, through the unmistakable gesture of affection, and the inconstant, fragmentary flickers emerging from the dark depths inside him, where their flashes almost immediately extinguish the tenuous and phosphorescent glow of consciousness, the frayed, mercurial recollections that assault him whenever they like, the tide of regrets, the turns of phrase, the nonsense, the doubts and ghosts, the lonely flux produced by the unaccomplished all come together, as we were saying, or rather yours truly, just now, was saying, and become a solid burst, a translucent, stable whole, almost a real but fragile object, like a smoke ring or a soap bubble, that occupies every corner of his body and radiates a euphoric sense of himself, him—Ángel Leto, no?—clearly defined and distilled among the things that, dispersed across the benign transparency, fill the morning. The force of that feeling is so strong that it suppresses its sporadic or transitory character, and when they reach the opposite sidewalk, as they step over the cable, the somewhat pedantic tone with which the Mathematician, recovering from his intrafamilial vexations, resumes his story, begins to gnaw at the edges of its short-lived stability: *As I was saying, with that response he assumed the conversation was finished*, says the Mathematician.

—Of course, Leto says. Obviously.

—Washington's reason for bringing up the mosquitos is explained in his response to Héctor, don't you think?, says the Mathematician, letting go of his arm after seeing the empty pipe in his hand and putting it into his pants pocket, then taking the folded up sheets of the Student Association's press release from his other pocket to verify that they are still there and putting them away again.

Leto takes advantage of the Mathematician's distraction to offer, without much enthusiasm, an affirmative response. What makes the whole thing troublesome, as they say, is that he can't remember just what the pivotal response from Washington had been that, according to the Mathematician, clarified the notorious subject which a while ago, despite their contradicting moods and versions, Tomatis and the Mathematician, without even suspecting his somewhat obfuscated confusion, seemed so in agreement on. However much he tries, Washington's response does not make what you might call an appearance in his memory—his memory, no?—or rather that maybe slightly concave mirror (or flat, what's the difference) where certain familiar images, through which the whole universe takes on continuity, are reflected, sometimes clearly and sometimes darkly, in an uncontrollable, fugitive rhythm all their own. And Leto realizes after a moment of frustrated effort, so to speak, that the famous response, the final explication of that string of allusions which from that night toward the end of winter would travel by means of increasingly variable and dubious recollections, that Washington's circuitous, vernacular sentence, apparently the solution to the riddle, must have been pronounced by the Mathematician, whose source was Botón, when he wasn't listening, most likely when they were crossing the last street, just before he—Leto, no?— absorbed in his thoughts, stumbled over the cable.

—Washington likes to draw out what he's thinking little by little, says the Mathematician. But everything is clarified when he reaches his conclusion.

—And that was where he wanted to end up? Leto says, trying out that vague question in order to obtain a better indicator.

—Right there, says the Mathematician.

—Set in motion by, Leto says slowly, in a thoughtful tone that simulates an implicit series of rationalizations.

—No. No. Not at all. Just the opposite, says the Mathematician with a kind of energy that could be of a pedagogical order.

—Right, yes, Leto says. Just another way to put it. More elegant.

—Why say it another way when Washington said it as clearly as possible? says the Mathematician.

—That's true, Leto says. And, disappointed, he takes a last drag from his cigarette and flicks it to the sidewalk.

Considering the issue resolved, the Mathematician says that, according to Botón, right after dinner they had given Washington his gifts: Basso, Nidia, and Barco had put them all in a big cardboard box, and Basso's girls, before going to bed, had taken out and given them one by one to Washington, who unwrapped them slowly to everyone's anticipation: Beatriz, a belt; the Bassos, a box of darjeeling tea; Marcos Rosemberg, a mechanical sprinkler for the garden; Cuello, a *mate* gourd with a silver top and base; Silvia Cohen, a book by Paul Radin; Tomatis, an album of erotic Japanese etchings from the eighteenth century; Dib had a case of wine from Salta in his car; and later on Héctor, Elisa, and Rita Fonesca brought him a super-expensive

179

illustrated history of modern art. The rest the Mathematician doesn't remember—ah, yes, Barco, a checked shirt of the kind Washington likes, and the twins a ham.

—A ham? Leto asks, less out of genuine surprise than out of a faked curiosity, which is aimed at distracting the Mathematician while he tries to remember, or in any case decipher from the Mathematician's words, the clarification of the story of the mosquitos that the whole world, except him in particular, seems to understand through lateral allusions and fragmentary, cursory precisions as conclusive and decisive evidence. But the Mathematician only responds with a quick, distracted nod, concentrating on what he means to say and not disposed to letting a secondary problem, the ham the twins gave Washington, disturb his mnemonic and rhetorical efforts. The sincerity with which the Mathematician seems to consider his full comprehension of the real meaning of Washington's words, as a result admitting him into an exclusive circle, produces ambiguous feelings in Leto, a mix of pride and guilt, as though he were slightly fraudulent, but the Mathematician, unaware of his contradictory states of mind, takes for granted his admission to a circle of people who are intelligent and well-intentioned, as they say, correctly situated in their politics and so, offering the first results of his internal elaboration, goes on: All the gifts, according to Botón, Marcos Rosemberg planned to take to Rincón Norte the next day. Washington was very happy with them. In fact, as they say, despite how mild the winter had been, as the night wore on it got increasingly colder and those who stayed outside, under the pavilion or simply out on the patio, had to cover themselves as much as possible in order to bear it, and on top of sweaters, overcoats, hats, scarves, gloves, and cloaks, the Bassos started bringing out ponchos and blankets to distribute among the guests who, sitting around the table, or coming and going from the pavilion to the house, or walking in clusters through the trees at the back, started wrapping themselves up and releasing streams of air that turned to vapor each time they opened their mouth to say something or just to breathe. According to Botón, says the Mathematician, at some point they went looking for mandarins at the back, the last of the year, from the trees where even in the morning darkness they could sense the appearance of the first shoots that signaled the end of winter, and the mandarins were so cold that biting them would hurt their teeth, until Sadi, the unionist, suggested heating them up around the last coals and ashes that were still warm, the way he did when he was a kid with oranges in a barbecue. And so they had put them in the ashes and embers for a while and had eaten them warm—and the Mathematician can't imagine how good those mandarins must have been. *I can't imagine what that's like. Ever since Botón told me about it Saturday on the ferry I've been tempted to recreate the experience.* Which is satisfying to Leto because he, on the contrary, as far back as his memory goes, can remember the warm mandarins and oranges they would take from the grill on winter nights, when he spent July vacations in his grandparents' town, and this is the first time since the Mathematician started relating the circumstances of the party that he feels ownership of one of the details of the events of that night last winter at Basso's ranch in Colastiné, which he's never been to and has had to piece together, as they say, from assorted images of various ranches, half real and half imagined. Like two towns on the river coast, the warm mandarin juice connects, one might say, his own life to the images evoked (if the expression fits) by the Mathematician's words: *Ah, the warm mandarins. Because they're always last, at the end of winter they're the sweetest. They're so full of juice that when you warm them in the ashes they taste like honey.*

The Mathematician looks at him. Like any good rationalist, he distrusts lyrical exaggerations—especially unfamiliar ones—and his look, blatantly scrutinizing, searches Leto's face for the gravity that's necessary to lend credibility to the description and for the indifference and absence of hesitation that would certify his rationalist certitude, which, in light of his somewhat indiscreet comparison, and conscious of having hyperbolized his description in order to amplify the importance of his experience, Leto struggles to maintain at all costs. Turning his eyes back to the street, the Mathematician seems to have concluded his inspection, with satisfactory results apparently, if Leto judges by the carefree bonhomie with which he resumes his stream of compact, well-turned phrases, at times elegant and not exempt from a kind of arch excess of precision, a certain refrigerant preciousness in the expression of emotions, and mostly ironic shades in the disdain of his assumptions. *Sometimes a general dispersal, sometimes a reunion under the pavilion.* They walked through the darkness covered with ponchos and blankets, holding a glass in one hand and a cigarette between the index and middle fingers of the same hand, the glow of red ends of their cigarettes growing slightly in the darkness, among the mandarins, if they took a puff. When they crossed the bands of light projecting from the ranch into the patio and between the trees, you could see the streams of whitish breath they expelled through their half-open lips. Sometimes, from somewhere in the darkness, they could hear a couple whispering, and in some cases, and despite the cold, the whispers sounded more like conclusive shudders than preliminary murmurs— *all this*, the Mathematician clarifies, *according to Botón*: branches shaking, voices, laughter and shouts that dispersed and faded in the dark, frozen air under the stars resembling pieces of ice formed yellow, or blue, or red, or green, that in the Mathematician's imagination are sidereal chemical memories in which each color is just evidence of this or that substance or of thermal relationships where the different colors are just the consequence of varying temperatures. As he speaks, the Mathematician imagines them, lighthearted and happy while he marched around Frankfurt, sees them coming and going across the dark patio under the sky loaded, one might say, with active substance. But these are private images belonging to what is intransmissible in his representations—those apparently arbitrary and senseless images that, nevertheless, were they diagramed, would reveal more of his identity than his fingerprints or the features of his face. *According to Botón,* says the Mathematician, *a few people sat around the table wearing blankets, scarves, hats, gloves—they smoked with the gloves on.* Until at some point the cold was so unbearable that the ones who were left, because most people had already gone, were forced to move inside. *The cold chased them from the patio to the house*, says the Mathematician that Botón had said happened. According to Botón, they had sat around drinking *mate* and at some point Washington had said that certain ritual positions in tantric yoga were revolutionary. *If Botón didn't hear wrong, which is highly likely*, says the Mathematician.

—This Botón's credibility seems to fluctuate considerably, says Leto, somewhat irritated by the continuous corrections he has to make to his general idea of Botón, and by the nagging feeling of having missed the crux of the Mathematician's story.

—His heart is big like a house. Unfortunately, its size sometimes seems inversely proportional to his intellectual faculties, says the Mathematician, simultaneously severe and tender.

—Isn't he also kind of a . . . ? says Leto.

The Mathematician discharges a short, resigned laugh to show that even on the defensive he is willing to get to the bottom of things.

—A liar? he says.

Making a vague gesture with his lips and his shoulders, half-closing his eyes and adopting an enigmatic, ambiguous expression, Leto declines to respond, so the Mathematician presents his opinion: If the descriptor includes even the slightest hint of moral judgment, he rejects it emphatically and pre-emptively. Otherwise—and here the Mathematician's timbre turns slightly pitched, a kind tone and singsong rhythm, as they also say—if it implies his inclination toward fantasy, his oversensitivity to bearing the steady bitterness of reality, his well-intentioned descriptions of things from an angle that will be most pleasant, calming, and enlightening to his interlocutor, his lack of, um, education and somewhat, um, limited culture, his malnourished capacity for rational thought, not to mention his intemperate consumption of gin, which don't exactly contribute to a clarification of his ideas and more than anything don't allow any certainty as regards the events to which he is an eyewitness or even a protagonist—if you bear all of these criteria in mind, the Mathematician continues, you could say that any statement from Botón, whatever its contents, presents itself *a priori* as slightly problematic. This said, he—the Mathematician, no?—isn't the only one who thinks that, among all his traits, his ingenuousness and simplicity are what make Botón so lovable. *Consider instead—or along the same lines maybe—the example of Noca, who might be regarded as a virtuoso of every variety or genre*, and straightening the fingers on his left hand one by one, to mark his enumeration, the Mathematician intones: exaggeration, omission, perjury, fabulation, contradictory statements—and having used all of his fingers, he folds them back against his palm, except the index, which ticks the sixth variant— slander—of approaches that are contrary to the truth, and then he resumes straightening his fingers one by one: chimeras, systemic distortions for obscure mercantile reasons, flagrant misinterpretations, *pseudologia fantastica morbosa*, etc., etc., says the Mathematician, circling both hands in the air to indicate the infinite varieties of falsification at Noca's disposal.

And then he falls, as they say, silent, and lets his arms drop to his sides. Two boys sitting in a doorway, seven or eight years old, gaze at a spot somewhere on the opposite sidewalk so intently that Leto looks toward it, not seeing anything, as does the Mathematician, who has not seen the boys yet but, intrigued by Leto's curious look, passes his over the same spot without seeing anything but the one- or two-story houses and the gray pavement covered with bright morning light. They are so abstracted, Leto observes, that they don't even see them approach or notice when anyone else walking down the sidewalk passes them, though the proximity to the government district generates a slight increase in movement along the streets. Just then the Mathematician recognizes—and is recognized by—two young men coming toward them on the opposite sidewalk, and they exchange, across the street where just then two cars are crossing, a quick greeting that consists in raising a hand, shaking their head a little, and smiling vaguely, a passing acknowledgment that dissolves in the bright air as quickly as it forms, so fast that Leto, because no verbal exchange follows, doesn't even notice it, intrigued as he is by the boys' indistinct but nevertheless attentive gaze. But as they pass alongside them and leave them behind, and he hears their conversation—*I spy, I spy. What. A thing. What. Shiny. What color.*—he suddenly understands the boys' extreme attention. He would have liked to hear the thing's color too, in order to find, somewhere in the spot, what they were talking about, but they've gone too far from the boys, and the one who was supposed to give the color stalls, possibly on purpose, in order to conceal the direction, disorienting the one who has to find the object and drawing out the game a little more. *I spy, I spy. What. A thing. What. Shiny. What color*, Leto thinks and, with somewhat childish disenchantment, can't stop himself from looking again toward the opposite sidewalk, motivating another pointless look from the Mathematician who, because he was distracted by his greeting didn't pay attention to the conversation, ends up slightly annoyed. Deliberately, Leto doesn't provide an explanation. Washington's notorious sentence, which the Mathematician must have referred to just before he stumbled over the guardrail, supposing that the allusions shared by the Mathematician and Tomatis were engineered to exclude him from the sphere where they moved effortlessly between the *trivium* and the *quadrivium*, as the Mathematician would say, the famous sentence that Leto continues to suspect was never spoken by Washington, sanctions his lack of explanation for his insistent interest in looking at the vague spot somewhere on the opposite sidewalk, prompted, so to speak, by a childish whim born, it's not clear why, in the fissures of his soul—a problematic object if there ever was one, as they say, and which yours truly—just now, no?—was saying seems not translucent but murky. And in that climate of what you might call tenuous opposition, they reach the corner.

The landscape, to put a word to it, has changed completely. The small, private houses with their bronze nameplates and balconies over the sidewalk give way, as they say, to the Plaza de Mayo, bordered, on its four sides, by the cathedral, the courts, the Jesuit college, the

185

capitol. From the long, three- or four-story buildings surrounding the plaza, suppliers of law, power, justice, and religion enter and exit with folders, briefcases, papers, alone or in small groups, men and women, the litigators, the faithful, and the public servants. Several pass, most likely on an errand from the curia to the courts, from the courts to the seat of government. Many cross, in different directions, the red brick paths of the plaza between the green flowerbeds bordered by bitter orange trees, rubber trees, or palms. The sky, bright blue, without a single cloud, spreads, you could say, over the plaza. The Mathematician slows down.

—This is my stop, he says.

Surprised, Leto looks at him, searching his expression for any resentment of his recent behavior. But the Mathematician's wide smile, and the sincere look that meets his, calm him.

—I have to drop the press release off over there, he says, vaguely pointing somewhere in the city beyond the plaza, the capitol, and the courts. And then, satirizing himself and the Students Association: It's not enough to travel through Europe. You've got to publish it too.

—I'm going straight, says Leto.

—Shame we missed the party, no? says the Mathematician.

—They didn't invite me, says Leto.

—It must have slipped their minds. Or probably they thought they didn't have to, says the Mathematician.

—So strange, giving him a ham, says Leto.

—It's Washington's favorite, says the Mathematician. But not to worry. In a couple of visits Tomatis will leave him with just the bone.

Okay. Time to say goodbye and finish it, Leto thinks, but as if he had guessed his thoughts, the Mathematician is already extending his hand. Leto holds out his. The look they exchange when they say goodbye, brief and polite, expresses many things that both perceive and register carefully, discreetly, and intuitively. Leto's look says more or less the following: *Frankly, when you whistled at me back there, I didn't have a single ounce of interest in having someone pester me for fifteen blocks, especially since I only knew you through Tomatis's patently unenthusiastic references, and your physical appearance and style of dress don't favor you much with the poor mortals you happen upon. But after our walk I have to admit that your personality, although not without its pedantries, is more or less pleasant, and things haven't gone badly. Furthermore, at some point I thought the whole thing was going to fall apart, but don't worry, to me, it's like the thing with the pants never happened.* And the Mathematician's—more or less as well, no?—and as we've said, without a trace of words: *I'm aware of your reticence. I'll try to understand it. And I'm aware of Tomatis's too. But that doesn't matter to me. The two of you, because I was born among uninteresting people, perceive uninteresting things in me, which is the cause, I'm sure, of that reticence. Let's take the pants, for example. I know I shouldn't let them be so important. But the feeling is stronger than me. At any point, if my white pants are in danger, my whole being feels in danger, because my whole being—who knows why, probably because of the uninteresting things that persist in me despite my efforts to eradicate them—though it seems strange, is concentrated in my pants. But I could offer some objections too, if I wanted. Tomatis, for example, wasn't so brilliant. And in your case, I'm not sure you've understood everything with so much patience, detail, and scrupulous respect for the truth I've been trying to tell you. More than once I caught you thinking of something else, and at one point I wondered if you were taking advantage of the thing with the pants. But why bother with all this—they're details that belong to the category of the uninteresting. Don't you think there are more important things for the time we've been given?* De rerum natura *or* Spinoza's Ethics, *for example, or the debate over the EPR paradox.*

And so on. When they let go their hands, the Mathematician, taking advantage of a favorable stoplight, crosses the street at a diagonal, toward the plaza, while Leto, hesitant, undecided whether to continue, watches with an inexpressive, almost inert gaze. The Mathematician's tanned, athletic, tall, and blonde-haired body, dressed in a white shirt, the blinding white pants that inspired a momentary enslavement in their owner, the white moccasins which Leto does not know were bought the month before in Florence and are worn sock-less with an excess of affected simplicity, the combination so stereotypical of the decade's aesthetic ideal that a rational advertiser would have rejected him from a billboard for fear that his exaggerated perfection, producing a refusal effect, would lower sales of the products he was meant to sell, the Mathematician—in a word, no?—or in two, to be more precise, leaves the street behind, and stepping into the plaza, and always at a diagonal, moves away from the corner on the red brick path between the green flowerbeds where, juxtaposed against the cloudless blue sky and a landscape of block-long public buildings three or four stories tall, grow bitter orange trees, rubber trees, *palo borrachos*, and palms. Leto's gaze follows him, more indolent than attentive and, unconsciously, at the level of thought that under layers of archaic rumination and delirium is always yoked to the essential, insolubly glued, so to speak, to the profound illusion of the external, watches as he is lost to the unreality of the morning, the translucent stuff of space and time that, with every step, swallows and returns him, over and over, with an impalpable rhythm, an absurd yet stable cluster of gradually diminishing radiation, less distinct as he moves away, a dense flux revealed and immediately erased again by the daylight. But when he reaches the center of the plaza, an acquaintance, coming in the opposite direction, intercepts him and they start to talk. From a distance Leto thinks he can imagine the conversation of which he catches only a few gestures and two or three head movements. He imagines hearing again the list of cities and the images associated with each—Paris, an unexpected rainstorm; London, a problem finding hotel rooms and some manuscripts in the British Museum; Warsaw, there was nothing left; Brussels, for *The Census at Bethlehem*; La Rochelle, sparkling white; etc., etc.—and, satisfied with the fresh rendering of the white image that had been losing its reality, recovering, through an illusory, conventional conversation, a somewhat more familiar humanity, he starts to cross the intersection.

The same lack of obligation that, some fifty-five minutes before, give or take, had compelled him to get off the bus and, instead of going to work, start walking down San Martín, now induces him to continue, though his decision is supplemented by the fear that, having told the Mathematician about his intention to continue straight, the white figure chatting with an acquaintance in the middle of the plaza might turn around and, seeing him still standing on the corner, killing time or undecided where to go, would suspect that what he had said was just a pretext for unburdening himself from him. But when he reaches the opposite sidewalk this apprehension disappears. Washington's birthday, the mosquitos, Noca's horse, the table set under the imaginary pavilion, at once persistent and inconstant, clicking along in a unique, complex order, now make up a carousel of memories more intense, significant, but nevertheless more enigmatic, you could say, than many others which, originating in his own experience, ought to be stronger and more immediately present in his memory. And the passing distractions, the opacity of certain allusions—apparently evident to Tomatis and the Mathematician—instead of diluting those images, clarify them, the way a crevice, by forcing a ray of light to pass through its tiny opening, contributes to a greater display of its richness in the concentrated darkness. Without realizing their fantastical aspect, Leto examines them, holds them—or accepts their persistence, passively—in the white circle of his attention, the way a traveler, projecting the artificial images of his recent trip, trying to gather together everything that escaped his attention just when the picture was taken, lingers a while studying the details of some slides more than others. The complete morning, including his body crossing through it over the gray pavement, and the intangible, ubiquitous "I" he carries inside him, disappear behind the images that, now almost definitive are, though they come from his memory, permanent and more indestructible, you could say, than the breath and flesh that contain them. They are, in any case, interwoven with them in spite of coming from the impalpable, articulate, and reverberant voice which, for several blocks, has been disseminated in the external transparency through the white, even teeth and well-formed, almost mythic superhero lips of the Mathematician. Until his death, certain associations, with greater or lesser force, will recall them, so dependent on each other that at some point he will no longer know which came first, the image or the association, and in some cases, as proof of their insoluble adhesion, so to speak, they will act upon each other without even reaching his consciousness, in the form of short sparks, pulses, and anonymous, shapeless signs that will wrinkle slightly the fissures, to put a word to it, of his being—his being, no?—or rather the incomprehensible formed into a continuous presence, a sensitive lump trapped in a nameless something, a slow whirlwind that it's simultaneously part of, a spiral of energy and matter that is at once the womb that produces it and the knife—neither friend nor enemy—that slices it open.

Leto looks back at the plaza. The white figure, at least a head taller than its interlocutor, speaks with distant and measured gestures, and as it forms part of a pleasant, blooming multitude, the plaza's flower-beds, the spring sun, the trees, and the blue sky, Leto thinks that it would definitely be nice to see the Mathematician again and have a conversation, less because of the Mathematician himself than because of the whole morning he is part of and because he is now a part of his life, but actually, in the coming years, they will only be together two or three times at parties where they exchange a few words and, when they meet on the street, will limit themselves to a greeting, polite of course, but without stopping to talk—and all of these encounters more and more sporadic and further and further apart. Little by little Leto will abandon his work, more and more involved in political militancy, with more and more radicalized groups, until eventually going into hiding, and not a trace will remain of the familiar Leto but for two or three brief reappearances, except with a few close friends like Tomatis, Barco, El Gato Garay, who he will visit every so often, always briefly and unexpectedly, not to discuss politics but to spend some time with people who are connected to him not just by principles, but rather, to say it again, by shared experiences and memories, since it's possible to fight against the same oppression, with the same principles even, but for different reasons. First he will leave his job—Isabel ends up marrying Lopecito—then his house, then the city, later the country, coming and going from Europe to Cuba, to the Middle East, to Africa, to Vietnam, until he disappears completely into the exacting, silent, clandestine life of the walking dead. For sixteen or seventeen years he will sink into an order governed by such strict, specialized, closed-circuit norms that, although they were created to form an association of people who intended to modify reality, will force him into an unreality so profound that, behind his so-called impenetrable mask, into which his face will be transformed, or inside the various costumes he will dress up in to enter and exit the same comedy like an actor playing several supporting roles at once, in his own life, behind the impenetrable mask—we were saying, or rather yours truly, just now, was saying, no?—nothing will be left after the rage, the faith, the daring, but a sardonic and not even self-pitying intransigence of someone who, chased by a torrential storm, as they say, or by an uninterrupted series of explosions, runs in a straight line, without caring, and maybe without even asking, whether the direction they are running in will lead them to safety or to a precipice. In any case, at some point he will start carrying, wherever he goes, a suicide pill, well-hidden against his body in one of his pockets, and every so often he will look at it to remind himself, not of his mortality, but of his freedom. Guessing the weight of things, he will tell himself with cold satisfaction that, placed on the opposite side of a scale as the little pill encased in plastic, the entire universe would weigh nothing, and that the little pill could dispatch the immeasurable weight of the known world and make it disappear suddenly and silently in spite of its iridescent, soap bubble feel. But all of this will come little by little, after successive stages of uncertainty, violence, and deception. At some point, in the last two or three years, he won't have anything left but the silence, the sardonic intransigence, and the pill. After confirming that the whole universe is inconsistent and futile, the pill, in its place, will become a singular object. And having realized after fifteen years that blind fighting against oppression can create more oppression rather than eliminating it, the way sometimes fighting a fire can actually increases the force of the flames, and having come too far to turn back, he will begin to trust, not in strategies or organizations or in so-called historical movements, not even in his own weapon, but only in the pill, in *his* pill, the way someone might refer, as they say, to his sixth sense or his lucky star. The way others think of their bank account as a provision against hardship, he will think of his pill. After a few years his physical appearance will change drastically. The messy hair on his head will thin and gray, making his forehead much larger, exposing the wrinkles. He will start wearing contact lenses in order to get rid of the glasses, and he'll grow a thin, silky beard, grayish, curly, and straightening out around the corners of his mouth, and in spite of his thin, almost frail shoulders and slightly crooked legs, a kind of taut thickness will build up at his abdomen, maybe because, having decided not to drink anymore so as not to lose his clarity or his reflexes, he will suffer, looking for a substitute, from a weakness, as they say, for soft drinks, cakes, ice cream, chocolate, and caramels. The change will be so drastic that after not having seen him for a few years, Barco, who he will go to early one day for the key to Tomatis's apartment—he was traveling in Europe at the time—Barco, we were, or rather, I—yours truly—was saying, seeing him appear between sheets of gray morning rain, won't recognize him for several minutes, until hearing him recall—his voice somewhat cracked by the cigarettes that in those days he lit with the one he'd just finished—their shared experiences. In fact, the sacrosanct pill will be given to him as yet another obligation, wrapped up with indoctrinatory discourse where the words *sacrifice*, *cause*, *victory*, and *republic* would easily stand out in any lexical frequency analysis, but he, secretly even to himself at first, will receive it as a promise, a privilege, an amulet. Later he will start to roll it over his tongue, not as a test of his invisibility to his enemies, but as a means of ridicule and contempt, behind his impassive face, toward his own allies. If by chance he finds himself yet again at a meeting where he doesn't agree with a single decision, he will catch himself thinking, slightly annoyed, sardonic: *Talk all you want, I have my pill.* It will be like his own portable nuclear bomb, his perfect weapon. At several dangerous moments, after realizing that they had been false alarms, he will notice that while his comrades had instinctively drawn their weapons, he had first reached for the pill and then, several seconds later, for his gun. He will learn to keep space, time, history, and matter itself at bay and as though in suspense with the pill. *No one likes going from subject to object,* he will tell himself more than once, laughing a little deep down because to the outside world he will be always impassive, so much so that his equals—after so many years of risk and violence he will have reached the rank of Comandante—his immediate superiors, mistrusted him, not having learned how to match, every day, his discipline and indifference to danger. *No one likes going from subject to object,* he will say, we were saying—or rather, no?—yours truly was, as I was saying. *No one likes going from subject to object, but with the pill, eh? With the pill what's lost in the transfer is still up for discussion.* He won't be far from thinking that just like the big bang was the start of existence, the almost inaudible click of his jaw closing and his upper teeth colliding with his lower teeth to crush the pill will end it once and for all. A few months before this click, he will visit Tomatis at his mother's house, where Tomatis has taken refuge after his third divorce. At the time Tomatis will be suffering from what people called psychiatrists call depression, which he will come out of intact a few months later, but when Leto visits he will be at what those same people call a critical juncture. Tomatis will spend every day being waited on by his sister—thrilled despite everything to have him home—while sitting in a chair in the living room watching television from noon until 2:00 or 3:00 in the morning, with a demijohn of Caroya wine on the floor next to the chair, and a glass, a plastic ice dish shaped like an apple with white bumps, and a stem-shaped corkscrew on the table. From the bedroom, his mother, blind and slightly senile, because she never gets up from bed, calls out to him every so often to often to give him a kiss, calls him baby, like when he was little, and whimpers a little. It will be midsummer. Since just before Christmas, Tomatis will have installed himself in the house, sleeping, by means of a meticulous ingestion of barbiturates and tranquilizers, in the room on the terrace, which his sister had to clean out because it had been turned into storage. Every morning, when the electric shadows, the garish simulacra, the bimbos, and miniaturized Barbies of cookie-cutter American shows, interrupted every five minutes by the commercials thought up by and for the retarded, the military propaganda inviting the unemployed youth to join gangs of murderers and torturers in order to save the nation from the cancer of deviance—every morning, no?—in the burning darkness filthy with the pestilence, you could say, of unmarked graves and decay, Tomatis will get up, breathless and somewhat brutalized by the Caroya wine, the barbiturates, and the tranquilizers, just to collapse on the same couch where, twenty years earlier, he had spent every night contemplating, joyfully, delighted, the carnal and the divine. Without recovering completely, he will wake up every morning around noon, and after drinking a couple of *mates* in the shade of the terrace, will sit down again, with a plate of cold cuts and tomatoes, the demijohn, and the ice dish, in front of the television, getting up every once in a while to take a piss or to get an irresolute kiss from his mother, who will call him baby again like when he was little and pat him on the wrinkled cheek that's covered with a hard, two- or three-day-old gray-streaked beard. The colored shadows will march across his inexpressive eyes, which will sometimes half close trying to understand the insipid jokes of the third-rate comedians, almost inaudible over the canned laughter and applause. Moving the chair between two open doors in order to take advantage of a nonexistent breeze, wearing only underwear and a pair of hemp flip-flops, from noon until 2:00 or 3:00 in the morning he will watch the cycle—sometimes losing the story lines and sometimes without even looking at the screen—of infomercials, educational shows, police dramas, or westerns, the kids shows, the soap operas, the folk stories, the shows written for housekeepers, picking his nose every so often, rolling a soft, dark ball with his snot and dropping it next to the chair. Once in a while he will have a jolt of rebellion: *What if I shove it in your mouth*, he will mutter to the host of a kids show who insists on speaking in the high-pitched, infantile voice people assume you should use with children. *If I shove it in your mouth, we'll see how fast you lose the baby voice.* And once in a while, to the government propaganda, out loud, but with a diluted hatred, sitting up a little and grabbing his flaccid bundle of genitals: *This, right here.* But deflating again, he will look toward the kitchen, afraid that his sister, convinced that he's having the most relaxing vacation in years, will be offended by the vulgar remark.

Leto will find him like this when, suspecting he might not have another chance, he decides to visit him. Tomatis will greet him with a weak smile, more visible in his squinting eyes than in his mouth, which will spread somewhat blankly, without his lips parting. For the first few minutes he won't even get up from his chair—his sister will be the one who lets him in—and his conversation will be disjointed because he will be looking anxiously at the television screen so as not to lose the thread of the show he is watching. But later, just when Leto begins to regret coming, with a superhuman effort, as they say, he will introduce him to his sister as an old book editor friend who has come from Buenos Aires, and will invite him up to the terrace to talk in peace. Tomatis will give Leto the plastic apple after filling it with ice, and carrying the demijohn and dragging his flip-flops while trying to hold up his underwear with the same hand that's pinching the glasses, will ascend the red staircase to the terrace. It will be the afternoon. Tomatis will offer him a glass of wine, which he will decline, but after some hesitation, in which he's not sure whether Tomatis isn't scared that his visit will implicate him, he will ask for a caramel, or a Coca-Cola, and Tomatis will stand up, barefoot, clutching the underwear that even his swollen paunch can't sustain, and, leaning over into the interior patio, ask his sister for a caramel. The sister will bring him a cellophane bag of fruit caramels, orange, yellow, green, red, each individually wrapped in little cellophane papers with twisted ends, which Leto will unwrap once in a while so as to pop the candy in his mouth and then toss in an empty tray next to his folding chair. Once in a while, Tomatis will look with vague curiosity at the canvas bag where he knows Leto has a gun. Night will come. Leto will feel confused, slightly disoriented: He has come to Tomatis to enjoy, maybe for the last time, his lethal jokes, his conversation, his somewhat nasal voice that's accustomed to discharging torrents of slightly stuttered words that are punctuated here and there with bursts of elegance, but finds instead an overweight, middle-aged man, his eyes teary, bright but bleary and alcoholic at the same time, his days-old beard more gray than black, his face swollen, feet dirty, and underwear dubious, a middle-aged man who mutters this or that irresolute and slightly weird question every five minutes, losing interest in the response almost immediately but repeating the same question a half hour later, as though he had never asked it, losing interest in the response again and drifting away into incomprehensible, labored ruminations. That fear is not what holds Tomatis back is proven by the fact that his questions refer, with the same detachment and the same indifference, to the most compromising and the most banal subjects, which, in normal times, they could have discussed in a lively, exhaustive way, but which on that winter evening Tomatis will mutter without conviction, uncertain and impassive, and to which he—Leto, no?—will most often respond with monosyllables, honest but incomplete. After a while his mistrust will transform into relief, and when he realizes that Tomatis's rare moments of good mood consist of a sanctimonious, mechanical rehearsal of television commercial slogans, into compassion as well. A couple of times, because the television was left on, Tomatis will get up, interested in the change in programming, in some sensationalist news story, in the plot of a police drama, yelling questions down to his sister through the interior patio, and then sitting down again in his folding chair, thoughtful a few seconds while serving himself another glass of wine on ice. Until, at a certain point, the pivotal question will reach Leto's ears, so sudden and unexpected that, in a violent rush of emotion, though he has spent years walking through gunfire unfazed and practically indifferent, he will feel faster and more violent beatings of his heart. *Is it true about the pill?* Tomatis will ask, leaning in, with the same complicit, delicate smile that he might have used to ask him about a pornographic photograph. Leto won't say yes or no. Looking Tomatis directly in the eyes, he will search for the complicit smile he just had, but to his surprise Tomatis's eyes, vacant of the least glint of humor, will be fixed on him, for the first time since he arrived, with a vivid, almost imperative stare. His eyes, which will have been moist and weepy during the whole meeting, will now glow so strong that Leto will think, mistakenly, that they are reflecting the lights in the terrace. In the end, Leto will slowly unbutton the safety pouch hidden under his belt and will remove the pill and, suddenly opening his hand, will make it appear in his palm, moving it toward Tomatis, and during that more or less quick movement, the plastic capsule containing it will reflect, in passing, one of the lights. Tomatis will lean forward to observe, with slow shakes of his head, of corroboration, affirmative at first, then negative, and finally affirmative again. *Of course, of course*, he will say, as though thinking of something else. And then he—Leto, no?—will put it away again.

A few months later he will take it out for the last time, in Rosario, in fact, and, in fact, in Arroyito. He will be alone in a house they've told him is secure, where, they've told him, not the slightest chance of detection exists. He will be laying on the bed, in the darkness, smoking cigarette after cigarette—lighting them, as he is in the habit of doing, with the one he'd just finished—not thinking of anything, examining the shape of the sparse furniture, the silhouette of the window, and the somewhat clearer darkness filtering in through the blinds of the shades. It will be around 11:00. An electric heater, placed at the foot of the entrance to the room, in the hallway, will give off a reddish glow, which the flame of the cigarette, brightening with every puff, will seem—to put it one way—to echo or metastasize. He will be fully dressed, since he has adopted, for years now, the habit of sleeping that way in difficult times, less to feel secure than to gain time, according to what you might call the principle of objective efficacy, in which his personal interests are not considered whatsoever. On the floor, within arm's reach, are his weapons. He will be just lighting a new cigarette with the end of the one he has just finished when, for a fraction of a second, he registers a large, very fast shadow momentarily imprinted on the parallel rays of clear darkness filtering gray through the blinds and, sitting up slightly in bed trying to listen for something, will put out the stub in the center of the ashtray and balance the one he has just lit on the notch so that, if it's a false alarm, the cigarette won't be wasted unnecessarily. Without making a sound, he will pick up his gun, turn off the electric heater to thicken the darkness, and approach the window. At first he won't see anything but the empty street, the stoplights, the trees, the sidewalks, the parked cars—everything tempered-looking, sharpened, full of dark reflections caused by the dry, hard-to-breathe air of the winter night. For one minute at least, he will remain motionless, looking through the blinds, and that minute will be so long and monotonous that, when it has passed, he won't even remember why he came silently to the window, since the street and the hard lines of the clearly outlined things in the frozen air will appear abandoned and even empty. When he is about to turn back and pick up the cigarette from the notch on the ashtray he will see shadows move slightly on the opposite sidewalk, less stable than the ones of the houses and of the naked trees crisscrossing those of streetlights on the sidewalk—*like a spider web*—he will think, a final literary reflex whose conventional, trite style will cast an ironic tint to his thought. And, the way someone developing a photograph perceives its details little by little, he will recognize little by little the outlines, the unmistakable silhouettes of armed men running hunched over to hide or protect themselves in doorways, behind cars or trees. Like the traveler who, before boarding a train, puts his hand in his pocket to check that he hasn't lost his ticket, Leto will reach for the thin pocket under his belt, will rub the capsule through the cloth, and, continuing to look through the blinds, will start to unbutton the pocket. Seeing two armed men cross toward the house, bounding silently across the asphalt, he will tell them, without uttering a word, with his thoughts, as he is used to doing: *You two, like the ones behind the cars and the trees, like the ones waiting on the corners, like the ones probably already at the front door, on the roof or at the back patio at least, you're not real, you're like ghosts or clouds or smoke, because I have my pill, I've just touched it with the tips of my fingers, the pill that with a single click will annihilate the big bang, the blind, senseless proliferation of its heavy metals and its ridiculous pseudoeternity.* And, groping toward the night stand and lifting the cigarette from the notch in the ashtray to take two or three more puffs before putting it out, he will bring the pill to his mouth in a motion so fast that, before biting it, holding it a moment between his teeth without pressing down, he will need to wait to exhale the last puff of smoke.

Reaching the corner, Leto turns his head back toward the plaza. The Mathematician's white figure, now separated from its interlocutor, has continued at a diagonal and reached the corner almost at the same time as Leto, one block away. And again almost at the same time as Leto, it crosses onto a parallel street, behind a government building, and disappears. In turn, Leto reaches the opposite sidewalk. Now, apart from the colonial building of the historical museum, with its tile roof, its gallery supported by columns of carved wood, its well—that's what they call it—painted white, in the patch of rare grass before the entrance, apart from the museum, we were saying—or rather yours truly, as I was saying just now, was, no?—apart from the museum building there are no others, and its front section and its green spaces occupy the whole sidewalk, until the next sidewalk, wide and deserted, beyond which, behind the *palo borrachos*, the blooming *lapachos* and *timbos*, the colonial church can be made out, white like the museum and the well—or so they call it—and also, like the museum, with its tile roof. When he reaches the corner, since he has to wait at the curb for a large bus from Rosario to pass, Leto observes a moment, to the east, of the ethnographic museum, built in a false colonial style that, trying to look like the others, only manages to accentuate its differences. The bus passes, turning south around the park, accelerating after having slowed through the intersection, and Leto manages to see its metallic side painted green and a row of pale, brief faces, a few of which return his gaze through the windows. Protected, restored, exhibited to preserve, contain, even represent and prolong the past, the church and the museums, wrapped in the insidious ubiquity of the morning light, nonetheless fail to escape the anonymous strangeness of the present—which may be, and why not, the name for it—exposed and dispersed in that light, already a museum maybe, or maybe since the beginning, with its perpetual display of objects without specific, or at least arbitrary, use, subject to what you might call the unique, monotonous variation of the fugitive and repetitive rhythm of mineral stability. Seeing the bus move away under the curved row of blooming *lapachos*, an intense red, bordering the park, Leto crosses, walking slowly, in full sun, stepping on his own shadow as it follows him, continuously smaller, over the large cement slabs, cracking in places and splattered here and there with oil stains scattered around the wide, deserted street that Leto leaves behind at touching, with the sole of his shoe, the cable guardrail.

Advancing along the park sidewalk, he leaves behind the grass and trees that precede the church and starts to parallel, under the first of the *lapachos* rising from the sidewalk, the lateral gallery of the convent. The sidewalk is covered in red flowers, flattened and rotten or fresh, almost intact, as though they've just fallen, and, lifting his head a little, he sees a few red stains that, detaching from the trees, fall through the air and land, softly, on the pavement. The flowered tops of the *lapachos*, without leaves, composed entirely of blooms, until the curve of the street disappears many dozens of meters ahead, emit a kind of rose-colored luminosity, whose proliferation, overflowing but contained in tops of regular, almost identical shapes that blend together to form a sort of large, curved, cylindrical cloud whose overflowing proliferation, as I was saying, instead of inspiring an aesthetic reaction in him, Leto, produces a kind of hatred, brief of course, that surprises him, that he would like to retain in his consciousness in order to examine it, and which he can guess the cause of, of course with nothing resembling words, beyond the innocence of the trees and the blind servility that makes them, an insignificant speck in the universe, bloom, puerile and repetitive, every year. Abruptly, discharging a short laugh because of his thoughts, he turns from the sidewalk and, taking one of the dirt paths, advances among the trees of the park, toward the lake. Beyond the cool shade that now dominates, the clarity of the morning and the blue sky shine over the open space of the lake. Suddenly, more fragile than its stone, iron, concrete, and plaster objects would have it appear, the city, with its prolific, almost primitive crisscrossing of straight streets and its diffuse clamor, seems to disintegrate behind him, itself likewise entering, with all of its unlikely presences, that anonymous place which the word *past*, of such fragile pronunciation, seems to denote so well, though without it having, on the reverse of the sounds uttered in speaking it or in the traces of ink left in writing it, any precise image to represent it.

But Leto is not thinking about this. Curious, he lends, as they say, his ear to a specific place—though it's always the same, no?—in the park, where agitated, sharp screeches are breaking, to put a word to it, the silence. Cutting across one of the flowerbeds, Leto walks toward the screeches, and when he discovers its source, stops, surprised, to look. A number of birds of a species he has never seen, ten or fifteen maybe, very large, black on their back and on their long, thin tail, yellow on their breast, with a long, black beak and a very strange silhouette that were it not for their size would resemble a paper kite, swarm and screech at a precise spot in the park, between the lower branch of a tree, a shrub growing at the edge of an embankment, and the space that opens between the embankment and the edge of the lake, which Leto, from where he is standing, is not able to see. The birds swarm, land, take off again, move away and return, screeching, flapping, gliding, and landing again on the branches of the tree or the bush, or even on the edge of the embankment. Their ridiculous paper kite silhouettes are not without, because of the increasing frenzy that agitates them, a sort of tragedy. Sometimes they plunge toward the water but almost immediately reappear, more frenzied still, closer to panic than to fury, rushing up as though terrified of having dared to graze the apparent cause of their agitation, they move away again, contaminated by its lethal essence or burned by its incandescence. So as not to scare them, Leto approaches slowly along the edge of the embankment, trying to figure out the cause of their flutter. But the birds do not even notice his presence. Observing them closely, he realizes that it's a foreign species, diverted, who knows why, from its migratory course. Agitation, terror, panic, the incessant, feverish swarming, the short, sharp, almost petrified screeches, and the plunging flight interrupted over and over by an abrupt change in direction, away from the object that impels them—Leto advances and gets so close to the birds that more than once he has to duck so that one doesn't graze him on its flight or knock him over. Now, from where he is standing, he can finally see the object: it's a large beach ball, made of yellow plastic, which some child must have left behind the day before and which, abandoned at the edge of the lake, tangled up in aquatic plants, rocks, slowly, with every imperceptible wave that arrives, periodically, to displace it. Between the more and more agitated screeches and the frenetic alarms of the birds, which are indifferent to his presence, Leto scrutinizes the yellow sphere that concentrates or spreads intense radiations, an incontrovertible but simultaneously problematic presence, a yellow concretion less consistent than nothingness and more mysterious than the totality of the existent, and then, with some compassion, seeing the birds' maddened swarm increasing around him, he, Leto, who is just starting to deconstruct his own, intuits the sense of loss, of awe, of wonder that are absent in a creature unable to raise, in the house of coincidence—which could just as easily be called something else—the sanctuary, in more than one sense superfluous, of what they call, apparently, their gods.

J uan José Saer (1937–2005), born in Santa Fe, Argentina, was the leading Argentinian writer of the post-Borges generation. In 1968, he moved to Paris and taught literature at the University of Rennes. The author of numerous novels and short-story collections (including *Scars* and *La Grande*, forthcoming from Open Letter), Saer was awarded Spain's prestigious Nadal Prize in 1987 for *The Event*.

S teve Dolph is the co-editor of *Calque*, a journal of literature in translation.

Open Letter—the University of Rochester's nonprofit, literary translation press—is one of only a handful of publishing houses dedicated to increasing access to world literature for English readers. Publishing ten titles in translation each year, Open Letter searches for works that are extraordinary and influential, works that we hope will become the classics of tomorrow.

Making world literature available in English is crucial to opening our cultural borders, and its availability plays a vital role in maintaining a healthy and vibrant book culture. Open Letter strives to cultivate an audience for these works by helping readers discover imaginative, stunning works of fiction and by creating a constellation of international writing that is engaging, stimulating, and enduring.

Current and forthcoming titles from Open Letter include works from Catalonia, France, Iceland, Poland, and numerous other countries.

www.openletterbooks.org